"Sergeant Hays, you may kiss your bride."

Darcy's breath caught in her throat. She hadn't bargained for this. This was only supposed to be a pretend wedding. But the handsome military man leaning in to kiss her was all too real.

Billy's lips touched her mouth, landing feather soft, like a butterfly lighting on a flower.

She should have let him lift off and be done, and that would have been that.

But Darcy kissed him back.

Then Billy pulled her closer, pressing her against his hard, strong chest. And Darcy felt almost...loved.

Heavens, she couldn't help wondering, what would it be like if they *weren't* pretending?

Dear Reader,

Harlequin American Romance has rounded up the best romantic reading to help you celebrate Valentine's Day. Start off with the final installment in the MAITLAND MATERNITY: TRIPLETS, QUADS & QUINTS series. *The McCallum Quintuplets* is a special three-in-one volume featuring *New York Times* bestselling author Kasey Michaels, Mindy Neff and Mary Anne Wilson.

BILLION-DOLLAR BRADDOCKS, Karen Toller Whittenburg's new family-connected miniseries, premiers this month with *The C.E.O.'s Unplanned Proposal*. In this Cinderella story, a small-town waitress is swept into the Braddock world of wealth and power and puts eldest brother Adam Braddock's bachelor status to the test. Next, in Bonnie Gardner's *Sgt. Billy's Bride*, an air force controller is in desperate need of a fiancée to appease his beloved, ailing mother, so he asks a beautiful stranger to become his wife. Can love bloom and turn their pretend engagement into wedded bliss? Finally, we welcome another new author to the Harlequin American family. Sharon Swan makes her irresistible debut with *Cowboys and Cradles*.

Enjoy this month's offerings, and be sure to return next month when Harlequin American Romance launches a new cross-line continuity, THE CARRADIGNES: AMERICAN ROYALTY, with *The Improperly Pregnant Princess* by Jacqueline Diamond.

Wishing you happy reading,

Melissa Jeglinski
Associate Senior Editor
Harlequin American Romance

SGT. BILLY'S BRIDE
Bonnie Gardner

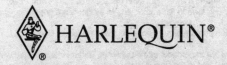

TORONTO • NEW YORK • LONDON
AMSTERDAM • PARIS • SYDNEY • HAMBURG
STOCKHOLM • ATHENS • TOKYO • MILAN • MADRID
PRAGUE • WARSAW • BUDAPEST • AUCKLAND

To Mud, as always.
To Sue, who reminds me that I am woman and can roar,
and Kathie and Kathy and Brenda. You know why.

To all the combat controllers and their families I have
known through the years and even those I haven't.
You all have tough jobs and manage to do them well.

ISBN 0-373-16911-6

SGT. BILLY'S BRIDE

Copyright © 2002 by Bonnie Gardner.

Visit us at www.eHarlequin.com

Printed in U.S.A.

ABOUT THE AUTHOR

Bonnie Gardner has finally figured out what she wants to do when she grows up. After a varied career that included such jobs as switchboard operator, draftsman and exercise instructor, she went back to college and became an English teacher. As a teacher, she took a course on how to teach writing to high school students and caught the bug herself.

She lives in northern Alabama with her husband of over thirty years, her own military hero. After following him around from air force base to air force base, she has finally gotten to settle down. They have two grown sons, one of which is now serving in the air force. She loves to read, cook, garden and, of course, write.

She would love to hear from her readers. You can write to her at P.O. Box 442, Meridianville, AL 35759.

Books by Bonnie Gardner

HARLEQUIN AMERICAN ROMANCE
876—UNCLE SARGE
911—SGT. BILLY'S BRIDE

Don't miss any of our special offers. Write to us at the following address for information on our newest releases.

Harlequin Reader Service
U.S.: 3010 Walden Ave., P.O. Box 1325, Buffalo, NY 14269
Canadian: P.O. Box 609, Fort Erie, Ont. L2A 5X3

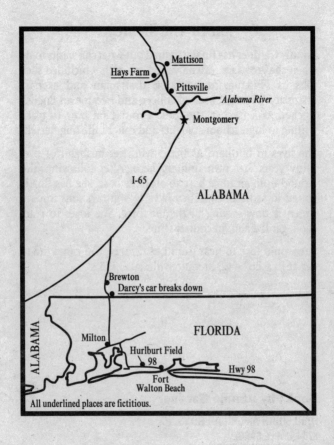

Mattison

Hays Farm

Pittsville

Alabama River

Montgomery

I-65

ALABAMA

Brewton
Darcy's car breaks down

FLORIDA

ALABAMA

Milton

Hurlburt Field
98

Hwy 98

Fort
Walton Beach

All underlined places are fictitious.

Prologue

Darcy Stanton sat in the bride's room in the chapel at Hurlburt Air Force Base and clenched her hands in her lap with a grip of death. She couldn't believe she was really going through with it.

She wasn't ready to be a bride. She didn't know what she was doing in this room getting ready to marry First Lieutenant Richard Harris III, a man she'd known all her life but wasn't sure she knew at all. At this moment, she wasn't sure she liked Dick, much less loved him.

She didn't want to be Mrs. Dick Harris, the daughter of General and Mrs. Harrington Stanton. She didn't want to play the role of the prim and proper niece of Colonel John Harbeson, the commander of the Special Tactics Squadron at Hurlburt. She wanted to be just plain Darcy. Not Tracy D'Arcy Harbeson Stanton, the namesake of four decorated generals.

She wanted to know how it would feel to work for a living, not to have to worry about protocol and which fork to use and what the other officers' wives were wearing and what they would think of her. She'd planned to put her degree from Duke University in North Carolina to good use after graduation, but Dick would hear none of it.

Darcy drew in a deep, shuddering breath and tried to still her racing heart. She was a registered nurse as of last Tuesday, and she knew the signs. She was in severe stress, verging on a full-fledged panic attack.

"Mom," Darcy whispered, her voice coming out in short, breathy gasps. "I'm not sure I can do this." There, she'd finally said it, she'd voiced the doubts she'd been harboring for weeks, months—almost from the moment she'd let her mother convince her that accepting Dick's proposal was the right thing to do.

Since her parents were out of the country because of Daddy's posting at NATO Headquarters in Belgium, Mom had transferred much of the mother-of-the-bride wedding planning duties to Aunt Marianne. However, even from long distance and via e-mail, Mom had ruled with an iron hand.

Mom had enumerated a list of reasons for marrying Dick Harris and joining the Harris family. The Stantons had had a long history of military service. Though Darcy was their only child—and not a son, much to Daddy's dismay—her parents believed that the Stanton military tradition, if not the name, would live on if their daughter married into another long-standing military family.

But Darcy wasn't ready for offspring to carry on the family tradition. The thought of bearing any man's child, much less Dick's, set her into a panic.

Her mother, just in from Europe, took Darcy by the hands and turned her away from the mirror. She brushed a flyaway strand of hair away from Darcy's face and looked into her eyes. "It's normal to have jitters, Tracy. I felt that way before my wedding. Once it's over, you'll be fine."

Darcy just looked at her and tried to blink the tears

of frustration and panic out of her eyes. How could she explain that the wedding wasn't making her nervous? It was the prospect of marriage...that was scaring the bejesus out of her.

Swallowing, Darcy forced herself to sit still in front of the makeup mirror. She had to do something before she made the biggest mistake of her life. She moistened her lips gone suddenly dry as the Sahara and looked at her mom. "May I have a few minutes to compose myself?"

Her mother nodded and shooed the bridesmaids out, then stepped out of the small room.

No sooner had the door closed behind them than Darcy leapt to action. She shot to her feet and locked the door. She knew what she had to do.

And it wasn't marry Dick.

Darcy rummaged through the drawers of the makeup table for paper and a pen or pencil. Finding none, she grabbed an eyebrow pencil from the new makeup case her mother had insisted she use and scrawled a note on the mirror.

She hated that she'd let it go this far, but it wasn't too late. There would be no wedding. She removed the engagement ring that had always weighed too heavy on her hand and left it on the dressing table.

Then, leaving her mother's bridal veil hanging on a hook on the wall beside the mirror, she grabbed the backpack that contained her wallet and her other important papers and stuffed her jeans and T-shirt inside. Then she pushed open the window.

Taking a deep breath, Darcy unhooked the screen, hiked up her long skirt and perched on the windowsill. Then she swung her legs up over the edge. It wasn't that far to the ground, and the bride's room was on the blind side of the chapel so nobody would see. She could be in her car, still in the parking lot from the rehearsal the night before, and on the road before anyone missed her. A quick change at an out-of-the-way gas station would remove any evidence of the wedding that wasn't to be.

Breathing a silent prayer, Darcy lowered herself to the ground and made her getaway.

Chapter One

In the sinking afternoon sunlight, Technical Sergeant Bill Hays pulled out of the parking lot of his apartment complex. As he drove onto Highway 98, he glanced at the clock on the new dashboard and frowned. Eight o'clock.

Surely the clock hadn't been properly set before he'd taken possession of his new Jeep. He glanced at the government-issue dive watch on his wrist and muttered a curse. He was running even later than he'd thought.

It was bad enough that the two-week field exercise with his Special Tactics Squadron's Silver Team had made him miss his regular trip to his family home in Alabama, but a maintenance problem on the C-130 transport plane bringing him back yesterday had delayed his departure for a week's leave by yet another day. And the long debriefing had made him even later.

Hurlburt Air Force Base might have been the closest Special Tactics Base to his home in Mattison, Alabama, but he might as well have been at his last assignment in California, as difficult as it had been to get home lately. Since he'd been in Florida, it seemed as if circumstances had contrived to keep him away from home.

His late start would keep him from arriving before

his mother went to bed. And the fifty miles or so of country road he had to traverse before he crossed the state line would make it impossible to save time. The roads wound and twisted enough in the daylight, but in the dark they were treacherous. He'd traveled these roads plenty of times, but as night had fallen, a thick, clinging fog had formed, making visibility next to nothing.

Hoping that each curve in the road would reveal a break in the fog and clearer conditions, he inched along.

Just after Bill drove into Alabama, he rounded a curve in the road and had to swerve sharply to avoid hitting something barely visible through the mist.

Muttering a curse, Bill slammed on the brakes and skidded to a halt some twenty or thirty feet beyond the apparition. He blinked and looked back over his shoulder to see what he had missed. A girl materialized and loped toward him with a duffel bag in one hand and a backpack slung over her shoulder.

"What the hell do you think you're doing out here in the middle of the road in the dead of the night?" Bill yelled as she reached the car. "I could have hit you."

She yanked open the passenger door without waiting for an invitation and tossed her bags over the seat to the back. "My old Volkswagen Beetle got me all the way through high school and nursing school, but it finally gave up a mile or so back. I was beginning to think that another car would never come along," she said breathlessly.

"You can't—" Billy stopped himself. It *was* late, and they *were* in the middle of nowhere. "Get in," he muttered.

"Hi, I'm Darcy," she said, sticking out her hand as

she slid onto the seat. "You aren't a serial killer, are you?"

"Bill Hays," he said, then laughed. "Hell, no," he finally managed between chuckles. "I'm one of the good guys according to Uncle Sam."

"Your uncle's recommendation works for me," Darcy said as she buckled herself in. "Where're you heading?"

Bill didn't know what to make of this unexpected passenger, and he wondered what had made her throw caution aside and hop into his car in the middle of nowhere, in the middle of the night. "Mattison, Alabama," he said. "About three hours up the road."

"You came from Florida, then? Me, too."

He nodded, then glanced sideways at her. Darcy might have said she'd been through college, but she didn't look much older than fourteen in that T-shirt and jeans.

Her hair was short, wispy, and flew around her face as she spoke using animated gestures and expressions. She was clean-scrubbed and fresh-looking, with a delicate mouth that seemed very kissable.

Now, where the hell had *that* thought come from?

Hadn't he just assured her that she could trust him? It might have been a long time since he'd been out with a woman, but he wasn't that hard up that he'd get the hots for the first one he came upon. The first one close enough to allow him to smell her perfume.

He had a hard-and-fast rule about remaining free of complications while he was in Special Ops, and this girl—woman—looked like a keeper. He had no room for a woman in his life. Hadn't he seen enough families torn apart because of the demands of the job? Not to mention families broken apart when the service member didn't come home. He would never leave a woman in the same desperate situation his mother had found herself in when his father had died too young and too poor. Or in the same dire straits his sister Lougenia was in when that skunk of a husband had left her.

Women were to be loved, protected, cherished. A man couldn't do a decent job of that if he was off attending to hot spots on the other side of the world.

He shook his head. If he continued to think about kissing her, he might not be able to trust himself. He drew a deep breath and cleared his throat, if not his thoughts. "Where were you going?" he finally managed after he realized that she hadn't said. She hadn't told him much other than that her car had broken down.

"Don't really know," she told him after what seemed to be a long, pregnant silence. "I just graduated nursing school, and I haven't quite figured out what to do with my life. I just knew I had to get away from my family and be on my own for a while."

Bill thought about that for a minute. Maybe her reluctance to talk about herself told him volumes more than if she'd prattled on. He shrugged. "I can take you to the next town," he allowed. "You can get a motel and somebody to tow and fix your car."

He wondered about this small woman who had apparently climbed into a stranger's car without a second thought. She was either desperate or stupid.

He glanced at her and decided that desperate was more the thing. He'd bet she was escaping an abusive family, and climbing into a car with a man she didn't know was probably preferable to going back to a situation she did.

"You sure you want to ride with me?" he wondered out loud before he put the car into gear.

She did what almost seemed to be a double take, then flashed a grin that seemed impossibly large from that small mouth. "I'm game," she said. "It beats walking."

Darcy settled against the seat and breathed in the wonderful, new-car scent. She had worried that she'd be picked up by some Friday-night liquored-up weirdo, and that she'd have to fight for her virtue, if not her life. But the minute she'd seen the clean-cut man in the driver's seat, she'd known she'd be fine. As soon as her gaze had settled on his face, her doubts had vanished.

One look and she knew she'd be safe in his arms.

In his *arms?*

What had made her think that? The last thing she needed was to be thinking about another man, considering the close call she'd just had. No, as soon as they reached civilization, she was going to thank Bill Hays sweetly for picking her up, then she'd get out of his car and do her best to get on with the rest of her life.

Darcy risked a glance at the man driving, his eyes trained steadfastly on the dark road ahead. It was hard to tell much in the dim glow of the dashboard lights, but what she could see was pleasing to the eye.

He was young, maybe a few years older than she. His clothes were clean, and he smelled like he'd just come from a shower. Was he hurrying to meet a sweetheart?

If he was, Darcy thought, she was one lucky girl.

Though he'd made that remark about Uncle Sam, he didn't look much like a soldier. He looked like the college boys she'd known in school, a little bigger, maybe, and rougher around the edges. He wore jeans, faded but not too worn. His pullover shirt stretched tight across a broad chest, not too muscled, but lean and taut. Physical activities were obviously a regular part of his life.

"Say, Darcy," Bill said, interrupting Darcy's thoughts. "I took off without eating. I could sure use a burger or something. What say we stop in Brewton for some eats?"

Why was he asking her? Darcy wondered as they rolled into the marginally congested area of a small, country town. He was the one doing her the favor. She spotted the brightly lit sign of a familiar fast-food chain looming above the trees. Though she'd recognized the fast-food logo, she had yet to see a chain motel she was familiar with. After all, he was just supposed to take her to a motel so she could arrange to have her car towed.

There was no harm in stopping for a bite, though. Sure, she wanted to get as far away from Hurlburt and Dick as she could, but a ten-minute delay to grab a burger wouldn't make that much difference in the scheme of things.

"Thank you. I'd like that," she finally said. "I skipped dinner, too." And breakfast and lunch, thanks to pre-wedding jitters, she didn't say. Darcy pressed her hand against her stomach to silence the rumbling that Bill surely must have heard. Maybe that's why he'd decided to stop.

She felt her face grow hot, and Darcy thanked the powers that be that the car was dark, and Bill wouldn't see her red face. Maybe he wasn't hungry at all, and he'd only decided to stop because of her noisy stomach.

"Let me buy your meal," Darcy suggested. "My way of thanking you for rescuing me. It's the least I can do."

She glanced over at him as they pulled into the parking lot. Hoo boy. His expression looked like a thundercloud on a sultry summer afternoon. She must have wounded his sense of macho. She shrugged. Tough. If he wanted to pay for his dinner, she couldn't stop him. But she wouldn't let him pay for hers.

Truthfully, she was too hungry to argue. She just wanted to eat. Anything to quell that empty feeling in her belly, not to mention her heart.

BILL WATCHED Darcy from over the rim of his cup. Now that he could see her in the bright light of the restaurant, he could see that she was old enough to have graduated from nursing school. She carried a certain degree of confidence that the girls he'd known in Mattison didn't.

He could see, however, how he could have mistaken her for a teenaged runaway in the dark. She was small and slight and wore a short-cropped do that seemed more pixie-like than sophisticated. He'd thought she was blond when he'd first seen her, but in the brightness inside, he could see that her hair was light brown.

Though she wore the uniform common to teenagers and college students—one that he favored, too—the figure that lay beneath the worn T-shirt appeared mature and well-developed. Darcy was tiny, but she wasn't skinny. She must be closer to his age than he'd originally thought.

Not that it mattered that much. He would never see her again after tonight.

In spite of his fatigue, he felt a stirring in his lower regions, but shrugged it away. He'd just met the woman, it was late, and he had promised that she had nothing to fear from him. He raised his cup to his mouth.

He wondered, though, if he should be careful of her.

She seemed safe enough on the outside, but it was what you couldn't see that was the problem.

"Penny for your thoughts."

Bill looked up, startled by the intrusion into his mental meanderings. "What?"

Darcy grinned, the expression making her look as young as he'd judged her to be. "Just wondering what you were thinking about." She nodded toward his drink. "You emptied your cup and didn't even seem to notice."

He put the cup down. Well, he damn sure couldn't tell her what he'd really been thinking about. "Nothing, I guess. And everything."

"Everything?" She arched an eyebrow. "That's heavy. Have you solved the problems of the world?"

Bill shrugged. "Hell. I don't even have a solution for my own," he said, grimacing. "I'd settle for that."

Darcy leaned against the red plastic booth back and gave him an assessing look that made Bill want to squirm. "You don't look like you could possibly have a care in the world," she said finally. "You look healthy, you've recently bought a new car—judging from the smell—and you're just back from Florida."

"It damned sure wasn't a vacation," Bill chuckled dryly. "I'm stationed there and just back from two glorious weeks playing war in the sand in Nevada on a field exercise with my air force combat control team. Now I'm on my way home to visit my dying mother."

Maybe the statement seemed harsh, but he'd had to say it that way at least a thousand times before he could do it without breaking down. It might seem hardhearted, but he had forced himself to face the reality. He was going to have to deal with it sooner or later. Might as well get a head start on it.

Darcy gasped, started to say something, but snapped her mouth shut. Bill wondered what had stopped her. Was it the cold way he had spoken about his mother's illness, or was it that he wasn't the kind of man she'd wanted him to be? Who *had* she expected him to be?

Darcy looked down and selected a cold, limp French fry, dragged it through a puddle of ketchup on the paper from her burger, then put it slowly into her mouth. She chewed thoughtfully as if she were using the exercise as a stalling tactic. Was she trying to decide what to say, or was she trying to avoid putting her foot in her mouth again?

Or was he just reading too damned much into the whole thing?

The silence between them grew awkwardly long.

It was hard not having anyone to talk to about it. It sure wasn't anything he could discuss with any of the guys on the team. Not even his roommate, Ski Warsinski, knew how he felt. He'd tried talking with the chaplain, but he'd only mouthed the standard platitudes. Bill didn't want comfort. He wanted to yell, to shout, to curse God. He couldn't do that with the chaplain. Maybe he could unload on Darcy, because after tonight, he'd never see her again.

He reached across the table and snagged one of Darcy's French fries. He wanted to talk about it, but he didn't know what to say.

"I'm sorry about your mother," she said softly. "Are you in Florida to be closer to home?"

Bill swallowed, then swallowed again. This time it was a lump of emotion he forced down his throat, not a morsel of potato. "Yeah," he said, his voice thick and husky. "We don't know how much time she has."

Darcy reached across the table and placed her hand

over his and squeezed. It was such a simple gesture, but so warm, so giving that it touched something deep inside him. "I'm sorry," she said simply. "Cancer?"

Bill shook his head. "Congestive heart failure. Every time I see her, she's weaker."

Nodding, Darcy spoke. "I understand. Sometimes, heart patients seem so healthy, it's hard to believe that they're sick. Other times, they can appear so fragile that you wonder how they've held on as long as they have. It must be quite a burden for your dad."

Bill drew a deep breath and let it slowly out. "Dad died when I was five. Momma worked hard to keep my older brothers and sisters and me fed and clothed, and now I want to make her last days easier," he said, his voice hoarse. He paused and swallowed, then moistened his dry lips.

"She used to be such a loving, giving person," Bill went on. "It so hard to see her this way." He looked down at Darcy's hand, still covering his. Her skin was so soft, the fingers so delicate, he should hardly have noticed that it was there. But the comfort she provided was enormous.

Darcy didn't respond. Maybe she knew that words weren't necessary. There was nothing to say, but her silence seemed to tell more than a Sunday sermon.

Bill glanced at the clock over the pickup counter. Almost ten. At the rate he was going, he wouldn't get home until midnight. He cleared his throat. "I reckon we'd best get on, then," he finally said, his voice strained, thick.

"Yeah. I guess so." Darcy lifted her hand, and in spite of the negligible weight she'd removed, his hand felt cold without it there resting on his.

DARCY GAZED OUT the window and tried to stay awake and on the lookout for a motel. So far, all she'd seen were local places that looked none too reputable. She might be eager to get away from Dick, but she wasn't that desperate. And Bill had agreed to let her ride along as far as Montgomery where there were more to choose from and the choices were likely cleaner.

In the meantime, she had to keep her eyes open. That had been easy when they were driving through the countryside on the small, back roads. She'd been riding shotgun, helping Bill to guide them through the dense fog, and the constant motion and the stops and turns had kept her alert. Now that Bill had pulled onto I-65 and the fog was gone, the never-changing scenery, unbroken by bright lights or towns, and the comfortable seat seemed to hypnotize her.

Bill turned up the radio and opened a window, to keep from going to sleep himself, she supposed. As it was, her long, sleepless pre-wedding night and even longer day, began to catch up with her. Darcy found herself nodding off and, she tried to think of something to keep her awake.

She yawned. "Do you have a girl waiting for you at home?" she said, trying to make conversation.

Bill shrugged. "Nope."

She didn't know why she cared, considering she was hitchhiking and she'd never see him again after tonight, but that small bit of information about him seemed sad. "Do you have other family in Mattison?"

"Yeah."

Darcy shrugged. Of course, he did. He'd already mentioned siblings. Obviously, he wasn't in the mood to talk. "Would you rather I be quiet or do you need me to talk to help you stay awake?"

"Naw, I'm fine. It isn't that late yet, and we're trained to do without sleep. It's part of the job."

"Oh. I'll just shut up then. When we get to town, you can drop me off, and I'll be out of your hair."

"No problem."

Darcy wondered how much company she could be, sitting there like a bump on a log. She felt about as useful as training wheels on a tricycle, but she was grateful not to have to make idle conversation. Just being in Bill's strong, silent presence was comforting.

The quiet companionship would be over too soon, she thought as they passed a road sign announcing that Montgomery was thirty-eight miles away.

Thirty-eight miles. At seventy miles an hour, that meant about thirty more minutes in his company. Thirty-eight miles and Bill would drop her off at some motel. Thirty-eight miles and she could get a good night's sleep and then figure out what to do with the rest of her life.

Montgomery was big enough to have several hospitals, she supposed. Hospitals were always short of nurses. Maybe she could get a job at one of them and start over free from pressure from her family. Free of Dick.

Then she wondered if it wouldn't be better to just keep going without letting anybody know where she was. Even Bill Hays knowing that she had ended up in Montgomery might bring Dick and her family to her.

No, she wasn't trying to hide from them. She just didn't want to deal with them for a while. She needed time to get her head together. She wasn't ready to face Dick, her parents, or even Uncle John right now.

She wanted to be just plain Darcy and to have the luxury of time to explore who that really was. Dick

Harris and the Stanton family with their long military tradition couldn't seem to understand that.

Darcy leaned back against the seat, pillowed her head with her bent arm against the window frame, and closed her eyes.

THE LIGHTS of the city loomed ahead of him, and Bill sighed. In just a few minutes, Darcy would be gone.

The roadside information signs indicated a wide selection of discount motels at the first exit, and he sighed again. He engaged the turn signal and started to ease into the right lane.

Then Bill looked across the seat to Darcy, sleeping on the seat beside him. Yes, he knew she expected him to stop at a motel in Montgomery, but she looked so peaceful curled up there that he didn't have the heart to wake her. What had made her so tired that she dropped off next to a stranger? He flipped the turn signal off and remained on the highway.

There were plenty of other motels on the road ahead before they got through Montgomery. Who said they had to stop at the first one? Darcy hadn't. She could get a room at the last one out of town just as easily.

Bill drove on through the sleeping city, then he drove past the last Montgomery exit, crossed the Alabama River and approached the first off-ramp for Pittsville just a few miles from Mattison. There were fewer motels here, but they were close.

Close to what? he asked himself. Or maybe to whom?

And why was he attracted to this woman he'd just met? It wasn't as if he were looking for a woman, even if he had time for one. Duty, physical training, night school and his mother kept him busy enough for three men. The last thing he needed was any distraction from his goals.

But what a distraction Darcy would be, he couldn't help thinking. He'd practically been a monk since he'd left high school and home. He'd wanted so much to pull himself out of the near-poverty he'd been raised in that he'd devoted all his time to the air force, to getting the education his mother couldn't afford to give him, to making something of himself.

If he could just get his degree, he could obtain an appointment to Officer Training School, become an officer and gain respect in the world. After almost ten years, the degree was in sight.

But there were times when he had a few minutes to himself that he couldn't help realizing just how lonely that climb toward the top had been. He looked at Darcy and wondered how it would be if....

No. He shook his head. He didn't have the time.

He realized suddenly that as he'd been woolgathering, he'd driven right through Pittsville. Now what? He looked at Darcy asleep on the seat and shrugged. He could save her the cost of a night's stay in a motel and put her up at Momma's. There might be a time later on when she would need that money.

He could drive her to Montgomery in the morning.

He yawned and stretched and looked for the familiar landmarks near his home. He saw the old Shell station on the corner, closed now, but still bearing the familiar orange sign. The station had once been adjacent to a motel, but the motel had been closed since before he was born. The interstate had gone through, and the traffic on the Mattison highway had dwindled to nothing.

There was Mrs. Scarborough's house three miles down the road from the little farm where he had grown up. He passed the Popwell's place and Maggie Montoya's restored house, then he saw the dirt road home. He eased on the brakes and steered onto the lane.

Darcy stirred. "Are we in Montgomery yet?" she said through a yawn.

"Hush, Darcy," he said. "We're home." And that simple statement seemed so right, that it needed almost no explanation; although he knew he owed her one. "You were sleeping so soundly, I didn't want to wake you. Momma'll have a bed for you, and we can figure out what to do tomorrow."

Darcy seemed to have heard his explanation, but she didn't react. Was he going to have to explain again? Would she be angry that he had taken her home? Now, he wondered if he'd made a mistake by not dropping her off in Montgomery as they'd planned.

"Oh. Okay," she mumbled, confirming his suspicion that she wasn't fully awake.

Bill wondered again what had exhausted her so that she'd succumbed so completely to sleep. Had there really been a car broken down by the road? Or had she hitchhiked all the way? That would explain her exhaustion.

As he parked in front of the house, he realized with alarm that the lights were still on. Was Momma sick? Or had she simply fallen asleep in front of the television?

The family had tried to get her to accept live-in help, but she always brushed them off, saying she didn't want a stranger in her house rearranging things, making it not her own. When she was ready for help, she'd tell them. Bill wondered if she was finally ready.

Then he looked up, surprised, when his mother flung open the screen door and stood at the top of the porch steps. She looked better than she had in months. Was she improving?

He knew better than to believe that, but a guy could always hope. He turned off the engine and climbed out of the car. He had to explain about Darcy before he brought her in to spend the night.

Darcy felt, more than heard, the car door slam. She struggled to rouse herself from the depths of exhaustion, but her mind refused to clear. Had Bill said they were home? She'd started to correct him, but it wasn't worth the effort.

She rubbed her eyes and looked around. They seemed to be in somebody's yard. Had Bill's car broken down, too? Had he had to stop to ask help from a stranger?

No. He seemed to know the woman, dressed in a worn housecoat, coming slowly down the steps from the homey-looking front porch complete with an inviting swing and a profusion of potted plants.

Then Bill's comment about being home started to make sense. This wasn't Montgomery, and it sure wasn't a motel.

He had taken her home to his mother's house.

Darcy stretched and yawned, then fumbled to release her seat belt. She had to get out and move around. She'd been sitting on this seat too long, and her neck was stiff. She needed to work the kinks out of her back and to get the blood circulating again. Maybe then she could think.

She and Bill could sort everything else out later. Or tomorrow, she supposed. She glanced at her watch. It was almost midnight. He'd said his mother would have a bed, and that's all she cared about for now.

She looked toward the house and couldn't help being touched by the mother and son reunion.

"What are you doing up so late?" Bill called as he hurried up the dirt walk to the house.

Mrs. Hays laughed, her merry tone belying her serious condition. She looked well enough, but Darcy's training allowed her to recognize the subtle signs that indicated her illness. "You said you were bringing me a surprise, Billy boy. You had my curiosity running so fast, I couldn't sleep."

Bill had forgotten about the comment he'd made when he'd called to say he'd be later than usual. He'd told her about ordering the new Jeep some time ago, but he hadn't told her that he'd finally gotten it. He'd said he was bringing home a surprise.

A brilliant smile lit up Momma's face, and Bill turned to see Darcy push open the passenger-side door and climb out, stretching after hours in the car.

"Oh son. It's the best surprise you ever could give me," Momma said, hurrying down the steps, her gait more steady than he'd seen in months. "I didn't think you'd find a bride before…before…. Well, you know." She smiled again and, arms outstretched, hurried toward Darcy.

He realized with horror what his mother must be thinking. Now, what was he supposed to do? Tell her the truth and break her heart?

Chapter Two

Bill's mother folded Darcy into a warm embrace. "Welcome to the family, daughter," she said, her voice thick with emotion. "It makes an old lady happy to know that her youngest son is finally going to settle down."

Fortunately for Darcy, the fact that she was enveloped in Mrs. Hays's frail embrace kept her from displaying her shock at what the woman had just said. Had she really just called her daughter?

What's going on here?

She glanced over Mrs. Hays's shoulder and saw the panicked look on Bill's face. At least he was as startled about this as she was. Darcy started to push herself out of Mrs. Hays's embrace and explain, but Bill shook his head and silently mouthed the word, *please*.

Darcy signaled her objection, but Bill just shook his head again. Considering the woman's health and the terribly late hour, she tacitly agreed to go on with the ruse. At least until morning.

They would have to explain then and make sure Mrs. Hays understood her mistake. As if she didn't have enough sorting out of her own to do.

She patted Mrs. Hays gently on the back and pushed herself out of the woman's embrace. "It's so nice to meet you, Mrs. Hays. Bill has told me so much about you.''

''Well, Billy surely hasn't said anything at all about you,'' Mrs. Hays said, shaking her head. ''If you're going to be in the family, you can call me Momma. Or, at least, Nettie. Mrs. Hays sounds so unfriendly, don't you think?''

''Yes, ma'am, I suppose it does. I'll be happy to call you Nettie.'' There was absolutely no way Darcy was going to call the woman Momma. That would just be too cruel.

It was bad enough that she and Bill were going to have to burst her bubble in the morning. She glanced up at Bill and raised an eyebrow and hoped he got the message.

She wasn't sure what the message was, but she did want him to know that she wasn't happy with the turn of events.

After all, she'd just escaped from one fiancé. She certainly did not need another one.

Darcy smiled at Mrs. Hays. ''It's awfully late, Mrs. H—I mean, Nettie. Why don't we get you settled, and we can chat in the morning.''

''I do look forward to that, hon. And you are right. I am tired. I guess all this excitement's done worn me out.'' She turned toward Bill. ''Help me up the stairs, son, so I can go to bed. I'll leave you to settle your fiancée in— Why, I do declare, you have not introduced me to my future daughter-in-law.''

''It's Darcy Stanton, Nettie,'' Darcy said, forcing a smile. She waved and Nettie smiled back, then took Bill's arm and allowed him to help her up the short flight of steps.

Wondering how they were going to talk their way

out of this charade without hurting the woman struggling up the stairs, Darcy stood outside in the glare of the security lamp and took stock of her surroundings.

The house was small, and Darcy wondered how the woman could have raised five kids in it. But the lawn was trimmed and the flower beds neat and cared for. Obviously, Bill's brothers and sisters were coming around to help. She thought about the strong love they must share and weighed it against her family's feelings about duty and tradition. They didn't compare.

She could see a couple of outbuildings beyond the small house: a chicken house, she supposed, and a shed or a small barn. Mrs. Hays might have kept some chickens and a few cows at one time, but Darcy doubted she was up to keeping them now.

It reminded her of something out of the Laura Ingalls Wilder books she'd loved as a child. Darcy suspected that it had been fun growing up here where the kids could run free and grow like weeds. Not like her own heavily restricted upbringing on military bases all over the world. She'd often had to be escorted to school by armed guards and had only dreamed of running free. The Hays family might have been poor, but her upbringing hadn't been any better. At least, Bill and his siblings had the roots and stability she'd always craved.

"What do you think?"

Darcy turned, startled, at the sound of Bill's voice behind her. "About what?"

She looked so much like an angel, Bill thought as he hurried down the porch steps to where Darcy waited outside in the yard. He shouldn't have left her there, but he had to take care of Momma first. Hell, he shouldn't have gotten Darcy in this mess in the first place.

He drew in a long breath and answered her question. "The Hays homestead, I suppose," Bill said. "It's gone to seed some since Momma's been sick, but it was a nice place to grow up." And for the first time in his life, Bill realized that it had been.

"That's exactly what I was thinking. I always dreamed of living in a place like this. I bet you had chickens and cows when you were growing up and had chores and everything."

"Didn't you?"

"Didn't I what? Have chickens and cows?"

"No, chores," Bill corrected.

"Oh, sure. Clean up my room. Dishes. I always wondered what it would be like to feed chickens, gather the eggs, and milk cows."

Bill shrugged. "Feeding chickens is no big thing. You just toss out feed, and the chickens come running. It was a little more exciting to get the eggs. Sometimes an ol' hen wouldn't want to part with hers, and I'd have to shoo her off. She'd go with feathers flying and clucking fit to beat the band." He chuckled and headed for his Jeep. "Can't tell you much about milking, though. We just had steers."

"Steers?" Darcy asked as Bill opened the back door to the Jeep.

Bill handed her the backpack and hoisted her duffel bag out along with his own, then slammed the door shut. "Yeah, we got bull calves free from the dairy farm down the road toward Pittsville and raised them for beef."

He smiled inwardly as Darcy grimaced.

"How can you eat anything that you've looked in the face?" she said, horror written all over hers.

"You can eat anything if you're hungry enough, I

reckon," Bill said as he turned toward the house. "You comin'?" He strode up the stairs. "It's been a helluva long day, and I'd just as soon hit the sack than stand out here and talk about butchering beef." He could stand around and talk with her as long as she could, but Bill could see that she was just as tired as he was. She might be wide awake right now, but he'd bet she'd drop off as soon as her head hit the pillow. Just as he would.

Just not together.

Why did he keep thinking about that?

He wouldn't mind sleeping with her, but he'd only known Darcy for a few hours, and tomorrow they'd say goodbye. It was nice to dream about, but in the morning he would wake up and face reality.

Bill stopped at the front door to reach for the knob, and Darcy collided with him. He paused, enjoying the feeling of her soft form against him, but she drew away quickly enough. He turned around. "I want to thank you for what you did back there," he said. "I know we're going to have to come clean with Momma in the morning, but it was more important to get her to bed tonight. It'll be easier for her to take when she's rested," he said.

"You're probably right," Darcy said. "But you will explain it to her first thing, won't you?" She yawned and rubbed her eyes. "And you'll drive me back to Montgomery?"

"I'll take you anywhere you want," he told her, but the only place he could think about taking her was to bed. His, not one in his sisters' room where Momma'd said to put her. He figured it wouldn't hurt anything to think about it. He was realistic enough to know it wasn't going to happen anytime soon. No, he told himself, firmly. It wasn't ever going to happen.

"Thank you," Darcy said and yawned again. "Now, could you show me where to sleep before I curl up on that porch swing over there?"

Bill chuckled. "I think I can show you something softer than that old porch swing. Come on inside. Momma said you could have Lougenia and Earline's room." He pulled open the screen door and ushered Darcy inside.

A ROOSTER CROWED, and Darcy roused briefly from deep sleep. She looked around the room, still colorless in the gray morning light, and listened for any sounds to indicate anyone in the house was up. Hearing none, she rolled over and burrowed her face into the pillow.

The next time Darcy woke, daylight was streaming in through windows unshuttered against the morning sun. She smelled bacon and coffee, and suddenly she was wide awake.

She was in Bill Hays's mother's house, and on top of that, she was pretending to be his fiancée. But only for a few minutes longer. Bill had promised to straighten it all out with his mother. Maybe he already had.

A girl could hope.

Darcy pushed herself up on her elbows and looked around the room she'd been too tired to study last night. It had obviously been a girl's room. Two girls. Hadn't Bill mentioned two names last night? There was another twin bed, the mate to the one she was in. Both were draped with pink chenille bedspreads, and a collection of dolls and stuffed animals watched her from the tops of both dressers and shelves on the wall. The toys were as dusty as the curling posters on the wall were worn.

Bill had mentioned that he was the youngest, so these

sisters must have preceded him by five or ten years. The posters were from the eighties. She recognized Kirk Cameron and a young John Travolta. She smiled with the realization that teenaged girls were pretty much the same no matter where or when they grew up.

A light tapping on the door caused her to jerk the chenille cover up over her chest. She hadn't packed a nightgown in her duffle bag and had slept in a T-shirt minus her bra. "Yes?" she managed, after her heart stopped beating a mile a minute.

"I've got breakfast ready. I didn't wake you, did I?" Bill asked from outside the door.

"No, I was up. I'll just be a minute." Darcy threw off the covers and tumbled out of the bed. She found her duffle and rummaged through it until she located fresh underwear and a clean T-shirt. She wished they weren't so wrinkled, but it couldn't be helped. She hadn't expected to be meeting her fiancé's mother.

She hadn't expected to acquire another fiancé on the same day she'd dumped the last one.

No, she reminded herself. In ten minutes or so, they'd straighten it out, and she wouldn't have to pretend anymore.

She pulled on the T-shirt, slipped on her shoes, then grabbed her toothbrush and headed toward the bathroom. She might as well put her best face forward when she faced the music. The best one she could, considering.

She just hoped that Mrs. Hays wouldn't be too upset about the truth.

BILL POURED his mother a glass of orange juice and watched as she drank it. It saddened him to see her so weak, and he felt so helpless not to be able to do any-

thing about it. She'd been so strong when he was growing up, and now she seemed so frail.

"Happy Birthday, son," Momma said. "In all the
excitement last night I plumb forgot about it. We'll have
your party tonight. Along with your birthday, we'll have
something else to celebrate."

"Something else?"

"Well, surely you want to announce your engagement," she said. "I called Lougenia first thing this
morning and told her all about it. She was so excited."

Damn, Bill thought. *Now what do I do? Why in the
hell did I think we could get away with it? We should've
told her the truth last night.* "Momma, I wish you
hadn't done that," he said, tempering his anger. After
all, he wasn't mad at Momma. He was mad at himself.

"Oh, did you want to save it till the party this ev-
enin'?" She looked apologetic. "I'm sorry, I didn't
mean to steal your thunder by telling your sister."

"It's all right, Momma. We'll sort it out later." The
sooner it happened, the better it would be for everyone,
Bill couldn't help thinking. At least, Momma hadn't
told his sister Earline. If she had, everyone in Pitt
County would know by now.

"Why didn't you tell us about your sweetheart,
son?"

Bill drew in a deep breath. Why didn't he just get it
over with now? He looked up and saw Darcy coming
down the hallway toward the kitchen. Might as well
wait until they could do it together. "We haven't known
each other very long. She's been away in school." It
was the truth, as far as it went.

"Why, good morning, Darcy. Did you sleep good?"
Momma's face lit up like a runway strobe light when
Darcy entered the room.

Darcy looked so fresh and beautiful in a well-scrubbed way, even after their late, late night and sleeping in a strange bed. Bill knew he couldn't have her, but he sure wished he could. Listen to him. He sounded like he was talking about a stray puppy, not a person with real feelings and needs.

"Yes, ma'am. Like a baby." Darcy shot a questioning glance Bill's way, and he shook his head slightly in answer to her unspoken question.

"Bacon's ready, and I'll have eggs scrambled in a couple of minutes," Bill said. Anything to change the subject.

Darcy smiled at Momma, then hurried over to Bill. She spoke to him in a low whisper. "Should your mother be eating eggs and bacon, considering her condition?"

Bill started to answer, but Momma answered for him. "Ain't nothing wrong with my hearing. I know I can't eat that high c'lesterol stuff, but I keep it on hand for Bill when he comes. Already had my oatmeal."

"Darcy just graduated from nursing school," Bill volunteered, perhaps as a way of explaining her...what? Concern?

"Well, that is so wonderful. Earline wanted to go to nursing school, but she married Edd instead. Did get her Licensed Practical Nurse Certificate at the vocational school. But she don't use it since the kids come along."

"Yes, ma'am." Darcy stood awkwardly between the table and the stove and hooked her thumbs in her belt loops while Bill scrambled the eggs. "Can I help with anything?"

At least he could give her something to do. "Here, put the bacon on the table." Bill didn't wait for her to do it, but poured the beaten eggs into the skillet. The eggs sizzled as they hit the hot surface, and he quickly stirred them up. "Coffee and mugs are on the counter."

"Will you be staying here the whole time of Bill's leave?"

"No, ma'am," Darcy said as she put the bacon down and reached for a mug and coffee.

"Please, hon. You make me sound like an old school teacher or something. Call me Nettie if you can't call me Momma."

"Yes, ma— I mean, Nettie. No, ma'am. I have to look for a place in Montgomery." She stirred some powdered creamer into her coffee from a jar on the counter, then settled at the table across from Momma. "I thought there might be some hospitals in town with openings for nurses, so I thought I'd apply. I'm so ready to get a job and live on my own after all the rules and restrictions of school."

He had to hand it to her, Bill thought. She was covering herself well. So far, she hadn't lied, but she hadn't said anything that would get him in any serious trouble, either. He scraped the eggs onto two plates and carried them to the table.

"Thank you," Darcy said. "I could get used to being waited on."

"Well, you'd best get what you can now," Momma said. "Once you start at a hospital, I reckon you'll be waiting on everybody else." She turned to Bill. "Son, get some silverware and set down before everything turns to rubber."

Darcy smiled. Bill had seemed so in command when she'd met him on the road. When they'd talked in the car and at the restaurant, even when he had allowed her that brief glimpse of his vulnerable side, she'd had the feeling that he was in charge. Now, she could see that his mother had him wrapped around her little finger.

"What's so funny?" Bill said as he plopped a fork down in front of her and took another chair.

"Nothing. I was just enjoying watching your mother boss you around."

Bill grimaced, the wry expression softening the angular lines of his face and making him look briefly boyish. "Believe me, I have people telling me what to do every day." He scooped up a forkful of eggs.

"You know something, hon," Nettie said abruptly, interrupting the pleasant banter. "Doctor Williamson in Pittsville is looking for a new nurse. I'd bet he'd hire you in a minute."

Darcy swallowed her eggs, almost choking on them. Every time she thought she was about to extricate herself from this mess, she found herself in deeper. "I was really looking forward to hospital work," she said. "They pay better. I do have to support myself, you know."

"Don't be silly. You can stay here with me. After all, you're going to be part of the family. Doc's my doctor, and he's just about ten miles down the road. You'd have much better hours, and you could save what you earn toward your weddin'."

"You think you have it all figured out. Don't you, Momma?" Bill said. "Darcy wants to live on her own for a while before she gets tied down with marriage."

"Psh. It's lonely livin' by yourself. I should know. And I know too darn much about working odd shifts. I did enough of that at the cotton gin when you were growing up." She smiled at Darcy. "At least, think about it, hon. I could surely use the company."

"Yes, ma'am. I'll think about it."

"Well, if you don't mind, I'm going to go on and set on the porch for a while. I do love to swing and smell the flowers while it's cool in the mornings." She pushed herself up out of her chair and slowly made her way toward the front door.

"I thought we were going to straighten out this mess first thing in the morning," Darcy hissed, the minute she thought Nettie was out of hearing range. "You can't keep lying to your mother like this. The longer it goes on, the harder it'll be for us to explain our way out of it."

"I know," Bill said slowly. "I tried this morning before you got up, but damn it, she's already gone and told Lougenia about it. Lou'll probably tell somebody else, and so on and so on. If she's told Earline, it'll be all over the county by nightfall. I don't know what to do."

"You tell your sister the truth," Darcy said firmly. "She's not old and sick. She can handle it."

As much as she hated lying, Darcy hated hurting Bill's mother more. She liked this gentle woman who, in spite of her obvious poor health, had welcomed Darcy into her home with open arms. She'd offered Darcy her home, her love, and Darcy felt like a number-one heel for leading Nettie on like this. "We have to straighten this thing out, now."

Bill just sat there, an impassive look hardening his face and making him look more like the trained military man he was than the farm boy she'd first supposed him to be. Had he even heard anything she'd said?

Darcy wanted to hit him.

His face brightening, he looked up and grinned. "Think about this," he said. "And I want you to listen to my entire proposition before you say anything."

"Something tells me I'm not going to like this," Darcy said warily.

"Just hear me out. It's important to me."

"Go ahead." Bill had done her a big favor; she might as well listen.

"You know about my mother's health problem. As a nurse, you know how precarious her situation can be." He took Darcy's hand, sending a tremor of... excitement?...running through her. "You with me so far?"

Darcy nodded, still wondering where he was going with this. "Go on."

"My family has been trying to get Momma to allow somebody to come in and help her out, but she will have nothing to do with the idea. Says she doesn't want some stranger in her house messing with her things. Earline does what she can, but she has her own family. She stops by on her way to work, and her daughter Leah—she's twelve—comes in to sit with her and do some light chores after school, but there's nobody here with Momma at night. Even with Leah here all day in the summer, we worry." He met her eyes. "As you may not have noticed last night when we came in...."

Darcy blushed, remembering how she had fallen asleep and slept all the way through Montgomery.

"Anyway, we live a good ways from town. If Momma needed help, it would be a long time coming from Pittsville. And then she'd probably have to be transferred to Montgomery anyway." He paused and looked at her as if trying to gauge her reactions.

"What are you getting at?"

"It would sure take a load off my mind if you stayed here. Momma wouldn't have a stranger messing with her things, and you would have a place to stay until you got on your feet.'' He looked at her, his face radiating hope. ''What do you say?''

Darcy stared at him, speechless. How could she possibly respond to this? Bill had promised her that they'd untangle this mess in the morning, not make it even worse.

''I know it's a lot to ask, but think about Momma. She needs you, even if she won't admit it.''

''I...'' Darcy struggled for some kind of response. The thing he was asking her to do was...was... preposterous. ''I'd feel like a heel for deceiving her. She deserves better than that.''

''She deserves to be well and healthy enough to enjoy retirement after working two or three jobs to feed us.'' Bill drew in a ragged breath. ''But she won't get that.'' His voice broke. ''At least, make her last days easier.''

Talk about a guilt trip. But why should she feel guilty about this? Nettie wasn't her mother. Why should she get involved at all? The last thing she needed was another fiancé when she'd just gotten rid of the last one. Even if Bill *was* only a pretend one.

Darcy tried to consider all the angles, not easy to do with Bill sitting just across the table looking at her. He'd given her some of the most compelling reasons to stay. But they couldn't justify lying.

She'd been living a lie for the last six months. She'd been pretending to be someone she was not. Darcy did not want to have to do it again.

Then she thought about Nettie Hays who had been so kind to her, so welcoming. The woman was ill. She didn't have much longer to live. If it would make Nettie's last days easier, maybe she could do it. After all, Bill would know that it wasn't real.

She knew it wasn't real. Nobody was fooling anybody.

Except Nettie.

And, the reality was that Nettie needed someone to be with her, and Darcy needed a place to stay. A place to think about what she wanted to do with the rest of her life without the distraction of her parents, her uncle and aunt and Dick. Maybe Mattison was the perfect place to hide while she got her head together.

She glanced out the kitchen window to where Nettie Hays sat swaying gently back and forth on the porch swing, humming a tune that Darcy couldn't quite catch. She looked across the table to Bill.

He must have sensed her wavering thoughts, for he reached across the table and captured her hand in his large, strong one. He squeezed it gently, almost seeming to telegraph his feelings through his touch. That's when Darcy knew she'd agree to do this foolhardy thing. Bill seemed to understand her unasked question. "I promise it will be nothing more than a business arrangement. I won't expect anything of you except to help Momma," he said huskily.

Bill needed her.

He needed her to be his eyes and ears and to take care of his mother when he couldn't. To be here for him when times were rough and he couldn't come. Bill had helped her out when she needed him. What else could she do?

Knowing she would probably regret this, she swallowed hard and looked at him. "All right," she said, feeling the warmth of his hand on hers. "We can try it. After all, who could it hurt?"

Chapter Three

Darcy hung up the phone and sighed gustily. What had made her think that she'd be able to find someone to tow her car out of that roadside ditch and repair it, when she didn't know the name of a single garage and tow company in south Alabama? And it didn't help that she wasn't exactly sure where the ditch containing her car was.

She'd already spent a huge amount of time calling long distance trying to get somebody to take care of the problem, but she'd gotten the royal runaround. And she'd thought military bureaucracy was hard to circumvent. She'd never tried to work within the system of a small Alabama town, and she was doing it blind from a hundred miles away.

At least she had been successful in getting an appointment for an interview with Dr. Williamson for the opening he had. It amazed her that he still kept his office open on Saturday mornings.

Darcy wondered if landing the job would be as easy as landing the interview. No, she told herself. Nothing had ever come easy for her before. She might as well be prepared for a long, hard haul. Still, it would be nice to have a job lined up right away.

She started to try again to find someone to tow her car, but stopped when she heard the sound of a car pulling into the drive. Had Bill returned from Barney's General Store, or had the first of the party guests begun to arrive?

When she'd agreed to pretend to be engaged to Bill, she hadn't known that the family was planning a party tonight. If they were really in love, she would have known that Bill had celebrated his twenty-eighth birthday alone while he'd been in Nevada on the last training exercise. It might be a birthday party, but it was too much to hope that the "engagement" would not come up.

Still, she hoped for a miracle because it was going to be hard to lie to his friends and relatives without having her partner in crime standing at her elbow. After all, they had to be able to keep their stories straight.

At least, for a little while.

Darcy breathed a relieved sigh as she heard Bill call from outside. "Come open the door. My hands are full."

She scurried to the door and let her "fiancé" in. She had been trying to force herself to keep thinking of Bill as her intended so she wouldn't slip up in front of his guests, but when she was alone it was hard to do. Now that she could see him again in the flesh, her breath caught in her throat. Any woman would be proud to be engaged to him. She could stare all day at his broad chest, showed off to perfection by the form-fitting T-shirt the color of Carolina blue skies. And those faded, snug jeans were bleached out in the most interesting places and made her wonder what lay beneath.

She almost wished she really was.

Darcy drew a deep breath and forced herself to speak.

"How did that short list grow to three full grocery sacks?" she asked as she took the bag dangling precariously from Bill's right hand and headed with it to the kitchen. "I thought you were getting milk and ice."

"Got two more bags in the Cherokee," he said as he lowered the two he carried onto the kitchen table. He shrugged. "You know how it is. You see stuff you need...." He paused and grinned. "And you see stuff you don't really need but you kinda want, and pretty soon your short list has grown a foot long." He turned to go back to the car, but looked back over his shoulder. "I saw Earline at the store."

"And...?" Darcy asked, hoping the comment wasn't prefacing bad news.

"She'd heard the news from Lou and was already blabbing to Barney. Who knows how many other folks she'd already spread the word to by then? Don't reckon we'll have to make much of an announcement tonight. Pretty much everybody in the county's gonna know."

Darcy sighed. "That's what I was afraid of."

FOR SOME REASON everyone was late this time. Bill stood by the front window watching for the first car to arrive. The lateness of the guests, family mostly, had given him a little more time to get his story straight with Darcy, he supposed, and it saved Momma from the stress and commotion of all the kids so soon.

Still, he couldn't help thinking that he wanted to get this over with as soon as he could. It was one thing to stretch the truth to his mother for a good reason, but another thing to announce it to half the town. If they weren't careful, they would find it in the local paper, and he sure wanted to prevent that.

And was it really a *white* lie?

It was one thing to let Momma think what she thought, it was another thing to carry it on as if it were true. Damn, when did life get so complicated?

"How do I look?"

He turned to see Darcy standing in the hallway to the back of the house.

"I don't have any party clothes with me," she said, smiling apologetically. "I wasn't expecting to be engaged quite so soon." She struck a pose, holding her arms out and doing a slow turn. "This was the best I could do."

Billy whistled, long and low. If that was short notice, he'd like to see what she looked like when she was really trying.

No. He wouldn't. This was make-believe, he reminded himself. They were pretending for Momma's sake.

Darcy was wearing jeans, and he wondered if she had any other clothes. This pair was newer, and instead of a T-shirt, she had on a sweater set in a soft blue that hugged her curves, yet looked delicate and demure. How'd she manage that? And why did he keep thinking about her as if she really were his fiancée?

"Oh, you look fine," he murmured, shaking his head appreciatively. "More than fine."

"Thank you," Darcy answered primly. "I didn't have anything dressy with me. I thought I'd be able to send for the rest of my clothes when I got where I was going and before I needed anything special."

She hadn't really thought that, consciously anyway, but she had sent most of her things ahead—to Dick's place—and had only brought the bare minimum with her. Mother and Aunt Marianne had enjoyed shopping for the honeymoon trousseau she hadn't really wanted, and she'd left that behind when she'd taken off. All she had were the clothes in the duffle bag she'd left in the car.

Strange, she thought, that she'd packed enough in her bag for the trip from school in North Carolina to keep her going until she landed on her feet. Even when she hadn't known she was going to run. Or had she?

She had an oyster-colored linen suit, badly in need of ironing now, her best uniform left from nursing training, and some jeans and T-shirts. She certainly had packed much more than she needed for the trip to Hurlburt Field.

"Will I pass inspection?" she asked him.

Bill whistled again. "You will do just fine. I might have to fight the other guys off my gir—" He suddenly realized what he'd said. "I'm sorry." Bill shrugged. "I know we're only pretending for Momma's sake."

"Apology accepted. After all, we have to make it look good." Darcy grinned. "Feel free to fight off any interlopers you feel like. It'll do my ego good."

"I don't know about your ego, Darcy. But it'll damn sure do mine just fine." Bill grinned. "I don't exactly have the reputation of a ladies' man around here."

Darcy arched an eyebrow. "You couldn't prove it by me. You sure did a good job of picking me up."

"Ha ha," Bill said dryly. "I might have come to your rescue, but it wasn't exactly on a white charger."

"No, just a dark green Jeep Cherokee. That was good enough for me." Funny, she hadn't noticed the color of the Jeep when he'd picked her up.

Now she noticed everything.

Like the way Bill's chest had expanded when he'd looked at her. And the way he cared for his mother, and his wide-open face, and his green eyes and the touch of his hand... No, she couldn't be thinking about that. It isn't real.

It isn't real, she reminded herself again.

She shook her thoughts away, and looked up at Bill, only to find herself drowning in his deep green eyes. She forced herself to look away before it was too late.

For what?

"What else do we have to do to get ready?" Darcy asked, though she knew they were as ready as they could be. She had to say something to change the subject. Anything. They were heading toward dangerous territory if they didn't switch to a different topic of conversation.

Bill shrugged and shoved his hands into his pockets. "Everything is pretty much under control for now. Lou and Earline are bringing the party. All we had to do was make sure everything was cleaned up and ready." He smiled crookedly. Odd that they were both acting like a couple of teenagers on a first date. But then, this *was* more like a first date than a birthday-slash-engagement announcement party.

At least on a first date, they would have been alone.

The crunch of tires on the gravel driveway saved him from any more deep thinking.

"Looks like the first wave is here. I reckon we better get to battle stations." He glanced out the window. "It's Earline and Edd and the kids." With Earline's kids around, at least, he wouldn't have time to think.

BILL WAS RIGHT when he'd told her they wouldn't have to make an announcement, Darcy thought as she assessed the crowd in the small living room. It seemed as if everyone who came in had already heard. It might have saved them from having to stand up in front of the group and tell a bald-faced lie, but it hadn't made it any easier.

Because everyone already knew, she found herself fielding questions that she and Bill had not prepared for.

Like, when was the wedding?

Since there wasn't really going to be a wedding, they hadn't thought that anyone would ask. Both of them had severely underestimated the curiosity of the residents of Mattison, Alabama.

"You really ought to set a date soon, girl," Ruby Scarborough, Bill's first-grade teacher, said as she cornered Darcy in the nook by the fireplace, far across the room from Bill.

Bill had told Darcy that Mrs. Scarborough considered herself a member of every family in the community since she'd educated all the kids and most of the parents as well. She attended every party, wedding shower and reception, whether she was invited or not.

"Gosh, Mrs. Scarborough, Bill and I hadn't even thought that far ahead," Darcy told her truthfully. "We've only just gotten engaged, and we want to enjoy that part of our relationship for now."

Mrs. Scarborough took her by the arm and pulled her farther to the side. "You know, Nettie doesn't have much more time," she said in hushed tones. "Perhaps, you should think of doing it sooner instead of later."

"Yes, ma'am. We know. But I've just gotten out of nursing school, and I want to work for a while first." Darcy knew her reply was lame, but what else could she say?

Bill came to her rescue. "You'll excuse me, Miz Scarborough, if I steal my fiancée away."

"You're excused for now. But I will not forgive you

if you don't set a date, and soon. Your momma needs to see you married and settled.''

"Yes, ma'am, I know. But, I'm going to be busy with several training schools for the next few months, so we won't be able to schedule anything until I'm done.''

"Until you're finished with them,'' Mrs. Scarborough corrected. "You're only done if you've been baking at 350 degrees for about five hours like a turkey,'' she added.

"Yes, ma'am. When I'm finished.'' Bill steered Darcy across the room.

"I'm sorry,'' he whispered quietly into Darcy's ear. "I hadn't expected the news to spread like wildfire. I could throttle Earline.''

Darcy turned and whispered back. "It's all right. We should have asked your mother to keep it quiet.'' Then she stopped. "But, that would have been unfair to her.''

"Yeah,'' Bill said. "I should've straightened it all out last night.'' Then he looked across the room to where his mother was seated regally in a chair, her attendant guests surrounding her.

No, he was glad he'd given her these few moments of pleasure. He and Darcy could pretend to have a falling-out later. He did have that long string of specialty schools coming up. It would be a perfect reason for the engagement not to work out.

Then he looked at Darcy, smiling down at Chrissy, Earline's youngest. It might be a perfect excuse, but everybody'd think he was a damned fool to let a keeper like Darcy get away.

Too bad she wasn't really his to lose.

DARCY'S FACE hurt from smiling so much, and it was still early in the party as far as she could tell. There were mounds of food on the table, and the huge sheet cake that Lougenia had baked and decorated herself had yet to be cut. It was going to be a long evening.

Lougenia banged on an aluminum cook pot with a wooden spoon. "Come on, ever'body. Food's getting cold. Grab a plate and fill it, then find a spot to set."

Edd stepped up to the table and reached for a plate, but Lougenia smacked her brother-in-law's hand with her wooden spoon. "Hold on, bubba. Where are your manners? Let's let the birthday boy and the guest of honor go first."

Edd backed up, looking duly chastened, but his hang-dog look soon turned to a grin. "Better get up there, boy. They's hungry people waiting."

Bill blushed, and Darcy couldn't help liking the man more. He took her by the hand and stepped forward, and as a shock of warmth ran up her arm, Darcy couldn't help thinking she liked that, too. It was a good thing that Bill was going back to his base soon. If she wasn't careful, she would be wanting to make this engagement real.

And the last thing she needed right now was another man in her life.

Bill handed Darcy a plate, a chipped piece of bone china in a beautiful old pattern that must have been in his family for years. "Better eat up," he said low, under his breath. "We don't skimp on food around here."

Darcy looked around the room at the well-fed group, and could see that that statement was true. Maybe too true. But that was a crusade she'd fight later. She hadn't done a cardiology rotation for nothing.

Lucy Carterette, the minister's wife, Darcy thought, stepped into line behind her as she debated the merits of deviled eggs versus carrot sticks. The eggs won. She could do an extra mile the next time she ran. She smiled at the woman and helped herself to an egg.

"It's so nice that Billy has found someone," Mrs. Carterette said as she, too, selected an egg. "How did you and Billy meet?"

"Darcy's car broke down, and I gave her a lift," Bill interjected. They'd decided to stick as close to the truth as possible without filling in too many details that could get them into trouble later.

"Isn't that sweet!" another woman, whose connection Darcy couldn't quite figure, cooed.

"Yes, ma'am. I was quite worried. I had just set out to walk when Bill drove up and rescued me." That much was true. She'd managed to keep her story straight, so far. Maybe, if people were busy eating, she wouldn't have to answer so many questions.

She filled her plate and followed Bill to a spot on the floor by the fireplace.

Bill held out his hand and took her plate while Darcy settled, cross-legged, next to him. They left the sofa and chairs for the older, less nimble people.

Chrissie squealed as Little Edd swiped a carrot stick from her. She shoved her plate at her mother and dashed across the floor and tackled the boy in a play that would have made any football coach proud.

Big Edd got up, crossed the room in two long strides, grabbed both kids by the shoulders and pulled them apart. "Go set with your momma," he told Chrissie sternly. Then he looked at Little Edd. "What do you mean, picking on your sister like that? You know we didn't bring you up to steal from girls."

The boy, head hanging dejectedly, dragged back to his spot on the other side of his mother.

"And you watch about letting people tackle you like

'at. It ain't no way to get to the University of Alabama if you gonna let a girl get the better of you.''

Little Edd looked up quickly, then swallowed. "Yes, sir," he said. "I know I shoulda been watching my flank." He picked up his abandoned plate and sat down.

"Starting a little early, aren't they?" Darcy murmured as she tried to hide a smile.

Bill looked at her. "Around here, one of the few ways a poor kid can get to college is to do good on the football field."

"A football scholarship's the only hope they have?" Darcy concluded.

"Got that in one," Bill answered grimly, then dug into a mound of potato salad with black olives and pickles. "That and joining the service."

Earline looked over the heads of her children, still giving each other dirty looks. "Momma said you just graduated from nursing school."

Darcy nodded.

"I got my LPN at John Patterson Technical College. Where'd you go?"

"Duke."

"Where's that?" Earline asked, her mouth full.

"North Carolina."

Earline swallowed. "If it's in North Carolina, how'd you meet Billy when he's in Florida?"

Now it was Darcy's turn to swallow. She swallowed again, but before she could answer, Bill came to her rescue.

"I went to jump school, at Fort Bragg in North Carolina."

"Oh. Lucky you."

Darcy didn't know whether Earline was referring to Bill or to her, but considering the good save, she answered, "Yes, it was lucky. If Bill hadn't come along when he did, I don't know what I would have done."

"That's enough poking your nose into Darcy's business, Earline," Bill said. "Let her eat."

"Well, I was just interested," Earline protested. "She *is* going to be a member of the family. I *would* like to know a little something about her."

Bill shot his sister a look, and she drew in a deep, aggravated breath and turned her attention back to her plate.

"Thank you, Bill," Darcy murmured under her breath. "It seems like you're always saving me."

"Wouldn't have it any other way," Bill said.

Darcy wondered what Bill meant by that, but she didn't make an issue of it. It was good enough that the questions had stopped, for now, and she could eat in peace.

BILL WOULD HAVE LOVED to have everybody leave so he could take a long nap after all the food he'd eaten, but he figured there were a good couple of hours before people headed home. At least he and Darcy hadn't been bothered too much since Earline's earlier inquisition. People had gathered into quiet clumps and the kids were outside chasing fireflies.

He turned to Darcy. "How you holding up?"

She shrugged. "Okay, I guess. I like your family and friends, but I feel funny about lying to them."

Bill let out a long breath. "I know that, but remember it's for Momma. And so far, we haven't really lied. We've just sort of left out a few details."

"What's the difference?" Darcy said, setting her empty plate on the floor beside her. "They all think we're engaged," she said in low tones.

"But we didn't tell them that. That's the difference."

"And we didn't correct them when they made the assumption," Darcy persisted.

Bill set his plate on top of Darcy's. "It's too late to do anything about it now. We're just going to have to stick with the plan."

"Easy for you to say. You get to go back to Hurlburt and business as usual." Darcy sighed.

"What you two lovebirds doing with your heads together like that? Making wedding plans?"

Bill and Darcy sprang apart, and Bill looked up to where Lougenia was standing at the plundered dining-room table, a cake knife in hand.

"It's time to honor the birthday boy and to cut the cake." Lougenia motioned toward Bill. "Come on up to the table, and bring the lovely Darcy up with you."

"They just want me to blow out the candles," Bill said, offering Darcy his hand. "And everybody wants to get a good look at you."

Bill loved the way her small, warm hand seemed to fit in his. He helped her to her feet. "Here goes nothing," he said as he led Darcy across the room.

Lougenia lit the candles and beckoned him forward. "All right, Billy. Stand here," she directed.

Bill had barely settled into position when everyone broke out in a chorus of "Happy Birthday." By the end of the song, even Darcy had joined in.

"Now, make a wish and blow out the candles."

Playing along, Bill closed his eyes and pretended deep concentration while he thought about his wish. Then, drawing a deep breath, he reared back and blew all the candles out at once.

"Yesss! That means you get your wish," Darcy said, falling into the spirit of the situation.

"What did you wish for?" Chrissie asked.

"It won't come true if I tell, sugar pumpkin," Bill said ruffling the girl's hair.

"I bet I know what he wushed for," Little Edd said, his voice dripping with disdain. "I bet he wushed we would all go home so he could make kissy face with Miss Darcy."

Darcy blushed, and Bill didn't know what to say.

"Well, brother dear, if that's your wish, I hereby grant it," Lougenia said. "Have at it."

Bill looked at Darcy, who was exhibiting nothing short of sheer panic.

"Kiss her," somebody said.

"Give her a good one," someone else chimed in.

"Kiss. Kiss. Kiss." Pretty soon the room echoed with the chant.

"Do you mind?" Bill said quietly, looking into Darcy's brown eyes. "I think that's the only way they'll quit."

Darcy drew in a short, quick breath and swallowed. "Okay," she said reluctantly. "If that'll be the end of it."

"Go on, Billy. It ain't no big deal."

Bill looked around the room. The noisy chant dwindled as the party guests saw that he was accepting the challenge.

"I don't usually do this in front of an audience," he murmured, more for Darcy's sake than for the people watching. In fact, it had been so long since he'd done it at all that kissing Darcy was a very big deal.

He swallowed and wiped his palms, suddenly sweaty, on his jeans. Then he drew Darcy into his arms, situated her in front of him, and lowered his mouth toward hers.

Chapter Four

Darcy's breath caught in her throat. She hadn't bargained for this. This was only supposed to be a pretend engagement, but the handsome man leaning in to kiss her was all too real. Yet, curiosity and more than a little desire had her closing her eyes and moistening her lips as Bill's face drew closer to hers.

His lips touched her mouth, landing feather-soft at first, like a butterfly lighting on a flower.

She should have let him lift off and be done and that would have been that, but Darcy couldn't. She wanted to know what it would be like to kiss this man standing so close to her, so steady, so real. She kissed him back.

Bill uttered a soft moan that only she could hear, or had she only felt it? Then he pulled her closer to him, pressing her against his hard, strong chest. Darcy's eyes fluttered open for a moment, but only a moment, then drifted shut again as she sank into the delicious sensation of being thoroughly kissed by a real man.

Her lips parted, and Bill accepted the invitation, plunging deep within her recesses. As he probed and tasted her, Darcy felt almost as if she had been well and thoroughly loved.

How would it be if they weren't pretending?

But this kiss felt too good to be pretense. And Darcy longed to satisfy her body's desire for more. For him. All of him. She heard herself whimper with need.

If Dick had kissed her like this just once, maybe she wouldn't have left him in the chapel.

"Come on you two. Get a room," Edd said from somewhere out in the real world.

Edd's comment and that brief reminder of Dick was all it took to break the spell. And that's what Darcy had to convince herself it was, a spell. An enchantment. There was no way she could have responded to this man she hardly knew if she hadn't been bewitched in some way.

She jerked away, fighting the urge to touch her tingling and sensitive lips. She felt unwanted heat rising to her cheeks, then willed her face to cool.

"Now that's enough, Edd. Leave those kids be. They don't need you teasing and taunting them," Nettie Hays said to her son-in-law from her throne-like position across the room.

"Yes, ma'am," Edd said. "Let's leave them to make out without a audience."

"Just thought we could give you a few lessons," Bill fired back over his shoulder as he loosened his grip on Darcy's arms. He turned back to her. "Do you want me to send everyone home?" he asked in an undertone.

Darcy glanced behind Bill to where Nettie seemed to be enjoying her company. "No, not yet. Nettie's having a good time, but if she begins to look tired, we should tell them that the party's over."

"Thank you," Bill whispered. "I owe you." Then he turned and grinned at his mother.

No, thank *you*, Darcy couldn't help thinking. Bill had shown her more about love today than she had seen in her entire life. She drew in a deep breath, pasted on a smile, and prepared to face the guests and the rest of the party.

IN SPITE OF the crush of guests around him, the only thing Bill could think of was that kiss. That wonderful, breathtaking, unexpected kiss. Maybe he should have anticipated the possibility—hell, probability—of kissing Darcy, but he hadn't. And now that he had kissed Darcy, he wanted to keep on doing it. But he knew he couldn't.

It wouldn't be fair.

Not to him, not to Darcy, not even to his mother, for that matter.

He and Darcy had to figure out a way to make this engagement look good for now and then make it come to an end without hurting anybody. Talk about an impossible task!

He wasn't used to lying. Pretending to be engaged to Darcy was a lie, even if he wouldn't mind if it were true.

Bill looked across the room to where Momma seemed to be sinking lower into her chair. He saw that she was tired. Excitement had been replaced by dark smudges beneath her eyes. He wondered how to ask the guests to leave.

"Hey, little brother, I've got one sleepy little quarterback here," Earline said, drawing Bill out of his thoughts and saving him from having to come up with an excuse. She guided a drowsy Little Edd toward the door while Big Edd followed with Chrissie in his arms. Leah, their oldest, brought up the rear.

"Hey, Uncle Bill, I like Miss Darcy. You got a real keeper," Leah said. She turned toward Darcy. "Can I be in your wedding? I'm the only girl in my class who hasn't been a bridesmaid yet.''

Darcy looked startled, but she recovered quickly enough. ''We'll have to see, sweetie. We haven't started to make plans,'' she finally said.

It seemed to satisfy Leah, and she left happily enough. Too bad they wouldn't be able to follow through.

Lougenia, announcing that Momma was tired, followed Earline and her family out. Soon the rest of the guests took the hint, leaving Bill and Darcy alone with Momma.

''I'll just take my bedtime pills and then leave you two alone,'' Momma said. ''I'd love to help you clean up, but I just don't seem to have the energy anymore,'' she said as she shuffled into the kitchen for a glass of water.

''That's all right, Nettie. We can handle it,'' Darcy called after her. ''You go ahead and get your rest.'' She started clearing the dining-room table while they waited for Momma to finish in the kitchen.

''I'm sorry Leah put you on the spot like that,'' Bill said as he watched Darcy stacking plates from the ravaged dining-room table.

''Me, too. I hate to disappoint her,'' Darcy said, piling flatware on top of the plates. ''She's a nice girl.''

''No nicer than you,'' Bill told her.

After Momma went up to bed, he followed Darcy into the kitchen and watched as she deposited the plates on the sideboard and filled the sink with sudsy water. ''I'll dry if you wash,'' he suggested, hoping for a way to be close to her without crowding. He knew that Darcy had been just as uneasy about the kiss they'd been forced into as he had, but they'd had to do something or they wouldn't have made their fake engagement look real.

Or ever heard the end of it.

"You're on. Though, I'd rather you'd wash and I dry," she said as she lowered the first glass into the water.

"I don't expect we ought to risk that slippery, wet china with these big mitts," he said, holding up his hands.

Darcy tossed a dish towel at Bill which he deftly caught. "Remind me to pick up some rubber gloves in town," Darcy said. "Or maybe a dishwasher," she mumbled just low enough that Bill had to strain to hear.

Bill chuckled. "We've tried for years to get Momma to let us give her one, but she wouldn't have a thing to do with it. Said she'd raised five kids without having one, so why'd she need one now?" He thought for a minute. "Now that it looks like there's gonna be a new Mrs. Hays, maybe we can swing one."

Darcy dipped a soapy glass under the running water. "No," she said, shaking her head. "I won't be here that long, and it's a big expense. I can make do. After all, you don't have twenty people over for dinner most of the time." Darcy looked up at him, her eyes wide. "This isn't a regular thing, is it?"

"Only for holidays. And most times Lou and Earline would've stayed to clean up." He paused and managed a crooked smile. "I think they were being considerate to give us some time alone."

"I see," Darcy said stiffly. "If they'd really been considerate, they'd have helped us get this mess cleaned up quicker," she muttered under her breath.

"Yeah," Bill answered huskily. "So we can be alone."

Darcy jerked her head up, a puzzled expression on her face. Then, just as quickly, she turned back to her work.

Apparently, Darcy didn't have the trouble separating fact from fiction that he did. Maybe she couldn't wait for the pretending to end, but he'd just as soon it went on.

No, he reminded himself. He'd like it to be over, too. He had no business thinking about it, even in the abstract. Not with the plans he had for the future.

He put the glass into the cabinet and stared into the darkness outside the kitchen window. He had to finish night school, then get accepted for officer training school, get commissioned as a second lieutenant and establish himself in his first real assignment as an officer. He wouldn't take a wife as long as he was in the air force. Military life was just too hard on families. Maybe, someday, when he'd retired and settled down, then he'd think about it.

In the meantime, he'd just have to settle for pretending. He glanced up at Darcy as she handed him another wet glass.

There were worse things he could be pretending about.

LATER THAT NIGHT, Darcy lay in the dark in the small twin bed, the pink chenille bedspread tickling her nostrils. She wrinkled her nose to stifle a sneeze, then rolled over, kneaded her pillow, and tried to make herself comfortable. Anything to help her get to sleep.

Last night she'd been too exhausted to think about what she'd gotten herself into, but tonight was another story. She'd spent at least an hour trying to count sheep or anything else to get to sleep, but her mind, or maybe it was her guilty conscience, kept bringing up memories of the party.

She compared it to the formal affair where she'd announced her engagement to Dick. Everything had been by the book down to the last dessert spoon. Aunt Marianne had selected the perfect menu of prime rib, steamed asparagus and new potatoes. The dessert had been tasteful—and tasteless—lemon sorbet. And, thinking back on it, her real engagement party had been entirely lacking in soul in comparison to the lively and friendly birthday party and impromptu engagement party she'd just attended.

If she had to be marrying into a family, she would have much preferred to be joining Bill's. These people seemed so genuine and caring.

So real.

She closed her eyes and tried to imagine what it would be like to be a real part of this big, happy clan. Not the stiff and formal family that she was a part of.

Smiling to herself, she lost herself in the fantasy. Soon she drifted off to sleep.

"YOU AREN'T PLANNING to bring Darcy with you to church?" Momma asked Bill at the breakfast table.

That was something he hadn't thought about and a question he hadn't been prepared to answer. And if it weren't for Momma, he'd probably skip church. When he'd talked Darcy into agreeing to play his fiancée, he hadn't anticipated they'd find themselves digging deeper into a mess he wasn't sure he would be able to get out of. He certainly wasn't about to drag Darcy into another situation that would put her on the spot.

Taking Darcy to church seemed wrong. It was one

thing to pretend in the safety of his own home, but
something else to do it in church.

"I'd like to go to church with you, Bill. I met Reverend Carterette last night, and I'd like to attend services
at his church." Darcy reached for a mug for coffee, then
turned to Momma. "Will the sweater set I had on at
the party last night be all right? I can put on the lower
half of a suit for a skirt. I didn't bring much in the way
of nice clothes with me."

"I'm sure you'll look lovely, Darcy," Momma said,
beaming. "The Lord don't care what you're wearing in
His house, only that you're there."

Their reasons for pretending to be engaged outweighed the lie, Darcy tried to convince herself. Otherwise, she wasn't sure she'd be able to show herself
in the church. Even if she had met most of the congregation—or so it seemed—in this house last night.

Bill touched her on the shoulder, squeezing it
slightly, and Darcy was warmed by his gentle gesture.
She liked Bill, she liked Nettie, she had to believe that
she was doing the right thing for everyone.

"Well, I'm right pleased that you are going to go
with us," Nettie said. "Most of the time, I have to nag
our Billy to death to make him come with me." She
put down her cereal spoon and pushed herself heavily
to her feet. "I'll just go get ready and leave you two
alone to eat your breakfast. Services don't start for a
couple of hours yet."

"Yes, ma'am," Darcy said, hoping she was doing
the right thing. It had seemed so simple yesterday morning when Bill had talked her into pretending. After all,
she was going to be helping by keeping an eye on Nettie's condition. Now, the reason didn't seem simple at
all.

It seemed very complicated, indeed.

She smiled up at Bill, more for herself than for him, as he scraped scrambled eggs onto her plate then sat down across from her. Darcy had thought that matters were complicated when she'd left Dick waiting at the altar two days ago.

If she'd known just how much more deeply involved her life could get, would she still have run? She scooped up a forkful of eggs and looked across the table to Bill and imagined sitting across from Dick.

Yes, she would have.

In Darcy's eyes, Bill seemed more of a man while serving breakfast to her than Dick had ever been.

HE FELT AS THOUGH he'd dodged a bullet. Bill breathed a figurative sigh of relief as he and Darcy helped Momma down the short flight of steps from the church and escorted her to the car. What he'd expected to be torture hadn't been so bad, and Momma seemed to have enjoyed showing off her son and future daughter-in-law as much as she had the service.

That alone outweighed the guilt he felt about their deception.

"Excuse me, Miss Stanton?"

Bill turned to see Darcy taken aside by old Doc Williamson. The doctor attended church about as regularly as Bill did, but Bill guessed that he had come to check out Darcy, just as about half of the less-regular members of Bobby Carterette's flock had.

He helped Momma climb into the Cherokee then stood watch outside the Jeep as Darcy and Doc Williamson engaged in a lively—and long—conversation. "I wonder what that's all about," he mused half out loud.

"I reckon the doctor couldn't wait till the morning to interview his new nurse," Momma said through the rolled-down window. "You saw how Becky Porter looked about to pop. I reckon he's afraid she'll have that young'un and leave him hanging without a nurse, and he wants to be ready."

"I suppose," Bill said, his eyes still trained on Darcy and the doctor.

"Don't worry, Bill," Ken Peterson, the high-school principal, said, waving as he passed the Jeep. "I don't think he has any designs on your woman."

"Uh, no, sir," Bill said, returning the wave. "Just waiting on her." If this was supposed to be a fake engagement, he and Darcy must be doing a pretty damned good job of playing their parts. Everybody seemed convinced.

Bill guessed that was a good thing, but maybe not. After all, if he wasn't careful, he'd begin to believe it, too. And marriage, especially to a woman he'd known all of forty-eight hours, just didn't fit into his plans.

While he had been distracted by Mr. Peterson, Darcy had disengaged herself from Doc Williamson. She all but skipped back to him, a wide grin on her face.

"I got the job," she announced enthusiastically, throwing her arms around Bill. "I'm so excited."

He didn't know whether to hug her back or step away, but Darcy seemed to realize what she'd done, and, blushing slightly, she quickly let go. Bill felt almost chilled from the loss of her touch.

"Sorry," she said under her breath, but she apparently couldn't control her enthusiasm for long, for she continued excitedly. "Doctor Williamson said his nurse is due any day now, and he doesn't think she'll make it to term. So he wants me to start right away so she can show me the ropes before she goes into labor.''

"Well, that must make you right proud," Momma said from her seat in the Cherokee. "That calls for celebration, don't you think, son?''

Bill turned, surprised by his mother's remark. He hadn't even thought that much about it when his mother had mentioned that Doc had the opening, and he hadn't realized that Darcy had followed through.

"I think it's a wonderful idea," Darcy said as she climbed into the back seat beside Momma.

"What did you have in mind?" Bill finally said, dragging his gaze away from Darcy. He turned and quickly rounded the Jeep and climbed in.

"We could stop off at the SaniFreez on the way to Lougenia's and get an ice-cream cake." She looked at him, her expression hopeful. "Now, I know I'm not supposed to be eating ice cream, and I do appreciate Lou fixin' me the right kind of food when she has me come over, but I reckon you young'uns would rightly enjoy having some ruther than fruit salad. And I do declare that I would just love to watch you eat it."

That was logic that Bill certainly couldn't argue with. And he also knew that one little serving of ice cream would make little difference in his mother's condition one way or the other in the long run. "Let's do it," he said.

THAT NIGHT, after they had returned from Lougenia's and Darcy had helped settle Nettie for the night, she found herself alone with her thoughts on the swing on the tiny front porch.

The night was warm and scented with honeysuckle, and fireflies danced over the lawn, entertaining her with their simple show. The only sounds were the chirps of crickets, the drone of june bugs dive-bombing the window screens, and the occasional creak of the swing.

Funny how her life had changed. In just a few days, she'd gone from a troubled, reluctant bride to a happy and contented woman. With a job!

This was the first thing she'd ever really done on her own. Besides running from her wedding. She was finally doing something for herself, and she was helping Bill with his mother, as well.

She still had a few reservations about staying in Nettie Hays's house when she wasn't really engaged to her son. She had always, in the back of her mind, imagined having an apartment of her own, but she rationalized that she was earning her way by keeping watch over Nettie. And, there would be time for an apartment soon enough.

The pretense couldn't go on forever. And neither could Nettie, for that matter. Darcy sighed and tried to push that thought out of her troubled mind. It was enough, for now, to try to make Nettie's life more comfortable. No matter how long or short it might be.

She wondered vaguely if there was anything that could be done. After all, they'd made great strides in cardiology in recent years. Perhaps, there was something that could be done to reverse Nettie's condition. She'd check with Doctor Williamson once she'd settled into her new job.

Bill stepped outside, leaned against the doorframe, and seemed to drink in the evening fragrances as she had. He said nothing, but Darcy was very aware of his presence.

She waited for Bill to say something or to sit beside

her or to do anything, but he seemed to be content simply to stand there, so near yet so far.

Darcy didn't know how long they shared the night like that, and the time wasn't important. She wondered if this was what it was like to be an old married couple, so comfortable with each other that words didn't matter. She wondered why she seemed so comfortable with Bill when they were involved in such a strange situation.

She drew in a long, deep breath of the warm, fragrant air. "Thank you," she whispered.

Bill didn't respond, and Darcy wondered if he had heard her, but whether he had heard her or not didn't matter. She was content to sit and listen to the summer symphony and soak up the peace and quiet. For now, her problems didn't matter. For now, this beautiful summer evening was hers to enjoy.

Finally, Bill shifted, and Darcy wondered if he was going back inside to leave her with the night. She'd like him to stay here with her, but if he went, it didn't matter.

"A while ago you said thank you," Bill said suddenly, startling Darcy with the abrupt intrusion into the serenity. "Why? I should be thanking you."

"You're welcome," Darcy said softly, knowing exactly why he was thanking her. She supposed she should explain. Maybe she couldn't tell him everything about her flight from the chapel and Dick, but she could help him understand.

She drew in a long, deep breath, then patted the swing seat beside her. She didn't care whether Billy joined her there or not, but it mattered to her that she had invited him. "For sharing your family with me," she said simply, knowing there was no way she could explain her own complicated situation. "I've never known such gentle, caring people.

"My family is nothing like that," she said softly, not really wanting to confess her parents' shortcomings, even though they might have been well-intentioned, even as she was happy to be free from them. For now. She closed her eyes, as if doing so would make the truth easier to admit.

"They always had a firm idea of right and wrong and what I should do with my life," she said finally. "They had my life all mapped out and planned in front of me, and it didn't matter that it wasn't what I wanted to do." Darcy gave Bill a moment to probe if he was going to.

"What did you want to do?" Bill accepted her opening, but the question wasn't the one she'd expected. She'd been prepared to explain about her family duty and expectations, not her own plans. No one had wanted to hear her dreams before.

Darcy sighed and took a few moments to formulate her answer. "I guess I just want to be myself," she said finally. "Not the woman my parents expected me to be. They lived a life of rules and great expectations. I never felt I could live up to them," she said, choking up. She smiled, forcing the lump from her throat. "I always knew I was a big disappointment to my father for not being a son, and my mother's idea of perfection was just not mine.

"I tried," she said, sighing again. "I really did, but I just couldn't do it any more."

"Is that why I found you all alone hitchhiking on that dark country road?" Bill laid his big hand over hers still splayed on the wooden swing seat. He squeezed gently.

Darcy nodded, unable to speak, her emotions overwhelmed by this simple gesture. His touch seemed so warm, so caring, that it made her heart ache. Maybe if even one of her parents had accepted her as Bill's family had, she wouldn't be here today. Then, she realized with a pang, if that had been the case, she would never have met Bill Hays.

Though everything else in her life had gone awry, sitting here with Bill seemed very right.

Chapter Five

Bill turned off the chain saw and took a moment to wipe the sweat off his brow. He wished he could take his leave time off to relax like the other men on Silver Team, but Momma needed his help. There'd be plenty of time to relax after... Well, he didn't want to think about that.

It had been a long time since anyone had cleared the brush around the old cowshed. Edd mowed the lawn, and Jim, his older brother, kept the house in good repair, but they each had their own jobs, their own lives and their own places to keep up with. Truth be told, Bill felt better doing something physical rather than sitting around and wringing his hands over something he could do nothing about.

With the dry conditions around here in the summer, it was better to clear brush away from around the house and outbuildings to make a fire break than to let everything go wild. Although this year seemed to be wetter than usual, he figured it was better to be safe than sorry.

Bill looked out over what had once been a thriving vegetable plot, now overgrown with weeds and blackberry brambles. Momma had always kept a big garden going, and what the family hadn't eaten in the summers, she'd frozen or canned for the winters. They'd never been rich, but they'd never gone hungry. He admired Momma for that, but he never wanted a woman he loved to endure the kind of hardship that Daddy's unexpectedly early death had caused his mother.

He'd seen what it had done to his mother. It had made her old before her time. Surely all that past struggle just to survive had contributed to her illness today. Maybe that's why he was so determined to save some other woman from the heartache by not marrying while he was on active duty.

It was one thing to work hard to provide for a family, but another knowingly to take on a job that could take him away from that family, temporarily, if not permanently. He was not going to let another woman struggle to support herself and her children the way Momma had done.

He started to rev up the chain saw again, but he wasn't ready to go back to work. One thing about this kind of farm work: it gave a guy time to think. And he had plenty to think about. Not the least of which was his temporary fiancée.

With Darcy up early and gone to the first day of her new job, Billy almost felt as though life had returned to normal. It was amazing how much easier it was to concentrate without her distracting him. And why she did, he didn't know.

Of course, now that he'd thought about her, she'd moved up to the front of his mind. Why did she bother him so? She was just a woman, and not even the most beautiful one he'd ever met. Compared to other girls he'd dated, she wasn't the prettiest. Yet, there was something about her that drew him like a moth to a flame.

He chuckled wryly. Yeah, that was a fatal attraction.
He sure hoped it wouldn't prove to be the same for him.
The last thing he needed along with everything else was
to crash and burn.

Just like this brush if he didn't get it cleared away,
he reminded himself. He reached for the insulated jug
of water he'd stashed in the shade of the shed and took
a long swig. Then, once his thirst was quenched, he set
back to work.

AFTER THE BUSY SHIFTS of her hospital training last
term, her duties with Doctor Williamson seemed far
from complicated, Darcy thought as she steered Nettie's
old car home after her first day on the job. She thought
vaguely that she needed to try again to retrieve her own
car, but since Nettie had given her free use of hers, it
didn't seem that urgent. After all, her VW Bug was
older than she was and would probably cost a fortune
to fix.

And she'd only kept it to irritate her parents and
Dick. They'd complained about it from the day she'd
bought it for $800 through an ad in the paper. Her father
had taken one look and declared the elderly woman
who'd sold it to her a thief, but Darcy had liked her,
and the old vehicle had taken her a lot of miles from
eleventh grade all the way through college with very
little upkeep. Perhaps it deserved a decent burial, but
she didn't think she needed to put it back to work. If it
had been a racehorse, she'd have put it out to pasture.

She paused at the intersection of the main highway
and waited for a produce truck to pass, then turned onto
the road toward the Hays place. She'd had a pretty good
day. Except for learning Doctor Williamson's rather
strange filing system and getting to know the patients,

this new job would be a breeze. She spent more time taking patient histories and doing triage than anything, and considering the number of bedpans she'd emptied in her hospital practicals, she was just as happy for the change.

Another couple of minutes and she'd be home, strange as that seemed. Nettie's small house seemed so much more welcoming than any of the military base quarters she'd lived in growing up. She didn't know why, unless it was the knowledge that these people had roots, something she'd longed for and never had.

Of course, she'd have to face Bill again and play the part she still felt guilty about.

As she pulled into the drive, she couldn't help thinking that she wouldn't mind being Bill's fiancée for real. As she turned the key and cut the engine, that thought was seconded as she caught a glimpse of the man, hard at work on the far side of the shed. There he was, clearing out the wild overgrowth, bare to the waist and sweaty and all too male.

Darcy opened the car door and stepped out into the thick, hot summer air. Feeling as though she'd been mugged, all she could do was stare.

Billy's back was to her, and he must not have heard her drive in over the noise of the chain saw, for he didn't stop. Darcy didn't mind at all. The longer it took him to look up, the longer she'd have to watch.

And wonder what it would be like to be involved with this man for real.

Darcy moistened her lips and swallowed.

He must have been working there all day. His skin shone with moisture, and though already bronzed by prior time in the sun, his shoulders shone pink from new exposure. His hair was moist and curled around his face. Darcy smiled as she noticed dirt on his cheek.

Bill turned off the saw and lowered it to the ground, the muscles in his back flexing and contracting. His motions were fluid and graceful, but sparse, as though he'd done this many times without having to think. He must have finally noticed her, for he stopped short. He looked in her direction, squinting at first, then shading his eyes against the bright afternoon sun.

Darcy forced herself to act as though she had just arrived. "Hi," she called brightly, hoping he wouldn't realize that she'd been watching. "You look like you've made a day of it," she said, instantly realizing that she must sound really lame. After all, he'd mentioned that morning that he was going to work on the brush. Had she just thought that he was going to trim the azalea bushes in front?

Maybe she had, but it was clear that he hadn't been doing anything as simple as yard work.

"Yeah," he grunted, wiping his forehead again and leaving a grimy smudge in his hand's wake. "I figure I've got another good day at this. Tomorrow I'll bush hog the area behind the sheds."

"Bush hog?" Darcy was an educated woman, but she had no idea what Bill was talking about.

"I hook an attachment to the back of the tractor, and it drags along the ground and roots up any low shrubs and stuff that could be a fire hazard. Works like a real hog, I guess." Bill stood there, arms hanging loose at his side as if he were waiting for her to make the next move.

Darcy didn't quite know what to say. She had to say something, if only to let him know that he could go back to what he was doing. "Well, I'll let you get back to work, then," she said, finally.

Bill shrugged. "I'm done for now. Don't have time to start bush-hogging this evening, and I'm gonna have to help with supper anyway."

"No," Darcy said, horrified. "You've worked out in the sun all day. You go take a bath or a shower and relax for a few minutes while I get supper ready."

"But you've been working all day, too. You must be beat."

"Piece of cake," Darcy said, grinning. "After my hospital practicals, this was no stretch at all. I fed myself every day while I was in school, and that was so much harder than today was. There's no reason why I can't now." She reached for her bag, left on the hood of the car, then turned toward the house.

Cooking dinner in an unfamiliar kitchen would be a challenge, but infinitely easier than trying to keep from staring at Bill as he stood in front of her in all his masculine glory. Darcy blew out a puff of breath, then pushed open the door.

BILL SAT ALONE in the swing on the front porch as the cicadas began to hum, the night birds began to call, and the june bugs began their evening suicide missions into the light bulbs. City people often talked about how quiet it was in the country, but they'd obviously never sat and listened to the sounds of a warm, summer evening.

He looked in through the kitchen window to where Darcy was finishing up the supper dishes. He'd offered to help, but she'd shooed him off, saying that he'd worked plenty hard today, and she'd just sat around Doctor Williamson's office, pretending to look efficient.

It was an argument he wasn't likely to win, so he'd respected Darcy's wishes and gone out to the swing.

As she had the past couple of nights, Momma had gone to bed early, leaving them alone. Bill didn't know whether it was because his mother was tired or trying to allow him more privacy with Darcy that he'd just as soon he didn't have.

He knew that his mother usually enjoyed watching television in the evenings. But when he'd said something to her about it, she'd brushed him off, saying that all her programs were in reruns, and she was too tired to watch them anyway. That worried him. How much energy did it take to watch television? But rather than nag her about staying up—to chaperon?—he'd let her go to bed.

So now he just sat in the swing and felt about as useful as training wheels on a tricycle. He leaned back and listened to the creak of the swing and breathed in the sweet scents of summer.

He must have dozed, for the next thing he knew, Darcy was speaking to him. He woke with a jerk. "What?"

Darcy smiled. "I asked if there was room for me on that swing. Or is this a private party?" She made a scooting motion with her hands, and Bill obliged.

"Dishes all done?" he asked, knowing that she wouldn't be out here if they weren't.

"Yep. Washed, dried, and put away," Darcy said as she settled down beside him. She leaned back against the seat and uttered a contented moan.

There seemed no need to comment, and if Darcy knew what he'd been thinking, she'd be more likely to smack him than appreciate it. Bill couldn't help thinking that he'd like to hear that moan coming from her as he pleasured her into releasing beneath him. He fought a tightening in his groin and tried to think of something less dangerous.

Not an easy thing to do with Darcy sitting so close beside him.

"I talked to Doctor Williamson about your mother's condition," Darcy said, breaking the awkward silence. "Do you mind?"

Bill sat up straight and looked at her. "Why should I?"

"Well, patients' histories are confidential," she said, but Bill shrugged and waited for her to go on. "If I'm going to be keeping an eye on her condition, I thought it best if I knew exactly what it is."

"And now you know," Bill answered grimly. There had been a time when Momma probably could have been helped, but poverty and lack of insurance had cut her options. Now, it was just a waiting game.

Darcy sighed. "Yes," was all she said. She rested her arm on the back of the swing and drew in a long, deep breath of the fragrant summer air.

Bill couldn't help wishing that he'd thought of that. That he could put his arm on the back of the swing, cup her shoulder in his hand and draw her to him, but he couldn't. It might be proper for a real engaged couple to sit out on the front porch and kiss, but they weren't a real engaged couple.

But, vow to remain single notwithstanding, Bill wanted more than anything to kiss Darcy. No, that wasn't true. The aching tautness in his groin told him more. If he kissed her now, he wasn't sure he would be able to stop with just a kiss.

AFTER A COUPLE of days, Darcy and Bill settled into a routine. Darcy would go to work at the doctor's office in Pittsville, and Bill would spend his day doing labor at his mother's house, then Darcy would come home, and they would pretend to be in love. Darcy wondered if Nettie knew how lucky she was to have a son like Bill Hays.

She was standing at the sink rinsing the last of the supper dishes when Nettie surprised her by coming in and sitting at the table.

"You know, you and our Billy don't have to hide your affection from me," Nettie said quietly.

Darcy stopped, a wet plate poised in mid-air halfway between the sink and the counter. "Oh?" she responded cautiously. What could she say?

"I know what it's like to be young and in love." Nettie chuckled softly. "It may have happened back in the days of covered wagons, but I do recall what it feels like when you can't keep your hands off each other."

"Yes, ma'am," Darcy managed in a strangled voice as she finally lowered the plate to the countertop.

"Just think about it," Nettie said. "I won't faint from shock if I catch you two kissing."

Darcy swallowed and turned to look at Nettie. "No, ma'am," was all she could manage. "I'll keep that in mind."

"You do that." Nettie pushed herself up. "I'll just get me a glass of water to take my pills with, and I'll head to my room to leave you and Billy alone." She filled one of the glasses Darcy had just washed and headed for her room. As she reached the kitchen door, she turned. "Just wanted you to know," she said quietly as Bill came in.

"What's that, Momma?" Bill said as Nettie patted him on the shoulder and brushed past him.

"I reckon your intended can fill you in. I'll just leave you two alone so you can talk." Nettie turned and blew a kiss their way, then made her way slowly to her room.

"What was that all about?" Bill asked, getting a beer from the refrigerator. He held the long-neck bottle up. "You want one?"

Darcy shook her head. "No." Grateful for the brief change of subject and a possible reprieve, she went back to work and tried not to think about the strange conversation she'd just had with Nettie.

Instead of going back outside to the porch swing as had been his habit, Bill stationed himself to her right, leaning comfortably against the counter. His closeness was unnerving, and Darcy tried not to look as Bill lifted the sweating bottle of beer to his lips and drank thirstily.

Maybe if she ignored him long enough, he'd go away. Darcy forced herself to turn back to the task at hand.

She had underestimated Bill's determination. Soon she'd washed all the dishes, but he was still there. She reached for a towel and started to dry a tumbler, but Bill took the glass out of her hand and set it carefully down on the counter. It was obvious that he was not going away.

"I think I've gotten to know you well enough in the past few days that I can tell when something is on your mind. Did my mother say something that upset you?"

Darcy shook her head, but she couldn't look Bill in the eye. She picked up another glass and started to dry.

Bill took it out of her hand and placed it on the counter next to the first. "I'm not going to let you finish until you tell me what's wrong," he said in a firm tone that brooked no argument.

Darcy swallowed, then moistened her lips. "Really. It's nothing."

"Then why won't you look at me?" Bill took Darcy by the upper arms and turned her around to face him.

Darcy looked down at the damp dish towel, shook her head then sighed. "It isn't important."

"It *is* important. If it wasn't, you wouldn't be avoiding the subject like this. Tell me." He tipped her chin up to look into her face.

Letting out a breath, Darcy closed her eyes. Maybe it wouldn't be so hard if she couldn't see him. "Okay," she said in a rush. "Your mother said she wouldn't mind if she caught us kissing now and then." There, once she'd blurted it out, it didn't seem so bad.

Bill looked at her as he digested what she'd just said, then muttered a one-word curse. "She said that?" Before Darcy could answer, he burst out laughing.

He laughed and laughed and laughed.

"I don't see what's so darn funny," Darcy protested primly. "What are we going to do?"

Bill swallowed a chuckle. "Well, darlin', I reckon we are just going to have to oblige her and put on a good show." Wagging his tawny eyebrows suggestively, he reached for Darcy. "We might need some practice."

She sidled quickly away. "What do you think you're doing?"

He just looked at her and grinned. He crooked a finger and beckoned. "Come here."

She retreated farther. "No."

"Listen here. We have to make it look good if we're gonna convince Momma." He moved toward her.

Darcy was less worried about convincing Nettie than she was about not convincing herself. The last time she'd kissed Bill, she'd almost forgotten that this ridiculous situation wasn't real. If they kept practicing, she wasn't sure she could continue to draw the line. Her brain might want her to stop, but her body had definitely been rooting for her to go. "I think that kiss from the other night was perfectly authentic," she said, backing farther away.

Bill stopped. "That it was, Darcy, my girl. That it was."

The homey kitchen that had always seemed so large seemed to shrink as Bill advanced on her. There was no place to hide. Darcy glanced around, but Bill had effectively backed her into a corner. She took one more step back and found herself wedged into the right angle between the counter and the stove.

Bill stepped forward, then stopped close enough so that one deep breath would bring them together. Darcy felt him tower above her. She breathed in the floral scent of his mother's Cashmere Bouquet soap from his shower as well as the tantalizing male scent the floral fragrance couldn't disguise.

Why was she shrinking from him?

Hadn't she spent the better part of the last couple of nights dreaming about this and more? Hadn't she, deep in the untamed recesses of her mind, wanted this to happen? She swallowed, then moistened lips gone as dry as a desert.

Suddenly, the beer Bill had left on the counter looked awfully good. She drew in a deep breath. "I need a sip of your drink," she said, hoping to create a diversion.

Bill reached for the bottle, hooked a finger around the neck and dangled it in front of her. "You want some of this?" He held the bottle just out of her reach.

Throat too dry to speak, Darcy swallowed and nodded.

"And what will you give me for it?"

"Give you?" she squeaked, her heart beating too fast.

"Surely you don't think I'd give it away for free?" Bill cocked his head and looked at her, one eyebrow arched questioningly. "I think this whole thing started with the mention of a kiss."

Darcy shrank deeper into her corner. She hadn't counted on that, but why was she playing coy? She'd agreed to pretend to be this man's fiancée for his mother's sake. She certainly should have expected that an occasional kiss would be part of the package. Why couldn't she just kiss him and get it over with?

It wasn't as if she'd never kissed a man before.

Because she wasn't sure it would stop with one kiss. Considering she was still one of the walking wounded after escaping from her aborted wedding to Dick, the last thing she needed was to get involved with anyone else until she had her head on straight.

And after kissing Bill Hays the other night, she knew that kissing him was the last thing she needed for head-straightening.

She was caught between a rock and a hard place, and for the life of her, she wasn't sure which was the rock and what was the hard place: Bill or...what?

"I'm waiting," Bill teased, one hand propped against the kitchen cabinet, the other still hooked around the neck of the bottle. His hips were pressed against her, and Darcy could feel his desire. "Beer's getting warm," he reminded her, his voice sultry as the summer night outside.

Darcy drew in a deep breath, and she could feel his

need pulse against her. She swallowed. She could do this, she told herself. It wasn't that she wanted the beer that badly, she just wanted to find a way to slide out of Bill's seductive trap.

If she stayed there, if she let him kiss her, she didn't know whether she could keep from following through with what her aching body was begging her to do.

She rose quickly up on her toes and delivered a quick peck to Bill's cheek.

"Oh, no, darlin'," he said slowly and grabbed her arm. "That ain't gonna do it." He touched the mouth of the bottle against his lips. "Here," he said. "One quick, little kiss right here. That's all."

That was all? Darcy didn't think so, but her heart was pounding like a jungle drum. Her breath caught in her throat, and something inside her fluttered like a bird trying to escape a cage. Holding her breath to see what Bill would do, Darcy stretched on her toes and quickly pressed her lips to his.

In a blink it was over, and Darcy leaned against the counter, her breath coming in quick gasps. Since Bill had done nothing, except tie her in knots, the kiss was almost anticlimactic.

"See, it wasn't so bad, Darcy." Bill offered the beer to her. "Just one little kiss for Momma's sake," he said, stepping back to allow her to take the bottle.

This was the opening Darcy needed. She pushed the bottle aside and, laughing, darted under Bill's arm. No sooner had she thought she could breathe, than a strong, calloused hand caught her elbow.

Her laughter died in her throat.

"That little kiss might have been for Momma," Bill

said, his voice low, seductive, as he reeled her in like a spent fish. "But I need something for me." He drew Darcy to him and all she could see was the hunger in his eyes.

Chapter Six

He wanted Darcy, and it had nothing to do with the part they were playing for his mother.

Bill knew he shouldn't push her, knew that kissing Darcy would be a huge mistake, but he couldn't help it. He might not be able to follow through to the satisfaction his body craved, but maybe one good kiss would quell some of his cravings. At least, for now.

Darcy had gone completely motionless, but still Bill drew her closer. He could feel the frantic beating of her heart as he pressed her against his chest. He could see the frightened, doe-like look in her dark-brown eyes. But he wanted her, and nothing would assuage that need except to have her. At least, her lips.

He lowered his mouth toward hers, and Darcy's lids fluttered downward. He closed in and took what he could.

Her lips were soft and firm, but as he pressed his mouth against hers, he felt a subtle yielding. He persisted and Darcy's tender lips parted, allowing him access to her sweet depths. She relaxed against him, and Bill knew it was all right.

He probed and plundered and tasted and explored. Time seemed to stand still as he satisfied his desire for her. He knew he had to stop it, that he couldn't take this further, but for now it seemed right.

Darcy moaned softly, a sound so sweet, so intimate that he almost lost it. He deepened the kiss.

He didn't know where this was going, but for now Darcy was his.

The only thing that mattered was this woman in his arms. He pressed against her, his need swollen and firm. Her skin was soft, damp and hot beneath his hands. Did she want him, too?

Bill loosened his hold on her and worked his hands around to the front of her blouse. He found the button at the top and struggled to work it free.

Darcy's body stiffened. She grew still, and her breath stopped. Then she thrust her hands between them and pushed him away.

Bill groaned, but he backed off.

"Stop. We can't do this," Darcy rasped, her voice breathless, panicky. She backed again into her corner. "You promised."

"I did promise it would be just a business arrangement," Bill admitted, his voice as hoarse and husky as hers. "I have never taken a woman against her will, and don't mean to start that now." But, he had been dangerously close to doing that not thirty seconds ago.

Darcy looked as if she wanted to say something, but she seemed to be at a loss for words. Her lips moved, but she didn't speak. Her wide, frightened eyes spoke eloquently for her.

"I'm sorry," he managed tightly, though he wasn't certain what exactly he was sorry for. Was it because he had pushed her too far?

Or had he just not gone far enough to satisfy himself? She blinked and swallowed, but still didn't speak.

She clutched at her neck with a trembling hand as if she were trying to catch her breath or still a racing heart. Did she feel what he was feeling, too? Or had he simply frightened her? He had to figure out how to be close to her without going out of his mind. Thank God, his week's leave was nearly over.

"I was out of line," Bill finally managed. "It won't happen again." He drew in a long, ragged breath. "We'll just have to figure out some other way to show Momma."

"That we like each other...?" Darcy managed a thin smile. "I do like you, Bill. Billy. I admire what you're doing for your mother, but I'm not in the right place in my life to get involved with anoth—with a man."

Had she meant to say another man? Bill shook the thought away. Why did it matter? He had no real claim on her. He'd known her only a matter of days, and he'd be returning to Hurlburt in just a few more. In the meantime, surely they could manage to keep their distance.

The charade depended on it.

He looked down at Darcy, who was busily trying to look anywhere but at him. Not easy, when he had her wedged in the corner in the kitchen. "I'll just go back out to the porch and let you finish up in here," Bill said.

"Thank you," she said, her relief evident in her voice. "I won't be long. Then I think I'll just turn in early. My day at work is catching up with me."

Bill backed away, and Darcy slid—her arms crossed over her chest and her back pressed against the counter—around to the sink. Only when he'd stepped out of the kitchen did she turn away from him and back to her dishes.

He desperately needed a long, cold shower, but Bill

didn't want Darcy to know that. He didn't want her to think that he couldn't control himself around her. He didn't want to frighten her away.

He uttered a wry snort. His air-force training had taught him to control a lot of his impulses. Why hadn't there been a course on how to control his need for Darcy? Or was it merely his need for a woman?

Any woman.

DARCY HELD her breath for what seemed like forever, then let it out in a long, slow sigh. She turned on the water and started to wash her hands, but stopped before she even got them wet. She wasn't certain what had upset her more: the intensity of her attraction for Bill Hays or the fact that she'd pushed him away.

In her mind, she knew that she shouldn't be reacting the way she was to the man, considering what she'd just been through with Dick. But, in her heart, she couldn't help wondering if this new depth of feeling, this sexual attraction she'd never felt with her former fiancé was something she wanted to—ought to—explore.

Why hadn't she felt that way with Dick? If she had, would she have left him waiting at the altar?

She shook her head. Then, realizing that she had left the water running into the sink, she turned off the tap. She didn't even remember why she had turned the water on, and she wasn't sure what she should do about Bill.

One thing she did know. If she couldn't untangle her confused thoughts about Dick and the growing attraction she felt for Bill, she wasn't going to be able to get on with the rest of her life.

She glanced over her shoulder through the door to where she could just see Bill sitting on the porch swing.

Darcy drew in a deep breath and moistened her lips. Bill would be going back to his base in Florida in just a few days. And considering the crazy, mixed-up way she felt at this moment, Darcy wasn't certain whether that was a good thing...or a bad one.

IT WAS BEGINNING to be a daily ritual.

Bill sat out on the porch swing while Darcy finished the supper dishes. Again. He hated staying out here when he could be inside helping, but he hated worse having to keep his distance from her. He figured the best thing he could do would be to keep himself as far away from Darcy as he could. At least, that way, he wouldn't be tempted, and if Momma was watching, he wouldn't have to try to pretend. Pretending wasn't hard. Not when the attraction was this real. The hard part was knowing that for Darcy it wasn't.

Mornings had been easy enough. He'd stayed in bed until Darcy had gone. Tonight had been a killer. They'd had to demonstrate the affection Momma expected, and it was agonizing to hold back. But then, Darcy stiffened every time he got close to her, and that was almost like being doused with ice water.

But only for a moment.

As soon as they'd get some distance between them, the heat of his desire would flare up again. Why couldn't she feel the same way about him?

"Is there room for me?"

Bill looked up, startled. How had the object of his thoughts, his desires, sneaked up on him like that? He swallowed and managed a smile. "There's always room for you, darlin'." He scooted over and patted the seat.

"Thanks," Darcy said as she settled down on the

swing—a little too far away for Bill's liking, but she was there, and that was better than nothing.

"I think I owe you a little bit of an explanation," she told him without preamble.

"No, you don't owe me a thing. I figure you've been doing me a huge favor, way above and beyond the call…and I shouldn't expect more than that."

She put her fingers to his lips, and Bill felt a sudden tightening in his jeans.

"Hush," she said. "I need to say this."

Bill held his hands up. "Okay, I give…"

"You and your mother have been nothing but kind to me since I've been here." She stopped and cleared her throat, then paused to think. "After all, I just sort of barged into your lives, and you took me in, no questions asked."

She paused again, moistened her lips, then went on. "Normally, I wouldn't have been so eager to let you convince me to mooch off you."

"You haven't been mooching. You're really going to take a load off my mind when I go back to Florida," Billy interrupted.

"Just let me finish," she said sharply, then softened her tone. "I'm glad to help, but you need to understand why I'm willing. Usually, I'm more cautious."

"You're not running from the law, are you?"

That made her smile.

"No," Darcy said, then swallowed a chuckle. "I was supposed to be married," she said simply.

"Did he walk out on you?" Bill couldn't imagine any man walking out on Darcy. That man must have been a fool!

"No, I left him. And, I didn't do it nice and neat. I left him standing at the altar, having to explain to all the wedding guests that there wouldn't be a wedding.'' She paused to moisten her lips.

"It's all right, Darcy. I'm sure you had your reasons.''

Darcy leaned back in the swing, causing it to sway gently. Bill rested his hand on the back of the seat to steady it, and Darcy didn't push him away.

She looked out over the yard, just being swallowed by the darkness. The fireflies were starting to come up as if responding on cue to the need to soften the night. Bill took a deep breath of the honeysuckle-scented air and waited for her to go on.

He could understand, now, why she was so skittish when it came to play-acting. Why she had been so shocked when he'd suggested they go along with his mother's assumption. He'd try to give her the space, the time, she needed.

It wouldn't be easy.

"I'd known the man since I was a kid. Our families had known each other forever.'' Darcy leaned her head back and rested it on his arm. Bill didn't move, but held his breath, lest the slightest motion remind her that he was there. He didn't want to frighten her away. He waited for her to go on.

"Our parents were so...so fixated...on us being united, that they didn't really notice that it wasn't what I wanted.'' She sighed. "And I was so used to being the good girl and doing what my parents told me to that I just went along with it. I thought I could do it.''

Bill muttered a curse. "Didn't they ask you? Didn't that guy ask you?''

Darcy managed a brittle laugh. "You know, looking back on it, I don't think I ever truly accepted his proposal. I told him I needed to think about it, but when I went to my mother for advice, she was so excited that it just seemed easier to go along with her grand plans.

"That's what I get for opening up to my mother, I guess," she said ruefully. "Anyway, I played along all the way up until the day of the wedding. Then I sat there in the church, waiting for the ceremony to begin, and I realized I couldn't go through with it.

"I couldn't imagine myself married to him, tied down to him, for the rest of my life. I want a chance to earn my own living, to go out and explore. To find out who I am, independent of my family's expectations." She looked up at him and shrugged. "So, are you sorry you got us mixed up in this mess?"

Bill thought for a long moment. "No," he said, finally understanding what was going on in her head. "I'm glad I could give you a place to figure things out, and I'm really glad I happened to pick you up that night. It almost seems like it was planned."

"I hardly think so," Darcy said wryly. "But, I like your mother, I like my new job, and I'm glad the arrangement is working out." She scooted around in the seat, turning to face him, and Bill mourned the loss of the feel of her skin.

"Whatever the reason, it'll take a load off me, knowing somebody who knows what they're doing is here with Momma. That'll make going back to Hurlburt a hell of a lot easier."

The hard part would be saying goodbye.

THE NIGHT was warm, in spite of the air conditioner, and Darcy lay awake in the narrow bed across the hall from Bill's room for a good long time. The cooling system droned, the crickets chirped outside, and the bugs continued to batter against the window screens.

Under normal circumstances, all the white noise around her would have guaranteed a sound night's sleep, but slumber eluded her.

And it had nothing to do with sounds coming from outside her window.

She felt better having told Bill about Dick. Well, she hadn't actually given him name, rank and serial number, but still…maybe if he kissed her, that would clarify her thoughts, make Bill seem more human and less damned attractive.

She laughed at that, softly in the quiet of the night. Bill Hays would have to work really hard to be unattractive. After all, she'd seen him sweaty and grimy after working all day in the hot sun, and she'd gone weak in the knees just at the sight.

Had that been merely a physical reaction that she should try to control, or was this the beginning of something…real?

Darcy sat up, punched her pillow, then flopped back down on the too-soft mattress. How many times had she gone through this ritual tonight? How many more would it take before she'd finally be able to sink into the silent oblivion of a good night's rest?

She glanced at the clock on the bedside table. If she didn't settle down soon she'd be exhausted in the morning. At least, she didn't have to go to work.

Was that a good thing? She wasn't sure.

Yes, she'd be free to relax, maybe go into town and do a little shopping. And if she were to go to town, she'd be away from too-hot, too-attractive-for-words Bill Hays.

Avoiding Bill wasn't her real reason for needing to go to town. She needed uniforms for work, and if she was going to stay here, she'd have to beef up her wardrobe. Her jeans and her linen suit would only work for her for so long.

She had plenty of clothes at her uncle's house in Florida, but she wasn't about to contact her family to send them to her; she didn't want to talk to them for any reason.

Not yet, anyway.

If she stayed—and she knew she would—she'd have to spend more time with Bill, pretending to be in love with him. Not that it was all that hard. Pretending for Nettie's sake was getting easier by the day. Not letting Bill know that she wasn't sure she was really pretending was going to be the real problem.

BILL YAWNED and stretched as he lingered over his breakfast plate. He wasn't tired. In fact, he was wide awake and ready to go. But he couldn't go anywhere until Darcy got up.

What was wrong with her? Was she sick? Was she having one of those female days his sisters always seemed to wallow in? Usually, Darcy was the first one up.

He chuckled as he poured himself another cup of coffee. He'd heard her get up early all week while he'd lain in bed waiting for her to leave for work. He'd felt like a champion slug for doing it, too. Hell, he thought as he added milk and sugar, you'd think he didn't get up at zero-dark-thirty every day when he was on duty.

But Darcy acted as if it were her job to wake up the roosters!

He'd heard that expression all the time, but he hadn't really understood it until now. She was a go-getter, all right. That was one of the many things he liked about her.

Bill guessed maybe Darcy deserved to sleep late after getting up so early all week, but damn it, he wanted to see her. He lived for her smile.

That stopped him. Had he really just thought that?

He shook his head. No, he had no business thinking about her in any way other than the relationship they'd arranged. Darcy was there for his mother. That was all. She wasn't there for him.

Even if he wanted her to be.

Bill raised his coffee mug to his lips. He hadn't really needed another cup of coffee, nor had he wanted it. He just needed a reason to linger in the kitchen until Darcy came in. He'd had it all planned that he would take her to town, buy her lunch at the Dinner Belle Diner, and by the time they came home, they'd have dispensed with all this shy awkwardness. But, he wanted it to look like a spur-of-the-moment idea, not a calculated plan.

He grimaced at the taste of the hot coffee on a day already too warm. It would damn sure be easier to pretend to be lovers if at least they were friends. And friends was all they could be, he reminded himself.

He had a good ten more years in the air force, and maybe more time after that before he'd be in a position to care for a wife and—dare he even think it?—a family. But, in the week he'd known Darcy, he'd begun to realize what he'd deprived himself of by pushing so hard to make something of himself.

A roll in the hay from time to time with a willing partner was fine, but it wasn't the same as having a woman who knew you and understood what you were all about and cared for you anyway. And now that Bill had begun to see what it was like to care for someone besides his family, he could see what he'd been missing. What he was not going to have for too many years.

He set his mug down, clenched his fist, then slammed it against the table. The dishes and flatware rattled and coffee sloshed out of his cup. Bill felt vaguely satisfied from venting his frustration, but it wasn't enough.

"Remind me not to get in your way in the mornings," Darcy said, her tone dry and ironic. "I might not live to tell the tale."

Bill jerked around, embarrassment staining his face. How had he let her sneak up on him and catch him in that one moment of bad temper?

There she was, fresh from a shower, and smelling like soap and flowers and woman, and he had shown her his worst side. Bill raised his hands in a submissive gesture and almost forgot what he wanted to say when he looked into her bright brown eyes. "I promise my bark is worse than my bite," he said. "Usually."

Darcy smiled. "You sure? I don't need my head bitten off first thing in the morning." She looked toward the stove. "Is there any coffee?"

"Yeah, plenty. I'll get it. It's been on the stove for a while, so it might be bitter." He pushed himself up out of the chair, upsetting it in his eagerness. *Nice move, bubba,* he couldn't help thinking. *First you come on like a rabid dog, then a gawky puppy. Way to impress her!*

"Thanks. I'll risk the bitter coffee as long as it has caffeine in it." She reached for a mug from a hook under a cabinet. "I love it when somebody else waits on me," Darcy said as she slid into a seat across from Bill's plate.

"I aim to serve," Bill said as he poured. "Can I fix you some eggs?"

"Why? Are they broken?"

"What?" Bill looked at Darcy. Was she making a joke this early in the morning?

"The eggs? Were they broken?"

Bill sat down across from Darcy. He still hadn't recovered from being caught in his fit of temper, and he was careful to avoid looking at her. What if she were laughing? "I got it, Darcy. May I prepare some eggs for you?" She must have spent too much time with Mrs. Scarborough the other night.

Darcy laughed and caught his hand.

Bill didn't know what he liked more, the sound of her laughter, or the feel of her touch. "Yeah?" *Yes, yes, yes, anything you desire,* he wanted to shout.

"You don't need to wait on me, Bill. I got up late, so I'm only going to have some cereal. Just sit with me and keep me company." She gestured toward the seat he'd just vacated as she got up to get a bowl and cereal.

That was an offer he couldn't refuse. And it worked right into what he'd intended to do this morning. Now, maybe he could ease that invitation to go to town with him right into casual conversation.

Funny. He felt anything but casual.

"You look like you have something on your mind," Darcy observed as she set the cereal box on the table. She sat down and looked at him expectantly. "Penny for your thoughts?"

A perfect opening if he ever had one. Why, then, did he suddenly feel so shy? Surely, Darcy wouldn't turn him down. "Just wondering if you wanted to go to town with me," he said. There, he'd done it.

"No!"

The speed of her answer and the force of it shocked him. "Why the hell not?"

Darcy jerked back and narrowed her eyes at him. "You don't have to snap at me. I thought somebody should be here so your mother wouldn't be alone. Isn't that why you wanted me to stay here with her?''

Relief washed over him. At least, it wasn't a rejection of him, Bill thought. Or was it? He shrugged. ''Momma won't be alone. My brother Ray's coming over.''

''Was he at the party the other night?''

Bill shook his head. ''Ray lives out in Alexander City, and he drives a truck, to boot, so he doesn't get over as much as he'd like. He's got a couple days off, so he'll be here any time now.'' He glanced at Darcy and tried not to look too hopeful.

Darcy gnawed at her lip as if he were a criminal and she had to decide his innocence or guilt. It wasn't that big a decision was it? He'd just asked her to go to town. He hadn't proposed.

Wishing he could kiss her to keep her from marring those lips he'd so much enjoyed kissing, he raised the stakes. ''I'll buy you lunch.''

What woman could resist a line like that?

Chapter Seven

What girl in her right mind could refuse an invitation from Bill Hays, Darcy thought as she tried not to drown in his earnest green eyes. At least, this morning he was fully dressed. If he had been sitting there shirtless, as she'd seen him so often this week, she might have been tempted to fall into his arms right then and there. As it was, he was still pretty darned attractive in a kelly-green polo shirt and khaki slacks.

She was still a woman on the rebound, she reminded herself. She didn't want to get involved with another man. After all, she'd demonstrated that she wasn't a good judge of husband material. Though she was certain Bill must have some flaws that would eventually turn her off, she hadn't seen any yet. He seemed too perfect, as had Dick right up to the day of the wedding. But instead of Dick's polished perfection, Bill's seemed raw, and so much more potent. Maybe, if she spent a little more time with him, she'd find his flaws.

No. She didn't need the complication no matter what the reasons while she was trying to figure out what to do with herself. Darcy glanced at Bill as if getting another look at him would make him less attractive. No, he still made her breath catch in her throat.

But Bill would be returning to Hurlburt tomorrow afternoon after church, another part of her mind countered. Nothing could possibly happen in a place as public, and as quaint, as the Dinner Belle Diner. Darcy had eaten there a couple of times this week, and she knew there was nothing romantic about the place. She had to smile as she poured cereal into a bowl.

"Your only reason for going to town isn't just to wine and dine me—without the wine—is it?" There was no way that she was going to let this feel like a date. "And I won't leave until your brother Ray gets here. I won't leave your mother alone if I don't have to."

"No, I'm not trying to wine and dine you," Billy said. Was that a hint of defeat in his tone? Had he really wanted it to be a date? "I have to get a haircut before I show up for duty first thing Monday morning." He raked his hand through thick, light-brown hair that seemed shades lighter from so much time working in the sun this week.

To Darcy, the slightly out-of-bounds look was quite attractive. She'd secretly hated Dick's impeccable haircut, but she never would have said a word about it. It was regulation, after all. She wished Billy didn't have to cut the thatch of hair she wanted to run her fingers through. Just once before...

She shook her head.

Bill's hopeful expression fell. "Is that a no?"

Darcy shook her head again. "Huh? What? Did you say something?"

"You shook your head. Have you changed your mind?"

"Oh, no." Darcy flushed with acute embarrassment. It was one thing to think about him, but another to le him see what she was thinking. "I'm sorry. My mind was wandering." Right over to him. She looked down at the dry cereal in her bowl. If she put milk on it, she'd have an excuse to eat and not talk.

"Let me eat my cereal before it gets soggy. Then I have to get ready before your brother gets here." She poured milk into the bowl. "I need to do some shopping," she said as if to prove it to herself—or to him?—that she was only going with him because she had planned to go anyway.

Bill didn't seem to mind. He just pushed out of his chair, took his breakfast plate to the sink, then left her alone in the kitchen.

HE HAD NEVER BEEN so glad to see his brother in all his life. Bill had shaken hands and introduced Darcy. Ray had already heard about the engagement. Was there anyone in Alabama who hadn't? They'd exchanged a few pleasantries about the weather and Momma's condition, and then he and Darcy had skedaddled out of there. His rapid defection was as much because he was eager to get to town as it was that he'd always felt awkward around his older brother.

Ray was the oldest and Billy the youngest, with fifteen long years between them. They hardly knew each other. Ray had gone off for three years in the army when Bill was three. His brother had come home with a German wife and a kid on the way, and grown-up responsibilities eight-year-old Billy couldn't begin to understand. Ray had been busy building his life and had been away most of Bill's growing-up years. Bill felt as though they were a couple of strangers who just happened to be related.

Bill breathed a long, deep sigh as he pulled out onto the Mattison-Elm City Road.

"Something wrong?" Darcy asked from her spot far across the front seat, all but mashed against the door.

"No. I just never have anything to say to Ray." Bill paused to think. "And sometimes I feel bad about it."

"I understand," Darcy said without missing a beat. "I feel like that about most of my relatives. We moved around a lot, so I didn't get to grow up with them like most people do." She looked out the window, a wistful expression in her eyes. "I always envied those kids who knew their cousins as well as their brothers and sisters. I envied their roots."

"Hell, I got roots, all right. And plenty of dirt to put them in," Bill said. "Too much dirt, sometimes. We've been trying to talk Momma into selling and moving into one of those Assisted Living Centers in town where she'd be taken care of and be closer to the hospital."

"Don't you dare!" Darcy said sharply. "How could you? I'd give anything for roots as old and as deep as yours."

Bill couldn't look at her, couldn't gauge her expression because he'd come to the turn-off onto the state road to town. "You know she won't have anything to do with the idea." He shook his head as he waited for a pickup truck to go by. "Sometimes we wonder if she cares more for that place than she does for her own good."

"She just knows how important it is to link the past with the future, that's all."

"I don't know why," Bill muttered. "That place has been nothing but heartbreak for her. Daddy died trying to run it single-handedly and work another job to feed all us kids. Died of heatstroke trying to get a week's worth of chores done on a Saturday.''

Darcy turned toward him and laid her hand gently on his shoulder. Even through the fabric of his shirt he could feel the way she seemed to care. "I'm sorry, Bill. It must have hurt to grow up without a father, but if he hadn't wanted to work so hard, he wouldn't have.'' Darcy smiled. "It's clear to anyone who looks how much your mother loves her home. Even after so many years, she doesn't seem to regret a moment of her life there." Darcy lifted her hand, depriving him of its slight weight and tremendous warmth. "Maybe you can't understand what they were working for, but I can. They wanted to give you what I never had. Roots. Tradition. A feeling of connectedness to a place.

"I know why that was so important to them. Your parents were from a generation that had very little. I think it was important to build something of their own, to have something to leave to their children." Darcy shrugged. "My family never lacked in a financial sense, but we never had that feeling of connection I see with you and your family. You may have regretted having to struggle for everything when you were growing up, but you were so much richer than I was in many ways."

Darcy had it nailed, Bill couldn't help thinking, but he didn't want to talk about it. Maybe, she hadn't grown up poor, maybe she thought it was romantic to wear hand-me-downs and scrape just to have the money to take a girl to a drive-in movie, but he didn't. "I'd just as soon not talk about this anymore," he finally said.

"Fine," Darcy replied and abruptly drew back into her spot, scrunched up against the passenger door.

Bill didn't like the way they'd left it, but it was something he wasn't ready to deal with. She hadn't had to do without. She hadn't had to leave home to earn for herself the things most other people took for granted.

He blew out a long, exaggerated breath. The rest of the drive to Pittsville was going to take forever with this stony silence between them.

THEY PASSED the big shopping center at the crossroads of the state road and Main Street and headed downtown to the uniform shop. Darcy liked the quiet, old-fashioned look of the small downtown area with its home-owned businesses and friendly people. Bill parked at the curb in front of the Dinner Belle Diner, then they split up, much to Darcy's relief. Bill went to get his hair cut at a place that looked like something right out of Mayberry, and Darcy headed for the uniform shop that the receptionist in Doctor Williamson's office had told her about.

Darcy breathed in the warm, summer air. Now that Bill was out of sight, she felt as if she could relax again. Even when they weren't speaking, the confines of that Jeep had seemed way too small. And not because they were upset with each other.

The car had been too small because she was too close to Billy Hays to think clearly. She still wasn't certain why. Had her feelings for Dick been normal, or was this the way you ought to feel about the man you were supposed to marry? Now she knew how women got themselves into trouble if that was the way their men made them feel. She could finally see how a woman could throw all caution aside and not really regret finding herself alone with a child when the passion finally burned itself out and the man had left.

That stopped her. She paused outside the uniform

shop, her hand on the doorknob. She couldn't believe what she had just been thinking.

She had to be more careful around Bill. It was bad enough that just looking at him made her weak in the knees. There was no sense in getting into a mess that she'd never get out of. After all, she'd just gotten herself out of one engagement, and that had not been pretty.

She and Bill weren't really engaged, she told herself sternly as she stepped inside the store. Just half the people in the county believed they were.

"I hoped you'd be coming in," a smiling young woman said from behind the counter as the bell above the door announced Darcy's arrival.

"Excuse me?" Was this one of the many people she'd met at Bill's birthday party the other night? At church? One of the doctor's patients? She didn't look familiar. "Have we met? I'm sorry I don't remember your name."

The woman, a ripe strawberry blonde with a figure Darcy would have killed for, was wearing too much makeup in a vain attempt to cover some of the freckles that peppered her from head to toe. "I'm Margaret Jean Smithfield," she said hurrying around the counter to take Darcy by the arm as if they were best friends, and leading her to a display of pastel-colored smocks.

"So, you've known Bill for a long time?" Darcy said cautiously a few minutes later, as she examined her reflection in the showroom mirror. A finger of jealousy stabbed at her as she wondered just how well.

"Since I was knee-high to a weed. Billy and my brother Jamey were like this." Margaret Jean held up two fingers pressed closely together. "I had such a crush on him, but of course, he never saw me as nothing

more than Jamey's ornery little sister.'' Margaret Jean
let out a huge sigh. "And now you've got him.''

Darcy didn't quite know how to respond to that, so
she didn't.

"Just because you have to wear a uniform don't
mean you have to wear the same thing day after day,''
the woman went on without stopping to listen. "And I
think the yellow and the pink will both look good on
you.''

The woman ought to be working at some expensive
boutique the way she was dictating clothing choices,
Darcy thought. "All right,'' Darcy said. "You've got
yourself a sale. And I'll need three pairs of white slacks
to go with.'' She told her the size.

The woman grinned and went to find the slacks.

"You might have to hem these up,'' Margaret Jean
said when she returned. "They might be a tad long.''

"I think I can deal with it,'' Darcy said, accepting
the package and turning toward the door. She wasn't
sure she liked being the constant topic of conversation.
And it didn't seem that Pittsville was small enough that
every newcomer would be instantly identifiable, but
here she was, recognized wherever she went. It gave
her the willies.

She shuddered as she left the store, the bell on the
door tolling her departure. Considering her experience
at the uniform shop, she wondered if she should risk
trying the dollar store two doors down, or wait till Bill
could take her to the giant discount store that dominated
the shopping center on the main road. She decided to
try this one. She needed her respite from Bill, even
though she missed him, too. And she didn't need him
hovering while she bought the nightgowns and other
personal items she'd come for.

Looping the handholds of the sack over her wrist, she pushed her way through the heavy doors.

BILL DRUMMED his fingers restlessly on the scarred tabletop in the corner booth in the Dinner Belle Diner. He hadn't thought to suggest a time to meet Darcy here. After all, how long could it take to pick up a couple of uniforms? They all looked alike. He'd been waiting for what seemed like hours.

The waitress came up and offered him a refill on his iced tea. "You don't reckon she stood you up, hon?" the woman said, the sympathy in her tone lost among the pops and crackles of her gum as she filled his glass—again.

He felt as though he'd drunk enough tea to float a battleship, or at least an inflatable rubber boat, but he had to do something while he waited. Bill forced a smile in the direction of the waitress. "Thanks. She'll be here. She just had more errands to run than I did."

"Well, if she stands you up, I get off at one," the woman said over her shoulder as she sashayed away, swinging her hips in a way Bill figured was meant to be seductive but missed the mark by a mile.

He grinned to himself. Had that been a come-on?

Bill looked around. The place hadn't changed much in the years since he'd started coming here in high school. This place had been the hangout until a couple of fast-food places had come to the shopping center on the highway. Still, he preferred this place. At least, here, he could linger over a glass of iced tea—or two or three—without feeling like he was taking up a spot a paying customer might need.

Not that the place was empty, by any means. On weekdays this little restaurant probably hummed when the workers from the courthouse, county offices and the bank next door came in for lunch. He glanced at a logo on the back of the uniform of one of the customers and grinned to himself. The feed store must still be open on Saturdays.

The jangling bell over the door announced the arrival of another customer. Darcy.

"I'm sorry I'm late," she announced breathlessly as she juggled shopping bags. "It took me a while to find what I was looking for. I had to go to several stores." Darcy piled her bags into the booth across from Bill and slid in after them. "It's good that I had a list or I would have forgotten half of what I wanted. As it was, I had to look and look until I found everything." She picked up the menu and made a big show of looking it over. "I must have walked a mile."

Bill took the menu out of her hands. "You know what's on the menu, Darcy. You've eaten here all week. Why are you avoiding me?"

With Billy touching her she found it hard to think...to breathe.

Darcy didn't think she'd been avoiding him. Not exactly. When she'd been wandering through all the stores in the tiny downtown section of Pittsville, that's when she'd been avoiding him. Now that she was here across the table from him, how could she avoid him?

He was there in front of her: as big as life and just as real. No, she couldn't avoid him or ignore him— even if she wanted to—no matter how hard she tried.

"What do you mean?" she finally managed. "I'm here." She reached for the menu, but Bill placed his hand firmly on top of it, anchoring it to the tabletop.

"You slid into this booth and ducked behind that menu so fast, I couldn't be sure it was really you."

If that hadn't been so close to true, Darcy would have laughed. She didn't know why she thought she had to have a wall between her and Bill, but she felt she needed some sort of protection. She'd come to like him too much in the past few days to clutter all that up with caring for him, too. Wasn't it enough that she cared for his mother?

She didn't know how to respond, so she didn't. She just looked down at his strong, square hand on top of the ugly, plastic-covered menu. She could think of better places for his hand to be.

How could she keep thinking these things? She wanted to sink down into the seat and die! And she'd thought sitting across from him in this diner would be safe...

She wouldn't be safe from these feelings of want and need and...what?...until he was safely back at Hurlburt Field. Darcy risked a glance over at him.

Maybe not even then.

"What's the matter, don't you have a snappy comeback?" Bill teased. "Good. I like it that I made you speechless." He moved his hand then gestured toward the menu. "Go ahead. Read away."

Darcy snatched it up before Bill could change his mind, opened it up and pretended to study it. She'd eaten here three times last week. She knew what was on the menu.

The waitress came over, a gum-chewing, slightly more shopworn version of Margaret Jean. Most of her hair was brittle blond and an inch of dingy roots showed in her over-sprayed do. "I see she made it," she said, directing her comment to Bill. Was that resentment in her voice?

"Yes, ma'am, she finally got done with all her shopping.'' Bill grinned up at the woman. ''Luverne, this is my fiancée, Darcy.''

Darcy started to bristle at the introduction, but this was one time she didn't mind Bill staking his claim on her. Not that she thought he was interested in the waitress. But, she sure could see why another woman would be interested in her Bill.

Her Bill?

When would her heart stop telling her mind what to say? She was an educated woman. A professional. She didn't need a man. She didn't need to be taken care of. She was perfectly capable of taking care of herself. Tracy D'Arcy Harbeson Stanton did not need a man.

''And what would you like?'' The waitress's nasal twang interrupted Darcy's private diatribe.

Remembering that the woman was working, even if it was Darcy's day off, she looked up and managed an anemic smile. ''I'll have an iced tea, no sugar, and the diet plate.'' Darcy closed the menu and handed it to Luverne.

She waited until the waitress had gone. ''And how is it that your old friend, Luverne, didn't know you were engaged like everybody else in this county does?'' Darcy muttered.

''My old friend?'' Bill looked at her, his emerald-green eyes seeming to bore through her. ''What the hell is with you today? One minute you can barely make yourself look at me and the next you act like you're jealous of a waitress. What's it gonna be? Either you're with me, or you're not. Make up your mind.''

If it had been Darcy giving that speech, she might have punctuated it by leaving, but Bill was too much of a gentleman for that. He just leaned against the booth back and seemed to shut himself off from her. Retreating to his cave, Darcy supposed. And she supposed she didn't blame him. She knew she was running hot one minute and cold the next. But, she didn't know what to do.

She wasn't supposed to feel like this.

This farce had been intended to be more of a business alliance than...than...what? She wasn't supposed to develop feelings for the man.

Darcy peeled the band off the silverware bundle and toyed with it. She should apologize to him, she thought miserably, but she didn't know how. Wasn't it enough that she'd spilled the whole stupid story about Dick and how she wasn't ready to get involved with another man? Did he think she owed him more?

She let out a long, tired sigh and wearily closed her eyes.

A warm hand covered hers, and Darcy couldn't force herself to pull away. The truth was she liked the way her hand felt in his. She liked the wonderful, frightening way Bill Hays made her feel.

But, Darcy kept thinking, she shouldn't be the least bit interested in another man. Not now. She wasn't supposed to be ready. It was much too soon.

"I shouldn't have pushed you, Darcy," Bill said, his deep voice penetrating her thoughts. "I haven't forgotten what you told me the other night." He paused, and Darcy looked up at him, waiting for him to finish.

There was something about that statement that needed an ending. It was like waiting for the other shoe to drop.

"Is there anything wrong with wanting to get to know you? After all, I am entrusting you with the care of my mother. I—" Bill stopped as Luverne approached with Darcy's glass of tea and a refill for Bill.

The waitress set the glass down almost grudgingly then shuffled away without saying a word.

"Looks like you broke her heart," Darcy couldn't help teasing.

"I promise, I never saw the woman before today," Bill said, holding up his right hand as if to swear.

"Then how'd you know her name?" she challenged. Why was she reacting like a jealous wife?

Bill rolled his eyes. "Darcy, Darcy, Darcy. If you hadn't been so busy memorizing the menu, you would have seen she was wearing a name tag."

"Oh." Darcy had to laugh. And to feel a bit ashamed, as well. She seldom noticed things like name tags, and it wouldn't have occurred to her to address the woman by name. To Bill, it seemed as natural as breathing.

No wonder she liked him so much.

"I'll try not to come on so strong," Bill said, only managing to make her feel worse.

That was her Billy. Genuine and true through and through.

Her Billy?

He wasn't really hers. When had she gone from thinking of him as Bill to *her* Billy? She didn't deserve a man like him.

But she wanted one.

No, she wanted him.

If he didn't go back to Florida soon, she didn't know how she would be able to continue to resist. Would tomorrow ever come so she could send him on his way?

Chapter Eight

He missed her already.

Bill hadn't driven twenty miles down the road before he'd realized that his pretend engagement to Darcy felt very real. As he crossed the Alabama River and drove through Montgomery, he thought about how he had procrastinated about finding a place to stop and drop Darcy off at a motel.

How different things would be if he hadn't.

And he wasn't sure if it would have been a good difference or a bad one. It would be good if he weren't being tortured by these strange feelings of need for Darcy. He had a plan, and damn it, this woman wasn't a part of it. But, if he hadn't nearly run over her in the dark that night, he might not have somebody to stay with Momma. Bill blew out a long breath.

Women were so confusing.

Or was it just Darcy?

No. He laughed bitterly. He was the confused one. Considering how standoffish Darcy had been, Bill was pretty sure Darcy was perfectly clear about their relationship.

He was damned if he was.

The only thing he knew was that someone he could

trust was staying at home with his mother. Not only did Darcy seem to be a good person, but the fact that she was a nurse was a real bonus. He was damned lucky to have happened on her. Even if she had his guts tied in knots half the time.

But he couldn't help thinking he was damned. Something in the back of his mind kept warning him to be careful. About what, he didn't know.

Would he be able to forget her when he got back to base? Would returning to the hectic, busy schedule be just what he needed to get his head back on straight?

Bill could only hope that if he put in a sixteen-hour day, he'd be too tired to think about Darcy. But for now, he had to keep his eyes peeled for Darcy's abandoned car.

He scanned the sides of the road all the way from Brewton—where they'd eaten—to the state line and he didn't see a car matching the description Darcy had given him. That probably meant the car had been found and towed. The tow company would track Darcy down through the registration. He figured he didn't have to worry about it any more.

DARCY COULDN'T BELIEVE how empty the house felt now that Bill was gone. She'd been so looking forward to the day he'd leave so she could be herself again. Now that it was here, she still wasn't the Darcy she thought she was.

She kept looking at her watch and wondering just where along the road Bill was. Had he located her car? Was he safe? She was a fine mess.

Nettie was out on the swing watching the fireflies dance, so Darcy decided to join her. She loved the smell of the honeysuckle and even the june bugs' whirring had become familiar and pleasant.

"What are you thinking about, Nettie?" Darcy settled down beside her and set the swing into gentle motion while she waited for the woman to answer.

Several moments passed before Nettie responded, but Darcy was in no hurry. Nettie smiled and patted Darcy's hand. Her fingers were cool in spite of the warmth of the evening and reminded Darcy that Nettie's time was short. Darcy closed her hand over Nettie's and waited. Sometimes the telling was in the silences, and she knew not to push.

"I was just thinkin' how proud I am of all my children," Nettie said softly. "I know I didn't have much to give them, but it does my heart good to see how far they all have come." She squeezed Darcy's hand and went on. "Even Lougenia's finally getting back on her feet after Dwayne leavin' her."

She smiled to herself, and Darcy knew that Nettie would finish in her own sweet time. In the meantime, there were all those fireflies to watch.

"You know, Lougenia was my smart one," Nettie said. "Always had her nose in a book. Had a scholarship to the University of Montevallo." She shook her head. "She met Dwayne there. Did you know that?"

"No, ma'am, I didn't," Darcy said. She didn't even known that Lougenia had gone to college. Much less anything at all about her ex-husband.

"He was a big ole senior and she was a freshman. He was from a rich family up yonder in Birmingham, and he just swept her off her feet. He went on to medical school, you know. Lou would have nothing else but to get married and work to put him through. She thought it was so romantic.

"But after Dwayne graduated, he'd outgrown her. Or so he said." Nettie sighed. "Said she wasn't up to socializing with the right kind of people. His kind of people. Told her she'd drag him down."

Darcy started to say something, but Nettie went on. "Billy was so angry at Dwayne when he moved out that he would've kilt him if he'd been there. Good thing he was still out in California." She laughed, the sound more brittle than merry. "He was furious that another Hays woman was left alone."

"But Lougenia has skills," Darcy protested. Lougenia hadn't put Dwayne through medical school by working a factory job; she'd become a medical transcriptionist.

"I know that, Darcy girl. I know that Lougenia is finally coming into her own, and that Dwayne leavin' her was probably the best thing that ever happened to her." She smiled. "I reckon she's happier now than she's ever been.

"Don't make no difference to Billy. He can't ever forget growing up with no daddy and not having the things that other kids had." Nettie looked out over the dark yard. "He swore when he was eighteen years old and leaving for basic training that he would never, ever put a woman in that kind of situation. He swore that he wouldn't marry until he was sure he could provide, and he was sure that he'd love her forever.

"That's why I'm so pleased that he found you." Nettie patted Darcy's hand. "I didn't think I'd get a chance to see the woman he finally settled on. And I sure didn' think it would happen so soon."

Tears stung Darcy's eyes. What could she say in response to that? She couldn't tell this wonderful woma who had worked so hard that she hardly knew Bil

They'd only gone along with her misunderstanding so Bill would know that someone with nursing experience would be here with his mother.

Darcy didn't know what to do. Their intentions had been good when they'd cooked up the plan, but she felt so darned guilty. She had thought it would be so simple to play along with Nettie's assumptions, but now she could see so clearly what they were doing. How could they lead Nettie along like this?

Darcy blinked back the tears, but she couldn't hold back a sob that had been fighting to come out. "I'm sorry," she managed, then pushed out of the swing and rushed inside.

She hurried to the solitude of her room and slammed the door behind her, not caring how it must appear to Nettie. Darcy flung herself on the bed. How could she be a party to such a horrible deception to such a kind and gentle woman?

Clutching wads of pink chenille bedspread in her hands, Darcy cried as if she'd lost her best friend in the world. And maybe she had. Hadn't she just realized that she'd lost her self-respect?

After a while, when she had no more tears to cry, Darcy lay in the dark in her room and tried to make sense of it. The tears might have dried, but she couldn't stop the sobs that still wracked her body.

Sometime between a sob and a sniff, Darcy noticed a gentle tapping on her door.

"Darcy, sugar. Can I come in?"

What could she say? It was Nettie's house. "Yes, ma'am," she managed.

Nettie stepped inside, letting the bright light from the hall in with her. "I know it's hard, you being so far away from our Billy, but the time'll go fast. He'll be

back soon," she said, her breathing labored from walking in from the swing. She lowered herself to sit on the
bed beside Darcy.

The words, meant to help, were like pouring salt into
Darcy's already raw eyes.

Nettie stroked Darcy's hair, and Darcy felt more miserable than ever. How could it be that she'd agreed to
stay here to help Nettie, and Nettie was here trying to
make her feel better?

How she hated that she and Billy were lying to his
mother. Even if it had been for the right reasons. How
she wished she and Bill could make it right.

How she wished he really were *her* Billy.

BILL PULLED into his designated spot in the apartment
complex parking lot and looked up to the front window
of his place. Used to be he liked the sound of that: his
place. Seeing it gave him a sense of pride, but now it
just seemed like another of the many dorms and military
quarters where he'd hung his hat.

Home was that little house in Mattison. Home was
where Darcy was.

And Darcy wasn't really even his.

Ski must be home because there was a light shining
in the window. Usually, Bill enjoyed his roommate, but
tonight the only thing he could think about was killing
the three weeks until his next scheduled visit home. To
Darcy.

He collected his stuff from the cargo compartment in
the rear, then locked the Jeep and headed up. Maybe
Ski would be a good diversion to keep him from thinking about her. Missing her.

Bill unlocked the door and shouldered his way
through. Ski was sitting in front of the television, wear-

ing one of his obnoxious Hawaiian shirts and drinking a beer. He was watching a soccer game, a satellite feed from some foreign country, and Bill shrugged. Ski had been born in Poland and had come to this country when he was a small boy. Bill figured he could be forgiven for preferring soccer over football, but Bill didn't get it.

He dropped his bag inside the door and headed for the refrigerator. He constructed a sandwich and grabbed a beer of his own and ambled back into the living room.

It was a commercial break, so he figured it was safe to talk. "Anything happen I should know about?" If there had been any real excitement, the first sergeant would have called him to come back. But, Ski had planned to go to Colonel Harbeson's niece's wedding. Maybe there was news from that.

"You know it, man," Ski said, putting his beer down and swiveling around to look at Bill. "The wedding was exciting."

Bill arched an eyebrow and made himself comfortable on the couch. He was just as glad that he had scheduled leave so he hadn't had to attend. He enjoyed the looser restrictions and family atmosphere of the combat control squadron that had allowed him an open invitation to the colonel's niece's wedding. But, he was just as glad not to have to witness another woman give herself to a man who might not come home.

He'd met the groom, a stuck-on-himself flyboy, and he'd felt genuine compassion for the poor woman he'd hooked. But, then the women who went for those flashy pilot-types were just as phony as Dick, so maybe there was an equal match. "What happened? One of the guys from Black Team get drunk and upchuck all over the bride's mother at the reception?"

"If only." Ski laughed. "The bride didn't show. She sky-dived out the back window, wedding dress and all, and took off in her car." Ski took a swig of his beer, and laughed again. "You should have seen the poor sucker. *He* drank enough at the reception—it was already paid for—to barf all over the bride's mother." The commercial ended and so did Ski's report on the fiasco.

"So, Colonel Harbeson's niece ditched the pilot," Bill muttered to himself. "It couldn't have happened to a nicer guy."

"You got that in one," Ski agreed, without taking his eyes off the screen.

But then Bill thought about another engagement and wedding that wouldn't come off. Of course, he wouldn't be left standing at the altar with egg on his face as Dick had. Both he and Darcy knew that there wasn't going to be a wedding. Still, he couldn't help feeling maybe a little bit like Dick must feel.

Disappointed about a marriage that would never be.

THURSDAY AFTERNOON, Darcy came home to find Leah at the door, a worried look on her face. Darcy hurried past her straight to Nettie's room. If Nettie's granddaughter looked worried, then something was very wrong.

Darcy found Nettie propped up on a pile of pillows. Her face was ashen, and she struggled for every breath. Darcy placed her palm on Nettie's forehead—clammy, but cool. Then she took her pulse—weak, but steady. She might not have had a coronary episode, but she was definitely ill.

Leah came in and stood quietly behind her.

"Go call Dr. Williamson and tell him we'll meet him

at the emergency room," Darcy ordered without turning.

Nettie began to cough, and Darcy could tell by the sound exactly what the problem was: congestion in her lungs. Whether it was from her heart condition or some other illness didn't matter. All that mattered was that she needed more medical attention than Darcy could provide.

"I...don't...want y—" Another round of coughing wracked Nettie's frail body, interrupting her protest.

"Hush, Nettie," Darcy said, perhaps, a bit too harshly. "Let us help you."

"But I...don't...want to be...a bother," she managed, her voice watery and weak.

"You're not a bother, Nettie," Darcy said as she bustled around the room, searching for Nettie's clothes.

Leah returned.

"Did you talk to the doctor?" Darcy snapped as she searched high and low for Nettie's shoes.

"Yes, ma'am. He said he'd meet us at the emergency room." She darted away and returned with a pair of white canvas shoes. "Were you looking for these?"

Darcy snatched them out of Leah's hand. "Yes. Now, go call your mother and tell her we're going to the hospital so she won't come all the way out here to pick you up and worry." She knew Earline would worry anyway, but at least she'd know what to worry about. "Tell her Gramma is in no immediate danger. It's just precautionary."

Leah scuttled away, and Darcy turned to Nettie. "You're going to have to help me. We're going out to the swing, then I'll pull the car around so you don't have to walk too far."

Nettie nodded. "Thank you," she murmured weakly

as Darcy hauled her up off the bed and looped the woman's arm over her shoulder. Nettie was frail, but Darcy was no weightlifter, either. She drew a deep breath and all but dragged her toward the porch swing.

Now Darcy could see why Billy was so concerned about having someone be with his mother. She'd bet her week's pay that Nettie had refused to let Leah call for help, and Leah, good girl that she was, hadn't known enough about the condition to do it anyway.

It was too far to wait for an ambulance to come all the way out from Pittsville. She had no time to waste in getting Nettie to the hospital.

"Momma said she'd meet us there," Leah said, her face so pale that her freckles stood out in relief. "Is Gramma gonna die?" she whispered.

"Not if I have anything to say about it," Darcy managed as she maneuvered her charge onto the swing. "Leah, sit here so your grandmother doesn't fall while I get the car."

"Yes, ma'am." Leah's voice trembled and Darcy wished she had a moment to reassure the girl, but time was of the essence. Leah's fears would have to wait.

She ran to the car, amazed that she still had the keys in her pocket. Someone up there must be looking out for her. She flung the door open, slid behind the wheel, and jammed the key into the ignition. She turned the key and held her breath until the engine of the old car caught.

Then she gunned it and threw the car into reverse, sending a shower of dirt and gravel flying everywhere and leaving an ugly set of ruts in the dusty lane. Ruts were the least of her worries.

Darcy pulled the car as close to the steps as she could get it, rueing the damage she'd probably done to the lawn. She could fix the lawn later. Nettie needed her now.

How she and Leah managed to get Nettie into the car, Darcy didn't know, but her adrenaline must really have been pumping when she all but carried the woman down the stairs. She buckled Nettie in, then herself, and barked an order to Leah to do the same, then she eased the car off the lawn.

Praying that she wouldn't encounter anyone from the sheriff's department on the way, Darcy headed for town.

They made the trip in record time, and Darcy pulled the car up to the emergency entrance of the hospital. She was afraid she'd have to lean on the horn, but an attendant with a wheelchair was there before she'd applied the brakes. She let him take Nettie inside, then looked for a place to park.

Her heart was beating so fast, Darcy thought it would explode, but she'd gotten Nettie here, and that was all that mattered. She found a slot and pulled in and shut off the engine, then rested her head against the steering wheel.

"Is Gramma going to be all right now?" Leah asked plaintively from the back seat.

Darcy had forgotten about Leah. She turned to the terrified girl, and patted her head. "I'm sure the doctor and everyone at the hospital will do all they can."

"Is she going to die?" the girl asked again.

"I don't know, Leah." Darcy closed her eyes and tried to will her racing heart to slow. "Why don't we go inside and wait for your mother?"

"What are we gonna tell Momma?"

Darcy fumbled with the latch and pushed her door open with trembling hands. She had to get inside before the adrenaline rush left her and she crashed. "I don't know, Leah. We'll have to see what the doctor says."

She made it across the parking lot and in through the automatic doors on wobbly legs. Darcy looked around for someone to talk to, but before she found anyone, her legs gave out, and she sank, boneless, onto a chair.

In all her haste to get Nettie to the hospital in time, she'd forgotten one thing. Billy.

How was she going to tell him?

BILL TRIED to ignore the persistent horseplay in the parachute shop and busied himself getting ready for the night practice jump. Though he enjoyed parachuting in the daytime, night jumps were a different matter. Not that he'd let on to anybody on the team.

A lot of guys signed on to Special Ops because they loved skydiving. He'd done it for the extra pay.

Danny Murphey strolled by and swatted him on the butt with the leg of his jumpsuit. "Hey, what's this business about you taking off every other weekend or so to go home? You'd think you had a girl up there or something."

Murphey didn't know how close to the truth he'd come. Bill felt the heat run out of his face, but he keep his eyes trained on his locker and hoped nobody had seen his reaction. "What's it to ya if I do?" Only the captain and Senior Master Sergeant Blocker knew the full story, and Bill intended to keep it that way.

"Leave the man be, Murphey. Don't you got something better to do than goose him? Nobody ribbed you about Allison," Sergeant Blocker said, a fierce scowl making his dark face even darker.

Bill didn't know what the deal was about Allison, but

apparently it was just the thing to shut Murphey up. The man blushed to the roots of his red hair.

"Yo, somebody's been in my locker," Ski yelled from the other side of the equipment room.

"What makes you say that?" Block strode to where Ski stood looking at his locker door.

"The lock's not closed."

"You sure you didn't just leave it undone?"

"Hell no. I never leave it unlocked. And look here, it looks like somebody picked it." Ski held the lock up to the sergeant. "See, there's scratches around the key-hole."

"I'll be damned. It does look like it's been messed with. You find anything missin'?"

Ski rummaged through the contents. "Doesn't look like it."

"Bus's here. Fall in," Lieutenant Marx called from the door.

"Maybe the scratches were there all along," Block said. "Just make sure it's locked up tight and let's go."

Ski grumbled, but he did as the sergeant told him. He slammed the locker shut, snapped the lock closed, then tugged on it to make certain it had caught.

"Come on, Ski. You can inventory your stuff when we get back." Bill pulled up the zipper that ran the length of his leg all the way up his jumpsuit to his chin. He hoisted his parachute harness to his shoulder and prepared to board the crew bus that would take them to the waiting aircraft.

"Hold it, Hays. You're not going," Lieutenant Marx said, barring Bill's passage with his arm. "Go see the captain in the shop."

"But, I need this j—" Bill protested.

"No, you don't," Block countered. "You just got

back from the Nellis trip. You got more than your share
of jumps for the quarter. You don't need no pay jump.
Go on," he said, jerking his head toward the captain's
office in the other building. "See what the captain
wants."

Bill didn't know whether to be angry or relieved. The
captain needing to see him was another matter. What
could he possibly want that would keep him from taking
off with the rest of the team?

Only one way to find out. He stowed his gear back
in the locker he'd just shut and set off to see the captain.

The expression on Captain Thibodeaux's face was
grim, and Bill wondered briefly what he might have
done, then another thought struck him. "Is it my
mother?"

He could barely breathe while he waited what seemed
like hours for the captain to speak.

"Your mother's been admitted to hospital. Pneumonia, they think. She's not in any immediate danger, but
according to your sister, her condition has not stabi-
lized."

Bill tried to speak, but his throat was too dry.

"I've arranged for you to take emergency leave,"
Thibodeaux said, handing Bill the necessary papers.
"It's for a week. If you need more, just let me know."
He smiled as if trying to make Bill feel better.

"Thank you, Captain. I'll leave right away."

"Take care, Bill. You don't need to worry your
mother more by having an accident yourself."

"Yes, sir," Bill said, then turned.

He was halfway to the car before he wondered if he'd
been properly dismissed.

DARCY WAS STIFF and uncomfortable from trying to
sleep in a plastic chair in the waiting room outside the

ICU. She had made Earline take Leah home and promised to call if there was any change, but so far the only change was the position of the hands on the clock on the waiting-room wall.

She yawned and stretched and got up to try to walk some of the kinks out. Her left foot felt as if she were walking on pins and needles, but the rest of her was wide awake. She peered through the glass windows of Nettie's cubicle and was rewarded with the steady blink of the cardiac monitor.

Doctor Williamson had started Nettie on a course of antibiotics and a diuretic to help clear fluid from her tissues. Barring any complications, Nettie would be home soon.

Still, Darcy couldn't help feeling that it was her fault. She should have noticed it sooner. How could Nettie have gone from a seemingly healthy cardiac patient that morning, to so seriously ill by afternoon?

A loud whoosh breaking into the eerie silence of the hospital after midnight announced that someone had come in through the automatic doors. Hoping it was somebody who could give her more information as to Nettie's condition, Darcy looked up.

Bill, clad in camouflage battle dress uniform and shoving a scarlet beret into his thigh pocket strode through the doors.

Without thinking about her reasons or the consequences, Darcy rushed into his arms.

Nothing could have felt better than the way he wrapped his arms around her in response. Pressing her cheek against his broad, hard chest, Darcy breathed in the scent of smoke and aviation fuel and Bill and warmed her chilled blood with the heat from his solid body.

"How is she?"

Darcy drew in a long, slow breath. This was the part she hated. Here was where she'd have to admit that she'd failed him. She pulled back and took his hands. Then she looked down and rested her forehead against his chest. Hoping he wouldn't push her away, she whispered, "Oh, Billy, I'm so sorry. I promised you I'd take care of your mother and I've let you down. I should have caught it sooner."

Bill said nothing for a long moment, but Darcy could feel him draw in a deep breath. She waited for him to do something, anything. Finally, he let go of her hands, and Darcy mourned the loss of his touch.

Would he ever hold her again?

She stepped back, steeling herself for whatever Bill would dish out.

He reached for her, tipped her face up and looked down into her eyes.

Chapter Nine

"Darcy, you did what you could," Bill said, his voice thick from exhaustion and emotion. "I didn't expect miracles. If you hadn't known what to do, it could have been so much worse." Billy drew in a deep breath and looked over Darcy's head toward the nurses' station. His eyes burned, and though he wanted to convince himself that the stinging was because of exhaustion and the long, tense drive here, he knew otherwise. He blinked frantically to clear his weary eyes.

"But, you counted on me…" Darcy still didn't seem to be able to look at him.

Bill framed her face with his hands and tipped it upward again. As he looked down into her tired eyes, he could see the fatigue etched on her face. He could see the caring. "No, Darcy. You haven't let me down. You did just what you were supposed to do. You were there. That's what she needed. Just to have you there," he said, his voice choking up. He figured it was best to shut up before he gave himself away.

And he couldn't help wishing he could get down on his knees and beg for her to be there for him. Always. Not just until this was all over.

He knew from looking at the hospital setup with the

tubes and monitors that he and Darcy wouldn't have to fake a breakup. Momma would be gone—long before that.

Bill drew in a deep, long breath and figured he'd had enough time to compose himself. "Can I see her?"

"You can look through the glass," Darcy said. "She's sleeping now, and she needs her rest."

A nurse came toward them from a room that looked like the cockpit of the space shuttle or, at least, command central with all the technology packed inside.

"You must be Mrs. Hays's son," the nurse said, her voice quiet, efficient, calming in an odd sort of way. She extended her hand and introduced herself.

Darcy stepped back, but hovered nearby as if she might be needed to help.

Bill nodded, noting that the woman did not let go of his hand. He liked that. It showed she cared. "What can you tell me about my mother's condition?"

"She's stable for now. She'll probably go to a regular room in the morning," the nurse said, squeezing his hand.

"And when can she go home?"

"That's not up to me to say. Dr. Williamson will have to make that decision, but I'd bet it would be the first part of next week." She let go of his hands and turned toward the cubicle where Bill's mother slept.

"You can go in and sit with her, if you like. "I don't know if she'll wake, but something tells me she'll know you're here." The nurse smiled, then turned back to her work station.

Bill turned to Darcy. She smiled and made a shooing motion with her hands. "Go on," she said softly. "Nettie needs you."

"Don't you want to come?" Was he such a coward

that he couldn't face his mother looking so tiny among all those machines without Darcy to hold his hand?

Darcy shook her head. "You go. She needs to know you're here." She turned toward the bank of chairs, then looked back over her shoulder. "Then I think we should both go home and try to get some sleep. Neither one of us is going to be much good to her if we're too exhausted to think."

Bill guessed she was right. And Momma was in good hands. He was beat, and it would be good to lie down in his own bed for a while. Even if it was only for a couple of hours.

Even if he didn't think he'd be able to sleep a wink.

Drawing a deep breath, he stepped into the room and sat down on a metal chair beside the hospital bed. He found the frail hand encumbered by tubes and tape and stroked it with his own. "It's all right, Momma. I'm here," he whispered.

She stirred and her eyes fluttered but didn't open. "I knew you'd come," she murmured, her voice gravelly and weak. "Now, go home and get some rest. I'll be here in the morning."

Bill didn't want to go. He held her hand, so papery white, so dry and brittle. He continued to stroke. He didn't know what to do. He was so damned tired he could hardly see straight, but on the other hand he needed to be here.

His mother's eyes fluttered again. "I told you...to go home..." she whispered. "Go on."

"Yes, ma'am." Bill could see clearly that his being here was making his mother even more agitated. And he knew she needed her rest. "All right, Momma," he said as he leaned forward. He kissed her forehead and was rewarded with the flicker of a smile, then he pushed to his feet.

It was time for him and Darcy to go home.

Home. He liked the sound of it. Not the place, but the thought that Darcy would be there.

Even if he would be sleeping alone in a bedroom down the hall, they would be together under the same roof.

Like the family they'd never get a chance to be.

DARCY AND BILL walked out through the emergency exit together, but Darcy stopped for a moment to breathe the cool, night air as Bill strode ahead. The darkness seemed so refreshing after the oppressive heat when she'd entered this place. Had it only been yesterday afternoon? She drew a long, deep breath, then started toward the car.

Strong hands caught her and Bill hauled her back. "Where are you going?" he growled.

She looked at him, confused. "To the car. Home. Where do you think?"

"With me," he said in a tone so proprietary that it reverberated down to Darcy's toes. "It's late. You're tired. I don't want you driving all that way in that rattletrap."

"Oh. But it was all right for your mother," she responded archly.

"My mother didn't have a choice. You do."

In spite of her weariness, Darcy bristled. "I drove it here. Who are you to say that I can't drive it back?"

Bill seemed to sag, his shoulders drooped. "Now don't go Women's Lib on me. I wasn't doubting your abilities. It's late. Let me drive. You can take the car home tomorrow." Without giving her a chance to rebut his statement, he strode away as if he expected her to follow.

Darcy, her hands on her hips, watched him go. She appreciated the view, though she couldn't say much for the sentiment that had preceded it. She wanted to argue, she really did, but she was so tired. And if Bill wanted to be macho and drive, it was okay by her.

This time.

Still, she wasn't going to let him get away scot-free, she decided as she trotted after him.

"Like you didn't drive all night to get here," she challenged as she climbed into the Cherokee beside him.

He made a face. "I had a night jump scheduled," he said tersely. "I slept in this morning. You probably got up before the rooster again."

Darcy sank wearily back against the seat. She held her hands up in a gesture of surrender. "Okay, I give up. You win. You've outmachoed me!"

Bill said nothing, but Darcy detected the hint of a smirk on his face in the murky parking lot light. His lips twitched as if he were trying not to smile.

She'd give him the benefit of the doubt, since he was trying. But, she wouldn't let him get away with it for long. She had to live with the guy.

Starting to buckle her seat belt, Darcy paused. What had she been thinking? They were just sleeping under the same roof. That was all.

Her brain seemed to have gotten the concept loud and clear. Too bad her heart was still a little slow on the uptake.

THE HOUSE was dark when they arrived and testified to the haste with which Darcy and Momma had left. Bill strode through the small house, glancing around to be certain that no intruders had been there before he would let Darcy come inside.

They didn't have a lot of crime in the Mattison community, but still, it never hurt to check.

He flicked on the light in Darcy's bedroom and made a cursory check. Everything seemed in order. Bill shrugged. He guessed it was safe to let Darcy come in. He turned to go out to call her, but collided with her instead.

His breath caught in his throat and his pulse raced at the sudden, unexpected contact with warm, soft flesh. "What the hell?" he muttered. "I thought I told you to wait in the car until I checked the house." He took her by the shoulders and set her at arm's length from him. Just that brief touch had awakened urges he should be too damned tired to even think about.

Darcy rolled her eyes, made a face, and stepped out of his grasp. "Bill, Billy, we're in Mattison, not some crime-riddled inner city. Your Jeep is the only vehicle out there. Unless a sneak-thief hitchhiked, there's no evidence that anybody's here." She stood there, her hands on her hips, and looked at him as if she had to explain in one-syllable words and very short sentences.

He should have thought of that. Bill didn't have a response, so he said nothing, just stubbornly set his jaw and looked down at her.

How could such a diminutive woman turn his knees to Jell-O and another part of his anatomy to stone?

"Oh, get over it, Bill. It's late and I'm tired." Darcy tried to brush by him, but Bill caught her by the arm.

He wanted to kiss her, but he didn't dare. After all, as tired as he was, they were alone in this house, and if he wanted to—and, oh, he wanted to—he could take her right then and there.

He let go of her arm.

"Good night, Darcy. And thank you again." He turned to leave, but this time, Darcy grabbed his hand and drew him back. "What?"

"You're a good man, Billy Hays," she said simply, then she rose on her tiptoes and brushed a quick kiss against his lips.

Bill was too stunned to react, and by the time he could think again, she'd ducked under his arm and entered her room. He stood there in the open doorway, watching as she drew a nightgown out of a dresser drawer. He stood there as she began to unbutton her smock.

She must have realized he was still there, for she turned and smiled. "Good night, Bill," was all she said, but that was enough. She put down the nightgown and crossed the room in several quick strides.

Bill swallowed and backed out of the doorway. "Good night, Darcy," he said huskily as she shut the door firmly between them. Then he turned and trudged to his empty room and his empty bed.

IN SPITE OF the late hour she'd gone to bed and the even later hour before she had finally succumbed to sleep, Darcy had gotten "up before the rooster" as Bill had so quaintly put it. She was by no means rested and not the least bit refreshed, but she couldn't lie in bed when she knew Nettie was still in intensive care.

Doctor Williamson had told her to take all the time she needed, so she didn't have to worry about calling in to the doctor's office. She headed for the shower and found evidence that Bill had been there before her.

Funny, she hadn't heard anyone stirring. Had she slept more soundly than she thought?

When Bill had gotten up was the least of her worries. She stepped quickly into the tub, only to pause when she considered that Bill had stood, naked, in the same spot only minutes before. As she soaped up, she wondered about the fact that this bar of soap had touched parts of his body that she longed to…

No, she shook her head. She had no business thinking about that. Nettie was lying ill in intensive care at Pittsville General, and Darcy had no right to be lusting after Bill. She quickly shampooed her hair, thinking about the song Nellie Forbush sang in *South Pacific,* humming the tune softly as she rinsed, she almost managed to forget why the song was meaningful to her.

Almost managed. Bill Hays came marching back into the front of her mind as soon as she stepped out from behind the curtain and spotted his shaving kit hanging from the towel rack. Darcy sighed and toweled herself dry.

Last night had seemed like forever when she'd been waiting for Bill. Now that he was here, the day promised to be longer still.

She dressed quickly—no need for a uniform today— in jeans and a T-shirt, and stepped out of the bathroom to be greeted by the aroma of coffee brewing.

At least, there was that.

Maybe after a stiff cup of coffee or two or three hundred, she'd be able to face the day.

And Bill.

Bill looked up as Darcy entered the kitchen, yawning and stretching and looking none the worse for wear after a night that had been long on tension and short on sleep. Even right from a shower and without a trace of makeup she looked more beautiful than any woman had a right to at this time of the morning. Her short hair was still damp, drops of moisture beaded on the back of the neck of her soft pink T-shirt and she smelled like his mother's Cashmere Bouquet soap.

"Why are you up so early?" Darcy murmured through a yawn. She reached for a mug and served herself a cup of coffee. "But I'm glad you are. I need coffee, and I need it now." She raised the mug to her lips and drank without doctoring it with her usual milk and sugar.

Bill shoved the milk carton and sugar bowl toward her as she grimaced and sank into the chair across from him. "I guess you'll still be needing this?" he said dryly.

"Thank you," she murmured, spooning a generous amount of sugar into the dark brew. Then she added an equally large amount of milk.

"Like a little coffee in your milk, do you?" Bill said wryly as he rose to turn the bacon. "I'll have breakfast ready in ten and then we can eat and go."

"I never liked the taste of the stuff, but sometimes I do need the effects," she said as she raised the doctored brew to her mouth. "I'd just as soon have a diet cola. It has caffeine in it, too."

"Yeah, but it won't put hair on your chest," Bill said, lowering the flame under the skillet.

"Like I really need hair there," Darcy said, producing the first real smile Bill had seen this morning. "You never did answer my question."

"What question?"

"Why you're up so early." She put the mug down and stirred, using the spoon as something to keep from looking at him, Bill suspected.

"Early? Hell, this is late for me," he said over the sizzle of bacon. "I'm usually up at zero-five-thirty. Have to eat, get dressed, and be at physical training by six-thirty." He yanked a couple of paper towels off the roll, laid them on a plate, then began to fish strips of bacon out of the grease. "I grew up in the country, remember."

"Well, you sure acted like a city boy when you were lounging around in bed until who-knows-when last week," Darcy commented wryly.

He couldn't tell her he'd been avoiding her, something he'd given her a hard time about at the Dinner Belle last Saturday, but that had been the reason. He shrugged. "I was on vacation. It wasn't the easiest thing to do, but I was trying to see how the leisure class lives." He poured the bacon grease off into a can, and reached for a carton of eggs. "It wasn't all it was cracked up to be."

Darcy looked at him over the rim of her coffee mug, but said nothing. She arched one tawny eyebrow, then took another sip.

"How many eggs?" Bill asked as he cracked a couple into a bowl.

Darcy shrugged. "I don't know. Truthfully, my stomach is just a little unsettled, but I suspect having a little something in it might straighten it right out. I never did get anything for dinner last night. You decide, and I'll make some toast." She pushed herself out of the chair and went to the cupboard where the bread was stored, and by the time she'd loaded and set the toaster, the eggs sizzled as Bill poured them into the pan.

Bill rather liked the domesticity of the moment. If it were always to be like this, sharing friendly banter and a quiet breakfast, he'd almost consider revising his decision not to marry. But he knew the demands of his job. He'd be sitting in some chow hall at some distant base while Darcy was stuck at home alone with all the responsibilities. He wondered how long she'd be able to take it.

And what the hell was he doing thinking like that anyway? He barely knew the woman, and he was thinking about her in terms of forever. He blew out a long, exasperated breath and shook the notion from his head. Hell, if the air force wanted you to have a wife, they'd have issued you one.

"What was that about?"

Bill looked up, startled at the question. "What?"

"You shook your head. What were you thinking?"

"Nothing," Bill lied. "I was just trying to avoid the steam from the skillet." He grabbed a pot holder and lifted the frying pan. "Here. Eat it while it's hot."

At least, as long as they were eating, they wouldn't be able to talk. And Bill was getting damned tired of having to watch his every word and thought. Damn, this woman was getting under his skin.

BILL HAD ASKED Darcy to inquire about Nettie's condition, claiming that she was more likely to understand the medical jargon than he, but Darcy suspected that he needed a moment or two to pull himself together before facing the hospital.

Watching a loved one hooked up to tubes and monitors could be unsettling to anyone, and Darcy didn't fault Bill for that. And she appreciated the chance to get the details before they tried to soften them for the family.

She stepped into the ICU waiting room and was surprised to see Earline and Lougenia already there.

Lougenia rose quickly and hurried toward her. "Good news," she announced, a smile brightening a face that otherwise looked far too wan for first thing in the morning. Obviously, she'd had trouble sleeping, too. "Doctor Williamson said she could go to a regular room as soon as she's had the rest of her intravenous meds."

"That's great, Lou. I'm sure Bill will be thrilled," she said, glancing into the cubicle where Nettie's intravenous fluid pouch appeared half empty. It wouldn't be long. She also noted that Nettie was awake and talking softly to Reverend Carterette. He bowed his head and in a moment raised it again to smile at Nettie.

Bill arrived as the reverend got up from the chair beside Nettie's bed.

"I'll see you in church Sunday week," Reverend Carterette said to Momma, then turned to Bill, clasped him on the shoulder, then shook his hand. "I hate that I'll be gone with the youth group to that church raising in Mississippi next week, but I've talked to the nurses and they expect your mother to go home in a matter of days. Lucy will come by to see her while I'm gone."

"Thank you, Reverend Carterette. I appreciate it, and I know Momma always enjoys Lucy's visits."

The reverend squeezed Bill's arm, then turned to Lougenia and Earline.

"It's good news, Bill," Darcy said, stepping forward. "Lou said she can go to a regular room as soon as she's finished receiving the medication in that IV."

Bill let out a long breath. "That's good to hear. I have to admit it scared me the way she looked last night with all those machines and tubes."

"Those machines and tubes are what is making it

possible for her to get better,'' Darcy told him, touching him lightly on the sleeve.

''I know, but still....'' His words trailed off as he looked up and realized that Doc Williamson had come into the ICU.

''Let me go talk to Doc and see what he says about her condition.'' He turned to go, but stopped, and looked back over his shoulder. ''Maybe you should come, too, to translate,'' he said.

He damned sure wasn't going to let on that he needed her for anything else.

DARCY LOOKED UP from the hard plastic chair in the ICU waiting room to see Bill stumble out of Nettie's cubicle. Looking as though he'd received a severe shock, Bill sank heavily onto the chair next to her. Panic raised the fine hairs on Darcy's arms.

Had Nettie had a setback? No, that couldn't be! Alarms would have been going off all over the place. Besides, she had just spoken to Doctor Williamson, and the news had been encouraging. The way Bill looked, though, he might well have heard something dire. Or seen a ghost.

She grabbed his arm, and he looked at her blankly as if he hadn't seen her or realized that she was there. ''What?'' he said in a tone so disconnected that it had Darcy worried.

''What's the matter with you? You look like you've had the wits scared out of you.'' He acted that way, too.

He looked at her again, and slowly shook his head. He blinked as if to clear his eyes, and then swallowed and cleared his throat. ''Nothing,'' he said hoarsely. ''My mother wants to ask a favor of you.''

Relief washing over her, Darcy smiled and released

Bill's arm. She didn't need the distraction of the warmth humming up her arm from his. "Is that all? You had me worried there for a minute. I'll do anything for your mom. You know that."

"You may not be so willing when you hear what she has to say," he said, still appearing shell-shocked, and looked around. "Where are Lou and Earline?"

"They had to go to work. You know they count on their paychecks, and since your mother is doing better, I told them they didn't need to stay. They'll both be back at lunchtime after your mother gets out of ICU."

"Oh," he said, still looking as fogged as he had when she'd first spoken to him. "I'll just sit and wait till you've talked to Momma." He turned his attention to the television set hung high on the waiting-room wall.

Darcy didn't know what to think. Why was he acting as though his world had just ended? And why did he seem to be so interested in the morning news? She drew in a long, deep breath and stepped into Nettie's room.

Nettie's face was pale and her eyes were closed, but they drifted upward when Darcy entered. "I didn't mean to wake you, Nettie," Darcy said. "I can come back later when you've rested."

"No. Please stay," Nettie said, her voice reedy and thin. "I was just restin' my eyes. Seems like such a waste of time to sleep when I have so little time left."

Darcy managed an anemic smile and settled on to the chair by the bed. She patted Nettie's hand. "Now don't be saying such things. Doctor Williamson tells me you're recovering well." She managed another smile, this one a little stronger, and squeezed Nettie's hand. It was papery and cool, and Darcy's smile faltered for a moment. "Remember, he can't fool me," she said. "I understand all his doctor talk."

Nettie smiled at that and motioned her closer. "Come closer, I have a favor to ask of you," she said, her voice still showing the effects of her flooded lungs.

Still holding Nettie's hand, Darcy did as she was asked. "You know I'll do anything for you."

"Hush, child. And listen. All this excitement is tiring, and I'd like to take a nap when we're done."

"Yes, ma'am. What can I do for you?"

"Take care of Billy. I know you and Billy told us you wanted to have a long engagement," Nettie said, then she stopped to catch her breath.

Darcy started to say something, but Nettie silenced her with a slight wave of her hand.

"But I know my time's almost come. Doc Williamson might pull me through this time, but I don't reckon that he's goin' to be able to do it too many more times." She paused again, and her breath came in long, painful gasps.

"I know it ain't what you planned, but it would sure make me go easier if I could see you and Billy happily married before I did."

Chapter Ten

Darcy gasped. How could Nettie ask this of her?

And how could she, Darcy Stanton, who had escaped from one ill-advised wedding with little more than the clothes on her back, actually be considering Nettie's request?

Now she understood the reason for Bill's dazed expression. He had to be as shocked as she was.

"Billy's gonna need somebody when I go," Nettie went on. "He's way down there in Florida all by himself. He might be a big, strong, strappin' man, but he's got a tender heart, and he feels things deep down in it. He's gonna need you to sustain him. You will comfort him, won't you, Darcy?"

Darcy couldn't believe she was about to agree, but she swallowed and answered. "Yes, ma'am. I'll do whatever it takes. I promise." She looked at her watch, the dial blurring in front of eyes filling with tears. "I think I've exceeded my five minutes," she said, then bolted from the room.

And right into Billy's arms.

The shock of landing so squarely in the middle of his hard chest knocked some of the panic out of Darcy. Bill put his arms around her and drew her closer to him. She could barely breathe. She didn't know whether it was because of what Nettie had just requested or Billy's closeness, but she took a couple more breaths and tried to collect herself.

Not an easy task with the reason for her confusion so close that she could hear his heart beat and could almost taste that warm, man scent unadorned with fragrance or aftershave. One sniff and she was hot and aroused and weak in the knees.

"Now you know why I was so shell-shocked when I came out of Momma's room," Bill said quietly, his voice seeming to rumble from deep within his chest.

Darcy swallowed and pushed herself away from him, out of the shelter of his arms. When she was so close to him she couldn't think clearly, and this was something she obviously needed to think about. She drew a breath, but she couldn't look at him. "What are we going to do?"

"I think we should think about it," Bill said quietly.

"No! Absolutely not!" Darcy jerked her head up and looked him square in the eyes.

That was a mistake. Every time she looked at him, her breath caught in her throat, and now that Nettie had mentioned the unthinkable, she'd even begun to think about it. Seriously? She was such a mass of confusion.

Oh, how she longed to spend the night in Bill's arms, but did she want to marry him?

She didn't know what she wanted.

Darcy looked around and realized that everyone in the Intensive Care Unit seemed to be looking at them.

"This was only supposed to be a pretense," she hissed under her breath. "This was only supposed to be temporary, but you keep dragging me in deeper and deeper. Look what happened the last time you drew me into one of your brilliant ideas!''

Bill took her by the elbow and led her toward the corridor.

"Where are we going?" Darcy asked with alarm as she shook free of his iron grasp. She was not about to let him tell her what to do! She stopped dead still.

"Come on," he said quietly, demonstrating far more calm than Darcy possessed at the moment. Of course, he'd had five whole minutes to think. "We need to talk about this," he said, glancing around. "This is not exactly the kind of thing you want to have make the evening news."

"All right," Darcy said reluctantly. She shook his arm away and started for the hall. "We'll go outside where we won't be overheard." *But do not think that you are going to be able to convince me of anything this foolhardy,* she thought.

Something deep inside her kept telling Darcy to think about it. If she actually said no, that would be the end of it. And she wasn't sure she wanted it all to end. Even if it wasn't real. Even if Bill hadn't as much as hinted that he might care for her as she did for him.

The air outside was warm and sticky and promised another humid Alabama day. Bill found a spot in the shade near a humming air-conditioning unit where they could talk safe from prying eyes and ears. At least he was thinking more clearly than she was.

"You can't ask this of me, Billy. You can't," Darcy whispered.

The place was secluded, but someone had left some webbed lawn chairs there. She settled onto one of the chairs and Bill took another one. He pulled it close to hers until they were sitting almost knee to knee. He leaned forward and their knees touched, sending a jolt of…something she couldn't describe rushing through her as he closed his large hands over hers.

"It wouldn't have to be a real marriage, Darcy."

She gasped and snapped her head up to look at him, and Billy wondered if he'd gone too far. She jerked her hands away.

"We could just go through the motions. For Momma. Nobody'd have to know."

Darcy sighed and closed her eyes, shaking her head slightly. "Where have I heard that before?"

"Oh, come on. We know where we messed up last time. We know what kind of precautions to take." Last time, they had acted too quickly, they hadn't had time to think it through. This time, they wouldn't agree until they'd worked it all out, Bill vowed to himself.

"I just…got…away from an unwanted marriage by the skin of my teeth. I'm not ready to get mixed up in another. No matter how good the reasons," Darcy said emphatically. She picked up a handful of loose dirt from the ground and watched it drift slowly from her hand in the turbulence from the air-conditioning fans. "I just can't.

"I can't."

Bill swallowed. Apparently, Darcy was going to be a harder sell than he'd expected. He reached for her hand and was grateful that she didn't yank it away again. He'd have to think this through a little longer. He'd have to figure a way to convince her. A way to make it happen and later a way out without injuring either of them.

He didn't want to hurt Darcy.

But, if it was the last thing he ever did, he wouldn't

break his mother's heart, either. He'd do anything he could to make her last days happy and worry-free.

Even if he did have to marry a woman he knew he couldn't keep.

"We have to think about this, Darcy. I have to think it through. If I can come up with a plan that would work and that we'd be able to get out of without a big fuss, will you, at least, consider it?" Bill closed his hands over her small one and hoped he could telegraph his sincerity to her.

He wasn't sure he could put it into words.

"I will think about it, Bill," Darcy said slowly. "But I'll make no rash promises. Been there, done that, got the fiancé." She let out a long, tired breath. "I'll listen to your plan, Billy. But you had better think this one through a lot better than you did the last one."

"Heard that," Bill said softly and drew back his hand. "Reckon we ought to go back inside? It might not be good if we stray too far from Momma this morning." He got up and offered his hand to Darcy.

As she accepted it and scrambled to her feet, Bill continued. "I can think back there in that waiting room as well as I can out here, and when I come up with a plan, you'll be the first to know."

"And you won't tell a soul until I've approved the plan?" Darcy said, letting go of his hand.

Bill felt briefly empty at the loss of her touch, but he had to get used to that, he told himself as they headed back inside. After all, he had made a business proposition. Not a proposal. It wasn't going to be a love match.

Still, he thought, as the automatic door whooshed

open for them and let them into the hospital and the refrigerated air, his heart couldn't help hoping it could be.

OVER LUNCH in a corner booth of the Dinner Belle Diner, Darcy tried to concentrate on her tuna melt. She'd eaten at the place enough to know what the food should taste like, but today everything tasted like cardboard and sawdust.

Bill had been quiet all morning since their little excursion to the rear of the hospital, so she knew he'd been trying to work out the details of The Plan. They'd left the hospital when Earline came in on her lunch break, and now Bill was digging into his lunch with appetite and enthusiasm, so Darcy assumed that he was close to something he thought might work.

She waited for him to announce it with the dread of an accused prisoner waiting for the verdict. No matter what it was, it would change her life forever.

No wonder she couldn't taste her food.

Still, Darcy forced herself to eat it, cardboard sandwich or not. She had a feeling she was going to need all her strength to get through the next few days.

"Here's The Plan," Bill said just as Darcy took a bite of potato salad.

She swallowed too quickly and choked. Coughing and sputtering, she grabbed for her water glass and knocked it over, sending a puddle of icy water spreading all over the Formica tabletop. Billy handed her his tea and she drank, while he swabbed at the spill. By the time Luverne arrived with a cloth, he'd averted the worst of the disaster.

Shaking her head and clucking her displeasure, Luverne made quick work of the rest of the mess, then left them alone. Had Luverne been there every other day

Darcy had eaten lunch? Had Darcy not noticed her until she'd seen the woman flirting with her man?

Her man?

Darcy shook her head, cleared her throat, and swallowed.

"I'm sorry," she said, finally allowing herself to look at Billy. "Next time, make sure I haven't just taken a bite. Now, you were saying…?" Darcy pushed her plate away—she'd lost her taste for sawdust—and crossed her arms and propped her elbows on the table. "I'm all ears."

Bill looked at her a long minute, then chuckled. "Not even close. But I have to say that you have the cutest little ears I've seen in a long, long time." He reached across the table and fondled her ear.

Darcy drew back and rolled her eyes. "Can it, Hays," she said. "Let's get this over with. The Plan?"

"We go over to the courthouse and apply for a license."

Darcy jerked her hand back and closed her fist tight. "No!"

"We get the blood tests."

"No-oh," she said even more emphatically.

"Then we hope that Momma comes to her senses when she starts to feel better, and we don't have to use them."

Darcy expelled a long, relieved breath. That was the first thing he'd said all day that made any sense. "Amen to that one," she said.

"But," Bill added, "If she still insists, we go through with it. As long as it isn't…" He paused for a moment and swallowed quickly. "…consummated, we can get out of it pretty quick."

"What about the ceremony? You know your mother

is going to insist that Reverend Carterette officiate.'' Darcy paused, trying to dredge up the right words for what she wanted to say. "Reciting our vows in front of Reverend Carterette in church would be the same as lying to God. I can't do that. I won't.''

"Got that figured out, too," Bill said. "He told Momma he was going to be away at a church raising next week. So, she won't think a thing about us going in front of a judge.'' He paused. "We'll tell her that we're doing it for her, and we want to do the church thing later for the whole family and the rest of our friends,'' he added.

"What's to keep her from telling somebody like she did last time?'' Darcy still couldn't believe how far the news of their phony engagement had traveled in one day.

Bill shrugged. "We'll tell her that we don't want to hurt anybody's feelings by making them think they'd been left out, so we'll ask her to keep it all a secret till the formal wedding. I think she'll go for that.''

"Are you sure?''

"Pretty sure.'' Bill took a long drink of tea. "At least this time, we'll have asked her not to tell, and we'll have given her a good reason.''

Darcy drew in a deep breath, then let it out slowly. "I don't know,'' she said. "It just doesn't seem right to play with your mother's emotions like that.''

"She'll never know. What isn't right is that a good woman who's had to work all her life might die with her one last wish not granted. A wish that I could grant her,'' Bill said with more force than necessary. "There are a lot of things that aren't right in this world, and I can't do anything about most of them. But, this is something I can fix. I just can't do it by myself," he said tiredly, as if exhausted by his attempt to persuade her.

"All right," Darcy said slowly. "But you and I know that this will not be real. Not in any way. We have to be able to get an annulment, clean and neat. When it's over we have to make it so this marriage never happened," she said, so softly she wasn't sure he'd heard.

Maybe it was because she didn't want him to hear. Was it because somewhere far back in the dark recesses of her mind, she really wanted the paper marriage to mean something?

Darcy closed her eyes and sighed. A few weeks ago she'd left a man at the altar because she couldn't picture herself married to him, and now she'd just agreed to pretend to be married to Bill. And it wasn't going to be really a pretense; she could see it clearly in her mind's eye. And in the eyes of the law it would be real.

At least until they proved otherwise.

BILL HUNG UP the pay phone and breathed a long, relieved sigh. He checked the coin box for change then turned to Darcy and made a thumbs-up sign.

"Good news," he said, feeling more optimistic than he had since his mother had sprung her request on them. He sank onto a chair in the waiting room outside Momma's room. Earline and Edd were in with her now, so he and Darcy had a moment alone.

Darcy looked as if she had steeled herself for the worst. She let out a short breath. "What exactly do you mean by that?"

"No blood test, no waiting period," he said, and he wondered if that was such a victory or not. Did he think that if they actually took out a license ahead of time, it would guarantee they'd go through with it? And why was he even entertaining the thought of staying married once it was over?

He'd made a solemn vow—if only to himself—that he'd never marry as long as he remained in the service. Leaving the air force now was out of the question, not when he was so close to his goal. He'd even applied for Operation Bootstrap, a scholarship program that allowed service members to attend college full time away from duty. He would finish his last few courses without the demands and distractions of duty to keep him from doing his best.

He didn't need a wife right now. He didn't want to put any woman—much less Darcy—into the same position his mother had found herself in. Yet, the thought of living without Darcy was beginning to loom larger than the fear that as his wife, she might have to live without him.

"Bill, are you listening to me?"

The touch of Darcy's hand on his arm yanked him out of his thoughts. "What?"

"I said," Darcy repeated, looking around to make certain they were still alone in the waiting area, "Why is no test, no waiting good news?"

"Because if Momma changes her mind, we won't have done anything that might catch up with us later."

Darcy raised an eyebrow. "Why are you so worried about it getting out?"

Bill didn't know what to make of Darcy's remark. Was she hurt? Hell, he didn't know whether to laugh it off or try to explain. Now was not the time for joking, if you asked him. "No. I... Oh, hell, I don't know what I meant by that. Just forget what I said, okay?"

"I'm sorry, Bill. I don't know what I'm thinking." Darcy drew in a deep breath and released it with a sigh.

"It's just...I...I just had myself all psyched up to do it, and then....'' Her voice trailed away as if she didn't know what she meant, either.

He could relate to that. He had no idea what was going on in his own confused head, and it was Momma they were thinking about. Darcy had no stake in this. She'd only met his mother a few weeks ago.

Hell, Darcy hadn't known him but a couple of hours longer. Why should either one of them be looking at this thing as anything more than a favor? What did they call it in those romance books Lougenia liked to read? A marriage of convenience?

It was only going to be a marriage on paper. A temporary one at that. But, as far as he was concerned it would be anything but convenient. How was he going to deal with being married to her and not touching her? Not being able to make her his wife in every way.

No, Bill told himself. You've got to stop thinking about your feelings. This is not about you. Though he didn't want to think about it, his mother had only a limited amount of time left on this earth. Doctor Williamson might have pulled her through this time, but what about the next? Or the time after that?

This was their way of making his mother's last days happier. This was about Momma.

It wasn't about them.

Bill risked a glance at the woman curled up in the seat next to him.

He just wished it were.

DARCY SAT in a chair pulled up next to Nettie's bed while Bill sat on the opposite side holding the hand that wasn't still encumbered by the IV line and sensors. At least in this room, Nettie'd been able to have flowers and gifts, and the counter behind her was veritably teeming with fragrant blossoms.

It amazed Darcy how efficiently the country grapevine worked, and it seemed as though everyone in the small Mattison community had sent or dropped by with some sort of love offering for Nettie. How wonderful it must be for her to know she had so many friends.

Darcy could count hers on the fingers of one hand, but she couldn't help thinking that could change if she ever had the chance to stay in one place longer than a few years.

Billy and his mother were chatting about somebody she didn't know, so Darcy tuned out their comfortable talk and let her mind wander.

What would it be like to actually be married to this strong, gentle man who tried so hard to hide his feelings? She'd lived around the military all her life, and she knew about the elite corps of men to which he belonged, the men who wore those scarlet berets. She knew that they were trained to defend and protect and…to kill. Yes, she could see Bill fighting for his country and even killing if it were necessary, but she'd seen the tender side of him as well.

She wondered if he had to hide it from his buddies, his teammates. She wondered if it ever caused him problems on the job?

What would it be like to run her hands over the toned and sculpted muscles she'd only seen from a distance? How would it feel to have his body pressed against hers, slick and damp with desire? Would he make love as well as he'd been trained to make war?

"Have you young 'uns thought any more about what I asked you this morning?" Nettie said suddenly, as if she'd just thought of it.

Darcy blushed because of what she'd been thinking, and Bill cleared his throat.

"We just figured you were doing so well that it wasn't necessary, Momma," Bill said, his voice strained. "I'm going to be too busy with duty in the next few months to give my best to startin' a marriage."

Darcy could have kissed him. That was exactly the right thing to say. She started to second his sentiment, but Nettie stopped her.

"Psh. If you wait till everything is just perfect, it won't ever be," she said. "You're young, but you're smart. I'm sure you could figure out a way to make it work.

"And you know, I ain't getting better. Doc might have pulled me through this time, but one of these days he won't be able to." She let out a shallow sigh, a sound so wistful, so poignant that it made Darcy want to cry. "The next time, the doctors might not be able to fix it."

Darcy swallowed and covered Nettie's hand with hers. The woman was right, of course, but it hurt too much even to think it. She swallowed again. "Now Nettie, you know they're making advances in medicine every day. They could come up with the cure next week, and then you could be dancing at our wedding— one that my mother would have time to plan and do up right."

Where had that come from? Did she really want to go through all that again? Or was she just clutching at straws to pacify a sick old woman?

Nettie shook her head. "I reckon you're just as married if a judge does it as if you have all the pomp and ceremony of a big wedding. Why, me and my Raymond paid two dollars down to the courthouse and had a judge say the words. I felt just as married then as I'm sure I would have if we'd had the Pope bless us.

"It ain't the trappin's that count. It's the meaning." She glanced toward the window. "Look here. It's almost dark. You two been here all day. You need to go home, get some rest. Think about what you really want in life. Do you want to waste money on some big dog-and-pony show, or do you want to do something that means just as much and have some money left over to start a life together?"

Hot tears scalded Darcy's eyelids, and she blinked them back. Nettie's sentiments had touched her. Was that why she'd fled from the chapel? Because Dick had wanted the show, and she had just wanted to be secure in the knowledge that he really loved her?

Maybe it had been with Dick, but love wasn't the issue here. She already knew Bill didn't love her. This was just a charade to humor a dying woman.

Why was she even thinking about love?

At least, she'd finally come to understand why she'd fled her own wedding. If any good were to come from all this, that was something.

Bill had gotten up and come around to her chair, and Darcy hadn't noticed. Not until she felt his strong hand on her shoulder. "Come on, Darcy. Momma's tired, and we've been here all day."

He looked at his mother and smiled. "I promise, Momma, that we'll think about it. But, it's Friday and the courthouse is closed till Monday. It's a big step you're asking us to take. Let us have the weekend to think on it."

"Done," Nettie said with a tone of finality. "Now, y'all go home and let me get some rest. I'll see you tomorrow afternoon."

Darcy drew her brows together. "Tomorrow afternoon? But you'll be all alone tomorrow."

"Shoot, Darcy girl, there's people a'comin' and a'goin' fit to beat the band. I won't be alone, and you need rest, too." She waved her hands in a shooing motion. "Now, git."

"Yes ma'am, Momma sir," Billy said, saluting smartly. "We'll see you tomorrow." He helped Darcy up, his hand slipping down to the curve of her waist as if it had always belonged there.

Darcy liked the feel of his hand at her waist, but she reminded herself that it wasn't about her. She managed a tired smile. "Good night, Nettie. We'll see you tomorrow."

"Go on, you two. Git," Nettie said.

Bill ushered Darcy toward the door, but he stopped in the open doorway. "One thing, Momma. We'd rather you didn't tell anybody about us maybe getting married. If we do this now, I think Darcy would still like to have a big wedding where we could invite everybody later."

"That right, Darcy?"

"Yes, ma'am. I think a lot of people would be hurt if they found out they'd been left out, so maybe it's better we just keep our plans quiet for now," Darcy said, a lump of emotion forming in her throat.

"I understand, I really do, and I'd purely love to be dancing at your wedding, but I'd ruther know you were happy than be able to dance a jig."

"Yes ma'am," Darcy said softly.

"Good night, Momma," Bill said again, and steered Darcy through the door.

Bill was quiet, too quiet, as they made their way

down the corridor to the way out. Darcy knew that meant he was thinking. She just wished she knew what it was all about.

Her future could depend on it.

Chapter Eleven

The ride home was long and silent. Bill wished they could have talked, but he wasn't sure what to say to Darcy. He wasn't sure what to tell himself. He needed to think. Long and hard. Even if this was only a temporary fix to ease an old woman's heart, it was still a serious step. One he didn't want to take lightly.

Darcy seemed to have withdrawn into her own silent world, as well. Funny, he thought. Normally, she would have tried to draw him out. She would have wanted to talk about it, examine every angle of the situation.

But, this time, she seemed too silent. That worried him. Did it mean she was seriously thinking about accepting the proposition? He certainly couldn't call it a proposal, but proposition seemed too contrived, too…mercenary?

That's what it was. Maybe it wasn't for money, but there would be a payoff. If it would make his mother's last days happy, he would do it. Even if it would hurt like hell to let Darcy go after it was all over.

Bill heaved a long low sigh as he steered onto the rutted dirt lane that led to his mother's house.

"I know, Billy," Darcy said as if she'd heard him thinking. "I know."

She didn't say what. She didn't explain it, but Bill knew exactly what she meant. They both understood the gravity of the situation. And it gave him a warm feeling inside to think that he and Darcy were so attuned.

And though she hadn't said it, Bill was pretty sure she was going to make the right decision.

Right for Momma anyway.

He wasn't at all sure if it would be right for him and Darcy.

"I'M GOING to go in to Doc Williamson's in the morning," Darcy told Bill as they were sitting down to a late supper of sliced tomatoes and cold cuts. She didn't wait for him to comment, but forged ahead. "He's short-handed with me out. It was supposed to be my turn to work Saturday, and I don't want to make somebody else work for me when they had other plans. I wouldn't be able to sleep late anyway." *If I get to sleep at all,* she didn't say.

It was difficult lying in bed under the same roof as Bill without wanting to go to him. He hadn't made a secret of the fact that he was attracted to her, and if she hadn't known it already, that stunt at her bedroom door last night had clinched it. Tonight, she would make sure her door was firmly closed before she went to bed.

"All right," Bill said, putting his fork down. He folded his arms across his chest and leaned against the ladderback chair that creaked in protest. "I'll drive in with you. You can drop me off at the hospital and I'll bring Mom's car home."

Darcy looked up. She hadn't even thought of Nettie's car still taking up space in the hospital parking lot.

"I reckon you'll have to come get me after work, so we can go back to the hospital together." His mouth quirked as if he were trying to hide a smile. "You'll have to come home and change out of your uniform, anyway."

Darcy started to protest, but Bill stopped her, "We promised Momma we'd get some rest. If you show up in your uniform, she'll know you didn't."

Bill was right, even if that smirk had turned a little too smug. "I had forgotten all about Nettie's car," Darcy said, unwilling though she was to admit Bill was right.

Bill shrugged. At least, he wasn't gloating over her lapse.

They ate the rest of the meal in silence as thick and heavy as deep winter snow.

Finally, after enduring more of the strained quiet than she could stand, Darcy rose to clear the table, and Bill yawned and stretched. "I'm calling the captain and let him know what's happening." He shrugged, then went on. "I want to see how the night jump I was supposed to be on when Momma got sick went. And I need to check on the dates for NCO Academy. It's a course to prepare higher-ranking non-commissioned officers for their new leadership responsibilities."

"That's probably a good idea," Darcy said, scraping the plates into the trash can. Neither one of them had eaten much, but at least they'd made the effort. And the cold cuts for supper tasted a great deal better than the cardboard sandwich she'd had at lunch. "There's not much to do here, you go ahead."

Darcy had had more than enough of Bill's silences for one day. She had a lot to mull over, and right now all she could think about was taking a hot bath to soak out the aches from her long days in the hospital waiting room. Then she could go to bed. She might not sleep, but at least she could lie down and hope some of the kinks from her two long days would settle out somehow.

She finished the light cleanup in the kitchen and dried her hands. As she hung the dish towel over the handle on the stove she caught a glimpse of Bill out of the corner of her eye.

He was hanging up the phone in what seemed to be slow motion, and something about it sent prickles of uneasiness down her spine. The expression on Bill's face was blank, almost unreadable. He walked slowly toward her with the vagueness of a sleepwalker.

"What is it?" Darcy tried to temper the panic she felt, but the expression on his face was frightening. "Is it your mother?" Had call waiting clicked in while he was talking? Was it bad news?

Bill shook his head, still showing that dazed, slow-motion effect. "No," he said, his voice strained, strange. "My roommate and another guy almost bought the farm the other night," he said, as he sagged against the doorjamb, a look of stunned disbelief on his face.

Darcy covered her mouth to stifle her gasp of shock. "They bought the farm?" *Went in* and *bought the farm* were paratrooper euphemisms for being killed when a parachute didn't open or when a parachute jump went disastrously bad.

"They're alive. Block's gonna be okay, he just screwed his leg into the ground, but Ski's critical.

"Back injury," he said, then he balled his hand into a fist and slammed it against the wall. "They don't know if he'll walk again. If I'd been there, maybe I could have done something."

"Ski is your roommate?" Funny, Darcy thought. She

ought to know that. But then, Bill probably hadn't told
Ski about her, either.

"Yeah," he said hoarsely. "I called the apartment
before I called the captain. Ski didn't answer, and I just
assumed he was whooping it up at some bar somewhere
with a girl on each arm." He drew in a long deep
breath. "I left a rude message on the machine for him."

Darcy reached for him, but drew her hand back. She
wanted to attend to his hand which surely hurt, and
wanted to comfort him. If it were her, she'd need a
shoulder, and she sensed that Bill did, too, but she
didn't know how he'd take the gesture. "I'm sure he'd
understand," Darcy finally said.

Bill closed his eyes as if shutting them would shut
off the recriminations that must be running through his
mind. "He'll never hear it. Thank God," he said. "I
will definitely erase it as soon as I get back."

He reached for Darcy and drew her to him. "Damn,"
he said. "Can things get any worse?" He tucked her
close to him and kissed the top of her head. "My God,
Darcy. I was supposed to be on that plane. I was supposed to jump that night, but…but that's when I got the
call about Momma. It could have been me."

Darcy stepped out of his embrace and looked up into
his clouded green eyes. "Now listen here, William
Hays, that has nothing to do with you. You're here
where you're needed. Where you belong. Don't you go
thinking you could have prevented it if you'd been
there. You don't even know what happened. Don't go
blaming yourself for something you had no control
over."

Bill managed half a smile. "Yes ma'am, Darcy sir. I
reckon you're right, but still. I wish I could have been
there. Hell, I just wish I knew the whole story."

"It's hard to sit around and not know the details," Darcy said, trying to be comforting. "But you are needed here. Focus on that."

"Yeah. I suppose you're right," Bill said. He heaved a big sigh, then pushed away. "I think I'll go for a run."

Darcy stood there as Bill went to his room to change into his running clothes and wondered if she should try to talk him out of it. She didn't like the idea of him out there alone in the dark, but she shook her uneasy feeling away. That wasn't a congested city road out there. Traffic was light and most of the time non-existent. She bit her lip to keep from saying anything.

Bill returned in short order, wearing running shorts and shoes and nothing else.

Darcy's breath caught in her throat. Every time she saw another layer of clothing peeled away from him, she wanted him more.

"Don't wait up," Bill said, then he pushed the screen door open and disappeared into the night.

THE RUN DID the trick. He'd gone all the way up the hill to Parson's Corner then walked the downhill stretch back. It must have been four miles to the top, but it had achieved what he'd been looking for. Release.

He'd been bottling up all his frustrations for too damned long. When he'd gotten to the top, he'd stood in the churchyard at the top of the hill and shouted out his anger, safe in the knowledge that no one would hear him.

Exhausted, he stumbled on the loose gravel at the end of the lane, but caught himself with his hands when he fell. Picking the dirt and gravel out of his palms, scraped and raw, he felt vaguely satisfied. He was alive. His hands hurt like hell, but he was alive. Maybe that was what all these trials were meant to show him.

They were supposed to tell him to stop putting his life on hold while he waited for everything to be perfect. Look what had happened to Momma. Look what had happened to Ski!

And, at least Momma had lived a full and happy life. She'd loved and lost and raised a family that loved her back. That was something to be proud of. She and Daddy hadn't sat around and waited for everything to be perfect, they'd reached for the brass ring and caught it, even if life hadn't quite been the tall cotton they might have dreamed about.

What would he have to show for it if he died tomorrow? Nothing. Not a damned thing.

He trudged up the steps onto the porch and sank onto the swing. He was still hot and sticky, and he needed to cool off before he stepped inside.

He would convince Darcy to marry him. He had to. That decision made, he got off the swing and went inside. Maybe Darcy would want to stay married once it was over; maybe she wouldn't. All he knew was that he was certain that this marriage was meant to be. For better or worse.

Darcy had already gone to bed by the time he stepped inside, so he didn't bother her. He'd have all weekend to work on her, to convince her to be his wife. After all, they couldn't get married until Monday anyway.

He showered quickly, then went to bed. He figured he wouldn't sleep, and that didn't bother him. He had plans to make.

As he tried to figure out the next step in his attempt to win Darcy over, he drifted to sleep, wondering....

DARCY DROVE BACK to the house after putting in her half day in Doctor Williamson's office. It had surprised her that the man still closed on Wednesday afternoons and stayed open on Saturday mornings when most doctors now tried to work only four days a week. But then, after going to school in urban North Carolina, working in Pittsville seemed like stepping into the past.

She hadn't spoken much to Billy this morning. He seemed to have something on his mind, and had answered in moody monosyllables. Of course, that was a no-brainer. He was still thinking about his mother's request to see him married before she.... And if that wasn't enough, he had to be worried about his friends back in Florida.

Darcy shook her head as she slowed down for a cow in the road. She hated to think about Nettie dying, but she had to face it. Bill's mother was going to die. And soon, if her frank talk with Doctor Williamson this morning meant anything. He'd taken her aside and told her without any of the sidestepping and whitewashing he'd done for the rest of the family just what Nettie's condition was.

Bill's mother's time on this earth was limited. If Nettie experienced another episode like the one she'd just gotten through, it wasn't likely that she'd recover. Or she could just not wake up some morning.

The thought was sobering, but Darcy was glad to know. Not that she hadn't already understood that reality somewhere in the back of her mind. She'd come to love the woman. Darcy hated that their time together was destined to be so short, but she was glad that their paths had crossed so that she could ease Nettie's final days.

But she still wasn't sure she could marry Nettie's son.

She wanted to make Nettie happy, but Darcy was already bothered enough about lying about being engaged to Bill. It wouldn't be any easier to go through the motions of a marriage that wasn't intended to be permanent or real.

Even if she did wish it would be.

That stopped her. Did she really?

Would it make a difference if she had any inkling at all that Bill might have some feelings for her? Feelings other than those of a healthy young man in close proximity to a woman for too long. Darcy sighed.

Kissing Bill had been more than she ever would have imagined a kiss could be. More than she'd ever felt with Dick. But was this electricity, this spark, this magnetic attraction love? Or was it just hormones and chemistry?

If Bill would just give her some little sign that he cared about her more than just as a means to make his mother happy, the decision might be easy. Well, easier. There was no way this situation was ever going to be easy.

And could she do it?

After all, she had left a man she'd known forever at the altar. Did she really think she could go through the motions with a man she barely knew?

She pulled into the drive and looked ahead to see Billy swinging idly in the glider on the front porch. Her breath caught in her throat.

After last night, she knew Bill better. She was beginning to get an idea about what made him tick. But she still didn't think she knew him well enough to marry him. Even if the marriage had an escape hatch built in.

She parked by the shed and turned off the engine. Bill had come down off the porch and waited for her in the yard. Darcy liked that, but she couldn't help wondering why?

"Lunch is ready. Do you want to change first or eat?" Bill announced as Darcy stepped out of the car. He offered her his arm, and escorted her up the steps.

Bill's odd behavior had her wondering, but Darcy decided to enjoy it, nonetheless. "Let's eat first. I'm hungry." What she didn't say was that just being close to Bill made her hungry, and not for food.

A NURSE STOPPED Bill in the hall before he and Darcy entered his mother's hospital room, and a vague feeling of alarm shuddered through him. Bill clutched Darcy's hand as they waited for the woman tell them what she wanted.

"I don't want to alarm you," the nurse said, doing exactly what she'd said she didn't want to do. "But I wanted to prepare you, Mr. Hays."

"Yes, ma'am. Go on."

The nurse splayed her fingers out in front of her in a gesture of supplication that Bill suspected was supposed to be calming. If it was, she'd missed the mark. "Nettie had a bad night and looks a little sicker this morning than she did last night. I didn't want you to go in there without being warned."

Darcy touched his arm. "Nettie probably just had a hard time sleeping because of the strange surroundings. The first night she was sedated. Now that she's feeling better, she probably noticed noises that kept her up." She smiled, but Bill was quick to note that the smile didn't reach the corners of her eyes. "I'm sure it's nothing."

Bill drew in a deep breath. "Okay, you've told me. Now can I go in?"

"Yes. Go ahead."

Bill grabbed Darcy's hand, turned and strode into his mother's room with Darcy in tow.

Compared to yesterday, Momma did look ill, but certainly not on death's door as he'd first imagined she might. She did look haggard, and blue-black circles rimmed her eyes. But when she saw who her visitors were, she perked right up, a grin brightening her pinched face. "Good morning, son. Daughter," she said.

Bill didn't see the need to point out that it was afternoon, but he kissed his mother's forehead, then took her hand as he settled into the chair next to her. "The nurse tells me you had a bad night," he said simply.

"Nothing new. I'm an old lady. Nothing's as easy as it used to be." Momma managed a chuckle. "Some nights I can't sleep a wink, and other days I just don't want to wake up. I just had some heavy thinking on my mind."

"Like what?" Darcy asked, situating herself on the other side of the bed.

"Thinking about my past. Your future. A little bit of everything." She sighed and managed a weak smile. "Life's been good to me, for the most. But, I've had my time. It's your time now to..." She let the words trail off, and Bill wondered if she had forgotten what she'd intended to say or whether she'd left it for him to fill in the blanks.

Darcy gasped slightly, then seemed to regain her composure. She patted his mother's hand and swallowed. "You still have plenty of time, Nettie."

Nobody in the room believed that. Bill loved Darcy for saying it. For at least trying.

"No, I don't. And you, of all my children, should

know it better than most,'' she said, directing her comment to Darcy. "My heart's failing me. I might go tomorrow, or I could hang on for months." She paused to catch her breath and coughed, the sound wheezy and wet.

"Just between you and me and the bedpost, we know I didn't have pneumonia. My body's tired. It's shuttin' down." She sighed again, her eyes bright.

"I don't mind goin'," she whispered, turning back to Bill. "I really don't. I just want to know that my youngest is happy." She smiled, a longing expression in her eyes. "I might not be able to dance at your wedding, son, but I would surely like to be there."

Bill's heart seemed to skip a beat, and Darcy drew in a quick breath. The following silence seemed to echo too loudly in his ears. What could he say?

He wanted to tell her yes. If it were only up to him, he would shout it to the rooftops.

It was no longer a matter of putting it off until later; it had to be done now. It was clear to him as a target in his gun sight that Momma had lain awake all night worrying about him...and Darcy...and that she wouldn't live to see their wedding.

Bill swallowed and glanced at Darcy. Seeming to be as uncertain as he was, she wrung her hands.

Why hadn't they told Momma the truth from the get-go? If they had, they wouldn't be in this fix now. Momma wouldn't even be thinking about whether or not he was going to get married sooner instead of later. Hell, she wouldn't be thinking about him in terms of marriage at all. And she damned sure wouldn't be lying awake at night making herself sicker by worrying about it.

Suddenly Bill's head throbbed, and he rubbed at his

temples, then scrubbed his hands down his cheeks. What were they going to do now? How could he and Darcy have known that their well-intentioned charade would backfire?

Darcy got quietly up from her chair and came around the foot of Nettie's hospital bed to stand behind Bill. She knew that what they said to Nettie in the next few moments might make the difference between her recovery this time or giving up too soon.

She'd come to love Nettie in the past few weeks, and she didn't want the woman to die, now, or later. But Darcy knew Nettie's death was inevitable. And she knew that granting this one wish would make her going easier.

She and Bill had set out two weeks ago on a course that they couldn't change. Every moment since she'd stepped out of that Jeep, yawning and stretching after her aborted wedding, had led them irrevocably to this moment.

They'd set the course. They'd have to follow through. Wherever that final destination might be.

Darcy moistened her lips and drew in a deep breath. She didn't know whether a marriage to Bill would be for better or for worse, but it probably wouldn't be forever. She let out the breath she'd forgotten she was holding. If she knew it going in, it wouldn't be so bad coming out.

And maybe it wouldn't end, she couldn't help hoping. Maybe they'd figure out a way to make it work.

To make it last forever the way Nettie wanted it to.

She'd known Dick all her life, but it had taken her years to realize that she didn't like him. She supposed she'd been more in love with the idea of love than with Dick.

At least she liked Bill. She admired the way he had been so good to his mother in her declining days.

It wasn't the sturdiest thing on which to base a marriage, but then this marriage wasn't going to be real for anyone but Nettie.

Darcy drew in another long breath, and took Bill's hand and squeezed it as she exhaled, for courage, she supposed.

"I'll make a deal with you, Nettie," Darcy said, focusing on the frail woman in the hospital bed. She was surprised at how much stronger and more certain she sounded than she really felt. "You stop lying awake at night so the doctor's medicine can do its work on you. Then, if you're well enough, you'll see us married on Monday."

Darcy couldn't miss Bill's sharp intake of breath. She squeezed his hand in hopes of assuring him that it would be all right.

Darcy turned to him and forced a smile. "That is, if that's what you still want, Billy." She paused, giving Bill a chance to stop her. He didn't, so she had no choice but to follow through. "Will you marry me on Monday at the courthouse? Will you have me as your wife?"

Chapter Twelve

Bill didn't realize he'd stopped breathing until he found himself involuntarily gasping for air. As his lungs filled and expanded, he tried to think of something as eloquent and as touching as Darcy's simple words with which to accept her proposal.

He knew that Darcy was only doing this for Momma, and Momma's happiness was the most important thing in all this. But he couldn't help thinking that it was the beginning of something else. It was also a way to get him and Darcy closer.

Even if he couldn't acknowledge it out loud, or let on to anyone else.

It was a wild idea, he was sure, but Bill couldn't help hoping that with his ring on her finger, Darcy might let him get to know her. She would learn to like him.

Maybe love would come later.

"Well, son. Are you going to give the child an answer? Or are you just going to keep us waiting here?"

Bill shook himself out of it. He had no business thinking about anything further than the ceremony. There was going to be no marriage, he reminded himself sternly. He'd known forever that he couldn't put another woman through what his mother had faced. This would only be a real wedding for Momma. For show. It wouldn't be real for Darcy. It wouldn't be for him.

The vows wouldn't be worth the paper he'd sign when the ceremony was over. He just had to remember that.

He couldn't count on anything more.

He swallowed and moistened his lips. "Yes, Darcy," he answered huskily. "I'll be honored to be your husband."

Momma clapped her hands together, a smile brightening her wan face. "Then it's settled. I'll call Judge Armistead, and we'll get it set up."

Darcy drew in a quick breath, but said nothing. What had she started to say? She'd already promised to marry him on Monday. She couldn't back out on him now.

Bill started to protest his mother getting too involved in the planning and tiring herself out, but he shut his mouth before voicing any objections. Already, his mother's color appeared brighter, and maybe it was his imagination, but the circles rimming her eyes seemed to be fading. If just thinking about the wedding was enough to do that, then he wasn't about to dampen her enthusiasm by objecting to her calling in a favor or two.

He just wondered when his mother had become so chummy with the Judge Probate of Pitt County.

"You know me and Theron go way back, don't you?" she said, seeming to be reading his mind. But then Momma had always been able to do that.

"No, ma'am. I didn't know that," Darcy said.

Momma giggled like a schoolgirl. "Why, Theron thought he had the inside track on my affections at one time," she said, her face brightened by a fond smile.

Bill hadn't known that, and he wondered with a brief

twinge of…what?…if this had been before Daddy or afterwards.

"He was a couple of years ahead of me in high school up at Mattison Consolidated. We dated some. He even took me to his senior prom. When he went off to college, he wanted me to promise to wait for him." She looked off into the distant past, a dreamy smile on her face.

"I knew it wouldn't work. After all, he was going to be a great big lawyer, and I had just been promised a job at the Five and Dime store in Pittsville. I told him no and broke his heart." She looked up then, a smile on her face. "It's a good thing. If I had saved myself for Theron, I would never have met your daddy," she said, patting Bill on the hand.

Then she shook herself out of her memories and drew in a long, deep breath. "I know you said you wanted to keep it between just us, but I surely could tell Lou and Earline?"

Bill, still holding Darcy's hand, felt her stiffen. He would have to deny his mother that one wish. "No, Momma. We don't want to hurt anybody's feelings about being left out. And you're going to have to tell the judge the same thing. We'll make it right in the end."

Bill hated saying that because, more than likely, the correction would be to end the paper marriage, not to celebrate it. But, for now, it was all he had, and he would take any morsel he could get if it made his mother's last days easier.

Even if it wouldn't do much for his next few months.

DARCY WAS QUIET on the way home. What could she say? Today, the silence between her and Bill seemed more strained than normal.

Could she tell him that she thought she might be falling in love with him, but she wasn't sure? And if they took their marriage seriously and actually worked at being husband and wife, she might just figure it out? She glanced Billy's way and smiled to herself. It would not be work at all.

Darcy turned and focused her gaze out the car window as the countryside flew by. She hadn't taken much time to look at the small part of the world where Billy had grown up, and the sheer beauty, flanked by such unimaginable poverty, sobered her. A woman in a faded house dress looked up from the washing she was hanging on the line beside her ramshackle mobile home and waved. Darcy had to look away.

Why did she think her life was such a mess when she had so much compared to so many?

And she and Bill had a wedding to plan. Even if it wasn't going to be for keeps.

Reminding them that they had important plans to make, Nettie had shooed them off when Ray and his wife arrived. Billy had shaken his brother's hand and introduced Anne-Lise to her before leaving. But not before Bill had given his mother a stern look of warning.

Darcy just hoped Nettie wouldn't let their secret slip. She sighed wearily.

"Are you sorry you got yourself into this?" Billy asked as they turned off the main highway onto the farm-to-market road that pointed toward the long-neglected Hays farm.

Darcy wondered if he was giving her the opportunity to voice her doubts, of which there were many. "No," she answered slowly. "Not really." She drew in a deep breath and tried to explain what she'd been thinking.

She couldn't. At least, not entirely. So she came up with something else. "It's just sort of ironic, don't you think? When I met you, I'd just run away from a wedding I'd been planning forever. Or, at least, my mother and my aunt had." She managed a wry smile. "Now, I fully intend to go through with this one, and on a moment's notice. Funny world, huh?"

Bill said nothing for a moment, then pressed his lips into a thin, hard line. Then he smiled grimly. "No. Not that funny. I think it was more like a miracle. You came into our life at a time when we needed you. Maybe it was fate."

Darcy shrugged. She drew in a deep breath and settled back against the seat. "I just don't know whether it's good or bad."

Maybe it wasn't exactly what Bill would have preferred to hear, but Darcy had to face it. This marriage would not be real for them.

It was for Nettie. Period.

And if she managed to convince herself of that, she knew about a bridge in New York City she could probably sell someone. Darcy sighed. She knew darn well that there was something in this marriage for her.

Billy.

She just wasn't sure how he felt about her.

If they'd met under different circumstances. If they really had met in North Carolina and fallen in love as they'd led everyone to believe, all this would be so much simpler. She wouldn't feel so guilty about tricking a sweet old woman, and she wouldn't be wondering why she was falling in love with Nettie's son.

FEELING AS RESTLESS as a caged tiger, Bill paced the confines of the small living room on Sunday afternoon. They'd been to see Momma, but she'd run them off, telling them that they had a wedding to get ready for and that she'd have plenty of visitors without them underfoot.

He was getting married tomorrow, and Bill was having a hard time getting a handle on that.

Now that Darcy had agreed to go through with it, the prospect of the wedding, even one as phony as a three-dollar bill, had him on edge. It didn't help that a summer storm was raging outside and he couldn't work off his tension.

Not that there was much work to do on a non-working farm at this time of year. But, he could have gone off to run or something.

Anything to take his mind off tomorrow.

"Have you given any thought to what you're going to wear for the wedding?"

Bill looked up, startled at the sudden intrusion into his chaotic thoughts. He hadn't even heard Darcy enter the room. Hell, the way he was acting, you'd think he didn't want to go through with this. "No," he said, realizing that figuring out what to wear would give him something to do. If only for a little while.

He felt so damned helpless. And he wasn't sure what he was helpless about. Getting ready for the wedding? Helping his mother?

Convincing Darcy to…what?

"I hadn't given it much thought," he said slowly. "I guess I should, huh?"

"The wedding might be taking place in the judge's chambers, but somehow I don't think jeans and a T-shirt will do," Darcy said dryly.

Bill frowned. Darcy was holding a rumpled, off-white suit in her hands. Was she planning to wear that? He felt a vague surge of disappointment that she wouldn't be in the traditional white dress and veil. Had he, somehow, been expecting it?

But why should she wear the customary wedding dress? And where would she get one? Why did he keep having to remind himself that the wedding tomorrow wasn't going to be for keeps?

"I don't know. Do you plan to wear that?" he said, jerking his head toward the suit. He had to say something to fill the awkward silence.

"Yes, what do you think?" Darcy said brightly as she held the jacket up against her to show it off. "They say it's bad luck for the groom to see the bride and the wedding dress before the wedding, but I guess, since this is not the traditional situation, we'll just forget about that one."

Hell, yeah. They'd ignored most of the other customs. And now that he'd seen it, Bill knew that the simple suit would be perfect. Darcy possessed such a sweet and simple beauty that she needed no ornamentation, no distraction from the glow that seemed to shine from within. "You'll look beautiful," he said thickly.

Darcy looked at him, a strange expression on her face. "Thank you," she finally said. "I need to get the ironing board out and press this. If you find something, I'll iron it for you, too."

He had forgotten that this conversation had started because she'd wanted to know what he was wearing to their wedding in the morning.

It was ironic, he supposed, that they were standing there in the house like an old married couple discussing what they were going to wear. They might as well be going to someone else's wedding, not their own. Then tomorrow night, unlike the married couple they'd be, they'd go to separate rooms to sleep.

Funny, he had no trouble thinking of Darcy as a bride, but the concept of groom connected with him was a real problem. He wasn't ready for this.

And he didn't know why he was panicking.

It wasn't as if this marriage was going to be forever.

"Bill? Are you going to go look?"

"What?"

"For something appropriate to wear," Darcy reminded him as she plugged in the iron. When had she put the ironing board up?

"I'll check in the closet and see if I have anything to go with that white shirt and tie I keep here to wear for church so I don't have to pack and unpack every time I come to visit." Bill expelled a long breath. Or maybe it was a sigh. No. It couldn't be. Special Tactics combat controllers don't sigh.

"Well, go on," Darcy said, making a shooing motion with her hands. "We might have to make a run out in this mess to town to buy a suit if you don't find anything," she said, then stuck her finger in her mouth, moistened it and quickly tested the iron. "Bill? Are you going?"

He was pretty sure combat controllers didn't let little slips of women no bigger than a minute boss them around, either. But he couldn't help thinking that when it was Darcy Stanton doing the ordering, he really didn't mind. "Yes ma'am, sir," he said, saluting sloppily.

Darcy rolled her eyes. "Go on," she said, shooing him out of the room. "You are definitely dismissed."

Watching him stride away, Darcy couldn't help chuckling. Special Tactics guys really hated to be bossed around. Yet, her Billy had let her. But, then he'd taken orders from a strong Southern woman all his life, so maybe it had come naturally.

She stopped for a moment to ponder what she'd just been thinking. Her Billy? She wasn't even sure when she had started thinking of him as Billy, as his mother called him. Much less, hers.

He wasn't hers to keep. At least, not forever. She was going to lend herself to Billy, to his plan, long enough to allow Nettie to die happy. But she'd only promised herself in name only.

She hadn't offered her body or her soul.

A clap of thunder sounded as the summer storm rolled on through and reminded her that she'd better finish her ironing before the electricity went off, a common occurrence here in the summer time.

Darcy shuddered and forced away any more thoughts of Billy or their life together after a wedding that was only for show. She pressed her lips together grimly and made short work of pressing the creases out of her suit.

Too bad smoothing out the mess she and Billy had gotten into wouldn't be as easy as ironing this suit.

"How will this do?"

This time, Billy had startled her out of her thoughts. "What?" Darcy shook her head, trying to shake loose the cobwebs that were befuddling her thinking.

Billy held up a plastic suit bag with the zipper pulled down to the bottom. "I'd forgotten that this was in the car the other night when I dropped everything to get up here so fast when Momma got sick."

In the bag was Billy's blue service dress uniform, complete with decorations. Of course, it would be perfect, but why was it here? He certainly didn't need it in Mattison.

"I had to go to the base photographer to update the photos in my service jacket the other day, and I didn't have time to take them back to the apartment before I had to report for the pre-jump briefing, so I left it in the car." He shrugged. "Who'da thunk it would come in handy?"

Was it more of that fate thing? Darcy shook her head. No, she shouldn't be thinking that.

"No?"

Realizing that Billy had misinterpreted her subconscious gesture, Darcy looked up. "I'm sorry. I was thinking about something else. Your uniform will be perfect. Take it out of the bag so I can make sure it's pressed."

She smoothed the dark blue fabric with her hands on the faded and worn surface of the ironing board, and Darcy couldn't helping wondering if the Fates were playing a joke on her. Here it was, just a couple of weeks after she'd run away from a traditional military wedding, complete with formal mess dress uniforms, and now she was preparing to marry another man in a uniform.

The uniform was different, and so was the man, but maybe this wedding had been preordained.

Was she destined to keep promising herself to men in uniforms until she finally got it right?

A SHARD OF SUNLIGHT streaked through the sheer curtains on the bedroom window and forced Bill awake. He yawned and stretched and tried to shake the cobwebs out of his sleepy brain. It was Monday, and morning had dawned fresh and clear after last night's storm. A lot clearer than Bill's head.

He hadn't slept well, anticipating today's events, and

if he had gotten three hours of sleep, he'd be surprised. He might have been trained to go without sleep, but this morning his training had been no help at all. He dragged himself out of bed, all the while wishing he could crawl right back in and pull the covers up over himself.

The morning birds were chirping as they usually did, but considering his aching, tired head, Bill wished they'd shut up. This was not exactly the way a guy was supposed to feel on his wedding day.

He felt as if he'd been to one hell of a bachelor party. Without having had any of the fun.

Bill glanced at the clock. It was barely past six. Too early, even if he had slept well. They didn't have to be at the courthouse until ten. How would they pass the rest of the morning until it was time to go to the court-house?

The smell of coffee wafted toward him from the kitchen, but considering the early hour, he figured he was the first one awake. Darcy had invested in a cof-feemaker with a timer, and he'd seen her put it on last night. At least there was coffee.

He stumbled toward the kitchen, only to pause out-side the closed bathroom door. The unmistakable sound of water running in the shower told him that Darcy was up after all. Visions of warm water sluicing over her slender body flitted through Bill's head, and his groin tightened.

He shook that thought away. He had no business thinking about Darcy like that. He wasn't really going to be her husband. Even after the wedding, he had no right to her body—even if he wanted her so bad he could taste it. He tried to will his nether regions to be-have.

"Gotta get yourself together, man," Bill grumbled to

himself, his voice gravelly from sleep, or lack of it. "If she sees you like this, there's no way she'll go through with it, phony marriage or not. He forced his feet to move and lurched toward the kitchen.

Maybe if he drank half the pot of coffee, he'd have made himself reasonably human by the time Darcy came out. Maybe if he drank the other half, he'd be able to fight the urge to sweep her into his arms and pass the morning exploring her body.

DARCY RINSED the soap away, turned off the water, then stepped out of the shower. She breathed in the sweet, floral scent of the old-fashioned soap Nettie used, not for the fragrance, but for the economy, and smiled. Maybe this particular brand was inexpensive, but she loved the subtle smell of the flowers that hinted at the life and warmth of spring. It seemed to make a promise.

And maybe it was appropriate for the day, she thought as she toweled herself dry from head to toe. She ran a comb through her short hair and briefly wished that she'd been able to get someone to style it for her, but she shook that thought away. She'd chosen the style for its ease and simplicity. It suited her.

And considering that the rest of today's ceremony wouldn't be real, she might as well be.

She dressed slowly in shorts and a T-shirt. There was no sense in putting on the white suit so early. The linen fabric would only wrinkle in the thick summer air, already muggy at this early hour.

Darcy stepped out of the bathroom, letting a cloud of steam escape into the hall. She wondered if she should wake Billy, but decided against it. Billy's door was closed, and he had no real reason to get up so soon. She shrugged at that. Neither had she, but she'd found herself waking at the crack of dawn like a child on Christmas morning.

She smiled at the irony as she headed for the kitchen and a cup of coffee to get her going. After all, with the exception that she and Billy were going to stand in front of a judge and Nettie to make promises they had no intention of keeping, this was just going to be another day. Why she was comparing it to Christmas, she didn't know.

Well, she did, but she tried not to think about it. After all, she shouldn't be as attracted to Billy Hays as she was. And there would be no wedding night.

She stopped short in the kitchen doorway, startled to find Billy at the table, hunched over, nursing a cup of coffee as if his life depended on it. He looked as if he'd just awakened after a three-day drunk, and she couldn't imagine why.

He looked up slowly, his eyes red-rimmed and bleary. If she didn't know better, she'd think he was coming down with something. And maybe he was: cold feet.

Still, her nurse's training kicked in, and she felt his forehead. It was cool. Or as cool as it could be in a poorly air-conditioned house on an Alabama summer morning.

"Are you all right?"

Billy motioned for her to sit, and nodded. He took a huge swig of coffee, swallowed, then spoke. "Yes. No. Hell," he muttered, his voice gravelly. "I don't know."

Darcy's pleasant spirits slunk away like a whipped dog. He'd probably spent all night tossing and turning and dreading the prospect of marrying her. Well, at least, she wouldn't have to worry about fighting him off tonight.

And after seeing him this morning, she was just as glad she wouldn't.

"THIS IS IT," Bill said, punctuating his statement with a deep breath, as he pushed his mother's wheelchair up the ramp and into the courthouse.

"Theron's office is over there," Momma said, pointing.

Bill steered the chair in that direction, and Darcy trailed behind. He knew Darcy must feel as if she were an afterthought, and he wished he could do something to make it better. But they had to remember that this wedding was not for them. It was for the woman seated so expectantly in the borrowed wheelchair.

They'd stopped by the courthouse earlier to apply for the license before they'd collected Momma from the hospital. So, all that was left was...to do it.

He sucked in a deep breath before knocking on the closed door marked Probate Judge.

In a few moments he was going to be a married man.

Even if it was in name only.

A portly man wearing a rumpled seersucker suit opened the door and smiled broadly. The lines around his mouth extended all the way up to wreath startling blue eyes that twinkled, making him look like a clean-shaven Santa Claus in a summer suit.

"Come in, come in," the man announced, with a welcoming gesture. "I don't expect you remember me all that well from when you were a boy, but I'm Judge Armistead."

He turned to Darcy. "And you must be our Billy's intended bride." He took her hands and kissed them in a courtly gesture that made Bill think of a scene out of a period movie.

"Yes, sir," Darcy said, smiling and looking as if she were resisting the urge to curtsey. "Pleased to meet you."

But the judge seemed only to have eyes for Momma. He stooped down and took her hands. "It is so good to see you, Nettie. And for such a happy occasion." He lifted Momma's hand, still wearing the hospital bracelet, to his mouth and kissed it. She blushed and giggled like a school girl.

Then Bill remembered. "Uncle Terry?" He had come around for a while after Daddy had died, bringing Momma gifts, helping her out. He hadn't thought anything of it then, but had the man, a lawyer then, actually been trying to court his mother? He couldn't help thinking that their lives would have been so much easier if Uncle Terry had succeeded.

The judge pushed himself to his feet, and clamped a meaty hand down on Bill's shoulder. "Ah, you do remember me." He looked down at Nettie and smiled fondly. "I tried so hard to win your mother's hand after your daddy died, but she'd have nothing of it. Said she was a one-man woman." He shook his head slowly. "My loss," he said with a hint of sadness. Then he clapped his hands together suddenly.

"Let's get this show on the road," he said, then he cleared his throat. "R.J.? Are you ready?"

A young black man wearing a crisp linen suit came in carrying a small bouquet of blue flowers. "I believe these are for you," he said, offering them to Darcy.

Darcy gasped as she accepted them and lowered her head to sniff them. Bill sucked in a deep breath. He hadn't even thought about flowers.

"This is R.J., my clerk. He'll be the other witness, if that's all right with you."

Momma's hand flew to her mouth. Was she going to object? "Oh, my goodness me. I almost forgot." She pulled something out of her pocketbook. "This is for you, son," she said. "I know you didn't have time to get Darcy a proper ring. So, I want you to use mine." She smiled fondly. "It's hardly been off my finger since your daddy put it there, but I'm not going to need it...."

Then she turned to Darcy. "And this is for you." She produced a tiny gold locket from that same pocketbook. "Billy gave this to me for Christmas when he was in grade school. This can be your something borrowed. I reckon the ring is old, the bouquet is new, and the forget-me-nots are blue. So," she said brightly. "We're all set."

Judge Armistead picked up a book from his cluttered desk, opened it to a marked page and began to read. "Dearly Beloved...."

Darcy stiffened straight enough so that Bill couldn't help but see it. Then she took a deep breath and managed an anemic smile.

Bill reached for her hand and squeezed. He whispered, "If you're not sure you can go through with this, it's not too late to back out."

Then he held his breath, hoping Darcy wouldn't take his offered out.

Chapter Thirteen

Darcy knew it the moment Bill stopped breathing, but Judge Armistead continued speaking.

Was it because Bill was anxious over what was about to come to be? Or that she might accept his out?

She returned his gentle squeeze and managed a timid smile. "I'm all right," she murmured.

The judge stopped.

"I'm okay. Go on. Just a little nervous."

"...to join these two people in holy matrimony."

Why did it all seem like a dream? As much as she tried, Darcy found it difficult to focus, to concentrate on the words of the pledge she was about to make.

She must have made the correct responses, for suddenly Billy gathered her into his arms.

"Billy Hays, you may kiss your bride."

"Hoo ah," Billy cheered softly, then pulled her yet closer.

Panic caused Darcy's heart to flutter wildly, but when she saw the expression of joy in Nettie's eyes, Darcy knew she had done the right thing.

She moistened her lips and tilted her face up to Billy, so handsome in his blue dress uniform. He bent down to kiss her. His hot breath excited her, and his clean man scent turned her insides into warm chocolate pudding. She melted into his arms.

How was she going to pretend she felt nothing for this man when her body was insisting that she did?

How was she going to stay alone with him in Nettie's house tonight, her wedding night, and not want to go to him? Why was she falling in love with this gruff, gentle stranger who'd been trained to make war, but seemed perfect for love?

Billy claimed her lips and branded her with a hot kiss. He started to draw away, but Darcy drew him back to her. They might have agreed that were going through the motions just for Nettie, but her heart, her body demanded otherwise.

If this was going to be all there was, then she was going to have all she could take. She heard a whimper of need escape from somewhere deep within her as Billy took what she offered and gave what she craved.

Why couldn't it work out? a portion of her mind asked.

Darcy gasped and pushed away, the spell broken. Her face grew hot, though the rest of her body felt cold as ice.

Nettie laughed and clapped her hands joyfully. The judge congratulated Billy, pumping his hand up and down for all he was worth. But all Darcy could think about was the sound of her heartbeat roaring in her ears.

She had done it. She was a married woman.

And though she might have promised herself that it was only for Nettie's sake, she knew from the bottom of her pounding heart, that she wanted it to be so much more.

"Best wishes, Mrs. Hays," R.J. said, and Darcy wondered briefly who he was talking to before she realized that he'd addressed her. "Now, if you'll excuse me, I must get back to my duties."

She felt her face grow hot with embarrassment, and hoped it didn't show. "Thank you," she said numbly, blinking as if to make the surreal moment clearer.

She and Billy were married.

The papers that the judge was beckoning her to sign would testify to it.

But even if their marriage lasted just today, Tracy D'Arcy Harbeson Stanton would always and forever, in her mind, be Mrs. Billy Hays.

Fighting giddy hysteria, she scribbled her name on the paper. Her right hand trembled, and she had to steady it with her left. Seeing the tiny band of gold on her third finger did nothing to calm her nerves.

How was she going to make it through the rest of the day? Through the night?

How would she be able to hold it all together until they checked Nettie out of the hospital and brought her home tomorrow morning? Until Billy returned to the combat control squadron and his teammates at Hurlburt Field?

She drew in a deep breath. She had to.

BILL STEPPED OUTSIDE and felt as though he'd been mugged by the thick, sultry air. He hated having to check Momma back into the hospital, but Doc Williamson, whom he had sworn to secrecy for the same reasons he'd given his mother, had only allowed her a short furlough for the ceremony.

She was to remain under observation for another night. Was the extra stay a ploy to give them time alone?

Time he didn't need—even if he wanted it so badly he wasn't sure he had the strength to stay away.

Darcy touched his sleeve. "Do you think we should stay out here all dressed up like this? What if somebody we know sees us and asks questions?" she asked quietly.

Bill hadn't thought of that. He'd figured once they got Momma checked back in they'd be home free.

Darcy was right, of course. As beautiful as she looked in her white suit, and in spite of the tiny blue bouquet she still clutched, they couldn't tell anyone what they'd done. They wouldn't be free until they got home.

He might want to shout it from the rooftops for everyone to hear, but he couldn't.

"We'd best get home and out of these clothes," he said, but he couldn't help yearning for the honeymoon that normally followed even the smallest wedding.

Darcy blushed, just like the bride she was pretending to be. Had his desires been so obvious that she could read them on his face?

"I've got to finish up some repairs around the house this afternoon before I go back to Florida tomorrow," he added gruffly, though repairs were the last thing he wanted to make. He didn't want Darcy thinking that the only thing on his mind was jumping her bones.

That hadn't been part of their bargain.

Maybe he could remind himself often that Darcy didn't love him, that he wasn't meant to have a wife, then he might be able to stay away.

He did want her, he might even need her, but he'd never take anything from her that she didn't offer willingly.

And hadn't he asked enough of her as it was?

"SUPPER'S ALMOST READY," Darcy called, looking up to the roof where Billy had been tacking down shingles loosened by the summer storm the night before. He had been banging around up there all afternoon, and she couldn't help thinking that he'd stayed up there longer and banged louder than necessary.

"I'll be right down," Billy shouted back, after another barrage of pounding.

Darcy sighed and stepped back inside. This was her wedding night, and so far it had turned out to be nothing like the romantic experience she'd dreamed of since she was a child.

Of course, as a child she hadn't expected that she'd be marrying a man for the reason she'd pledged herself to Billy. As a child, she'd believed in happily-ever-afters. Now, she wasn't so sure.

She smelled something scorching and hurried back into the kitchen to find the pasta for the spaghetti boiling over. Darcy lowered the flame and sighed. So much for impressing her new husband with her culinary abilities.

Why she should be worrying about impressing Billy, she didn't know. They weren't married for keeps. But real marriage or not, this was going to be her only first meal as a married woman. Even if she did, someday, fall in love with a man who loved her back, it wouldn't be the same as the first time, the first kiss, the first...anything. It might not mean anything to Billy, but it mattered to her.

She'd pulled out all the stops and cooked the one fancy meal she knew she could pull off. The one meal that she could count on everybody to like, and the one she always got raves for. And she had scorched the pasta.

What a way to impress a man! Darcy shrugged and dumped the noodles into a colander and ran cold water over them to stop them from overcooking. Now, all she needed was someone to eat it.

Billy came in, bare to the waist, shiny and slick with sweat, and stopped in the middle of the living room. Darcy's breath caught in her throat. Then he sniffed the air appreciatively, and Darcy smiled. Maybe she had impressed him after all.

"Do I smell spaghetti?"

"You smell the sauce," Darcy said. No need to point out that you really couldn't smell the noodles. "It'll be on the table by the time you wash up."

"I'll hurry," he said, and Darcy grinned. Maybe the way to a man's heart really was through his stomach.

Then she reminded herself that she shouldn't have expectations. This marriage was only supposed to be real to Nettie, and for Nettie it was real enough as it was. Darcy let out a small sigh and turned back to the kitchen.

In her childish daydreams, she had imagined roses and candlelight. In reality, she had daylilies plucked from one of Nettie's perennial flowerbeds and it was still broad daylight. No need for candles, and there was no point in bothering with them anyway. This meal was merely to satisfy their bodies' needs for nutrition.

But what about her other needs?

Darcy shook the thought away. She had to stop thinking about what should have been and focus on the way things were. That wasn't easy to do with Nettie's wedding band weighing so heavy on her left hand.

Glancing involuntarily at the finger adorned by the thin gold band, she wondered if she should put it away.

If it were out of sight, would the marriage be out of mind?

She tugged at the ring, but her finger, swollen by the heat of the kitchen wouldn't release it.

"What are you doing?"

Darcy looked up to see Billy, damp and rosy and obviously fresh from a fast shower, standing in the doorway. She let go of the ring and blushed. "Nothing. Are you ready for dinner?" she said brightly. "I made my world-famous spaghetti and meat sauce." It wasn't exactly spaghetti weather, but…

"I love spaghetti. There was a place I used to go to when I was at Fort Bragg in parachute training that really made great spaghetti." He laughed as he took his place at the table. "It almost made jump school bearable."

He was probably talking about Luigi's, but Darcy thought it prudent not to mention that she'd been there, too. He still didn't know that she'd spent her life moving from one military base to another. Billy didn't know that her father was a general in the army and her uncle was the colonel in charge of his squadron back at Hurlburt Field. Darcy knew she ought to come clean about her background, but somehow, her wedding night, such as it was, didn't seem to be the right time. There would be plenty of time to explain all that later on in their married life.

If there was a later on.

No, she told herself sternly. There was only now.

Darcy forced herself to think of the present. "I'm not sure it's up to the standards of an Italian restaurant, but I've never had any complaints," she said, wiping her hands on a dish towel. "I'll just get the bread out of the oven and the salad, then you can tell me what you think.''

Why it mattered so much to her, Darcy didn't know. After all, it wasn't as if their marriage would fail if he didn't like her cooking, she reminded herself as she removed the garlic bread from the oven.

Their marriage was going to end. Period.

She might as well get used to the idea now, and stop thinking as if she had forever.

They only had until... Darcy swallowed a lump in her throat. They only had until Nettie was gone.

Darcy set the salad on the table and seated herself across from Billy. It seemed strange to be sitting there like that, as man and wife, yet familiar as well. After all, they'd eaten at this same table together many times before. "I usually serve wine, but I..."

Billy covered her hand with his. "You didn't know today was going to be a special day. It's all right, Darcy. I'm amazed that you were able to produce this...this feast when you've been too tied up with my mother to shop." Billy lifted her fingers to his lips and kissed her hand right over his mother's wedding ring.

Darcy felt the heat of his lips on her hand and all the way down to her toes.

Bill felt the way Darcy trembled, but she didn't jerk her hand away. She withdrew it slowly, tentatively.

Had she wanted him to keep holding her hand?

Maybe it was too intimate, considering the circumstances, Bill thought, but it seemed right. Darcy had made a great sacrifice in taking him on, and he wanted to show his appreciation.

If he couldn't love her in the physical sense, he could at least demonstrate that he cared.

What he didn't understand was his strong attraction to a woman he'd only known for a short time.

Hell, he'd dated one girl all the way through high school, and he hadn't felt this strongly about her. When he'd joined the air force, she'd forgotten him soon enough. She'd been engaged to someone else by the time he came home for his first leave, and he couldn't have cared less.

So much for true love.

"We'd better eat before the salad gets warm and the spaghetti gets cold," Darcy said, bringing him back to the here and now.

"Yeah," he said huskily. "I'm sure it'll be great."

She smiled, a look that made him think of pictures of the Madonna from his one night-school art appreciation class. It made him think that she had a secret.

And he couldn't help wondering what it was.

DARCY WATCHED with silent pleasure as Billy uttered a satisfied sigh, then pushed himself away from the table.

"If I'd known the cookin' was going to be this good, I might have considered gettin' married s—" Billy stopped.

He must have realized what he'd said and had second thoughts about it. After all, their temporary marriage wasn't the real thing, Darcy thought.

She swallowed a lump. Was it because he hadn't finished his compliment or for some other reason? "It's all right, Bill," she said softly. "I know what you mean."

He reached for her, but Darcy pulled away and made a show of reaching for his empty plate. "I'd better get this mess cleaned up. If the sauce hardens, it'll be hard to get off." That was a lie, but she didn't need Billy watching her. She needed time to compose herself. To get herself together. "You go on. This won't take long."

"I could help, and it would go that much faster," Billy offered. His tone sounded almost eager. Hopeful? Should Darcy dare think his reasons might be something other than getting the kitchen cleaned?

Darcy shook her head. "No. Thanks for offering, though. This kitchen is small, and it'll be easier if I do it myself." The kitchen was too small with him in it, and she wouldn't be able to concentrate on what she was doing. Of course, she couldn't tell him that.

"All right," Billy grumbled cheerfully. "Just don't ever say I didn't offer."

"Wouldn't dream of it," Darcy answered flippantly. "Now, would you just go," she told him, more sharply than she should have.

He stood there for a long minute, and Darcy wondered if she had hurt his feelings. She tried to ignore him, but he stood there, silent as a boulder, and just as immovable. Darcy didn't know whether to relent and to let him help, or to shoo him off. As much as she wanted him to leave her alone, she also wished he would stay.

Fortunately, Billy took the decision out of her hands. He sighed sharply, turned and, saying nothing else, left.

Darcy felt more alone than she ever had. More alone than when she'd finally decided that she couldn't marry Dick, or when she'd hiked along that dark country highway.

But then, she knew she had to get used to not having him. He would never be hers to keep. She was borrowing him as her last gift to a dying woman whom she had come to love as much as her own mother.

Tears welled in her eyes, and Darcy tried to blink

them back. What was the point of crying when you didn't even know why? Was she weeping for Nettie who would soon be no more, or was she weeping for herself...and the marriage that would never be?

No, there was no use dwelling on that, she told herself sternly as she filled the sink with hot, sudsy water. She and Billy had married for good reasons, but they were not the right ones. They had not married for love. They had wed for Nettie. There would be no more of a future for them than there was for her.

Darcy tried to lose herself in the routine monotony of the everyday task. Washing dishes was no more out of the ordinary than cooking the meal had been. She'd wash, she'd dry, and she'd put them away. Just as she did every night.

Before she knew it, the dishes were done, and Darcy could find no more reasons to stay in the kitchen. There was nothing to watch on television but reruns. It was too early to go to bed, especially alone.

Normally, she and Nettie would sit together on the porch swing and watch the fireflies. The june bugs had retreated for another year, but crickets had taken up where they had left off. Nettie would tell stories about her beloved Raymond and their children, and Darcy would listen raptly until Nettie grew tired and went to bed.

Sometimes she'd go inside with Nettie. Other times she'd stay out on the porch, breathing in the sweet summer air, until she, too, was tired. Darcy loved that routine, and there was no reason she couldn't enjoy the porch tonight, as well. She dried her hands, hung up the towel, and headed outside.

Billy stood on the top step, staring out into the night. His shoulder was braced against one of the porch supports, and he was chewing on a twig or a sprig of grass. He seemed to stiffen when Darcy opened the door, but he said nothing.

Taking that as his way of saying he didn't want to be bothered, Darcy silently settled onto the swing and began to sway gently back and forth. The only sounds were the crickets, the occasional call of a bobwhite and the creak of the porch swing.

Darcy knew better than to expect anything of this night, her wedding night, but she couldn't stand the depth of the silence. Yes, the night was alive with all manner of fauna, but it was the silence of the man so close to her, yet so far, that preyed on her mind.

"It's a beautiful night," she murmured quietly, hoping to break the icy stillness.

He didn't turn, but he answered. "Yeah."

One word was better than none at all, Darcy supposed, though it wasn't what she'd been hoping for.

"There's room on the swing," she tried again, patting the seat for emphasis.

"I'm fine."

Two words. It wasn't exactly a conversation, but it was an improvement. Darcy sighed. She wished she knew what Billy was thinking. Was he worried about his mother? Perhaps, he was thinking about his return to duty tomorrow afternoon. Was it too much to hope that he might be as frustrated about the situation as she was?

Did she really want Billy to act as though he wanted her? What would she do if he did?

"I miss the june bugs now that it's July," she tried again.

Billy chuckled. "Yeah, it seems quiet without them."

Darcy smiled. "Be still, my heart. A complete sen-

tence,'' she murmured wryly. ''I must be making progress.''

''I don't mean to be ornery, Darcy,'' Billy said, turning. ''It's been a long day, and tomorrow's going to be
even longer.'' He plucked the twig from his mouth and
tossed it out into the darkened yard. ''I'm gonna turn
in. See ya.''

It wasn't the worst brush-off Darcy had ever gotten,
but it was a brush-off. She didn't know whether to laugh
from relief or cry from disappointment. She sat there
on the swing in the dark for a long time.

Then she finally went inside. To bed. Alone.

So much for her first night as a married woman.

BILL LAY AWAKE for hours alone in the bottom bunk in
the room he'd shared with his brother Jim when he was
small, listening to the silence. It was hell knowing full
well that Darcy was lying just as alone in Earline's twin
bed across the hall. He lay there, hard and aching,
knowing that there were only two ways to relieve the
pain. He could go to Darcy and take what the law said
he was entitled to, or he could take a cold shower.

He couldn't go to Darcy because he'd promised that
this wouldn't be a real marriage, no matter how much
he wanted her. There was no way he'd get up in the
middle of the night and turn on the water in the bathroom just outside her bedroom door. He'd wake her. If
he woke her, then she'd know.

That he wanted her.

Three steps across to the door, three more across the
hall, and maybe another six to the bed. Twelve steps to
Darcy. Twelve steps and he could make her his.

But he wouldn't take those few steps.

She wasn't his. She wasn't anybody's.

Tomorrow, he'd go back to Hurlburt, back to his real life, away from the woman he'd come to love.

Away from his wife.

It was a hell of a way to start married life.

Bill turned and punched the pillow again. He wasn't married, he told himself. Not the way that mattered. He and Darcy had only recited some words to make Momma happy. They were only playing their parts until the time came to go back to the way it was before.

He let in a deep breath, then let it out. He didn't want things back the way they were.

He wanted Darcy in his life.

And, something about the way she'd acted tonight made him believe she wanted the same thing, too. How could he know for sure?

There was only one way to find out.

"God help me," he muttered. He tossed the covers aside and went to her door.

Chapter Fourteen

Bill stood in the quiet hallway, hand raised and poised to knock. Then impulse failed him.

He couldn't do this.

He couldn't force himself on her or put her in an awkward position that she might feel required to oblige. Even if she seemed to come to him willingly, he would never know if it had been because he'd come to her in the middle of the night and wakened her from a dream. He'd never know if she'd been too sleepy to think.

He would never know if she would have turned him down in the light of day.

Bill opened his fist and lowered his hand, then, let out a long, low sigh.

He might have been able to satisfy a temporary need, but he would never be sure why she'd allowed him to make love to her. As much as he wanted her, he couldn't do it this way. He wanted to know that she loved him, too.

He slipped back into his room, quietly closed the door, and lay back down in the tiny, empty bed.

He must have slept, for he didn't remember seeing the night turn from black to gray to full sunlight. When he awoke, the sun was bright and clear and trying to burn through his sticky, swollen eyelids.

Yawning and stretching, he climbed out of bed, and steeled himself to face the day.

His second as a married man.

DARCY STOOD at the stove, turning bacon in the heavy, cast-iron frying pan. She sighed, or maybe it was a yawn. She'd gone to bed early, but she doubted she'd slept for more than a couple of short catnaps the whole night through. Yesterday was supposed to have been just another day.

Why then, had she been so disappointed when Billy hadn't come to her?

She'd thought she'd heard his footfall in the hall outside her door, but she must have been mistaken. If he had really wanted her, he would have found a way to make her his. Instead, he'd probably slept like a baby in his childhood bed just across the hall.

So near, but so far.

Yawning and stretching, Billy stumbled in, scratching his chest and looking as if he'd been out carousing with his buddies instead of sleeping just across the hall. Had his night been as restless as hers?

Darcy tried not to hope. After all, he could have been sleepless because the notion of marriage, even one as sterile as theirs was supposed to be, terrified him. Maybe he didn't want her but wanted out. As quickly as possible.

The one shred of hope that she'd been clinging to fluttered away on the summer breeze.

Well, she couldn't give him his out. Not yet. After all, they'd married for Nettie, but she could make it easier for him to get away today. There was no sense in her making him hang around here when he was, apparently, miserable.

She drew a deep breath and forced a bright smile. "Did you sleep well?" Obviously, he hadn't, but Darcy was determined to be pleasant.

"Yeah," he muttered, his voice gravelly and thick as he poured himself a mug of coffee.

"Your mother called already," Darcy continued brightly. "She'll be discharged as soon as we can go to get her."

"Good," Billy grumbled over the rim of his mug. His lids appeared puffy, and his eyes were a roadmap. "I'll go get her as soon as I've eaten and showered."

Darcy swallowed a sob and turned back to the stove. It was worse than she'd expected. He didn't even want her to go with him to pick up Nettie. It didn't take a scientist to tell her he couldn't wait to get away. She swallowed again. "I think Nettie would expect us to come together," she said, pouring off the grease. She added the eggs she'd already beaten and listened to them sizzle as they hit the hot pan. "It being our honeymoon and all," she added.

"Yeah, our honeymoon," Billy said, and Darcy tried to interpret his meaning as she stirred the eggs.

"I've already showered," she said quietly, hoping not to show her hurt as she turned the cooked eggs onto plates. "I'll be ready to go by the time you are." Then she set the plates on the table, sat and tried to force herself to eat.

It was going to be a long day, and she needed all the strength she could get to make it through.

"DO YOU THINK you should leave Momma at home by herself all day while you go to work tomorrow?" Bill asked Darcy after they'd seen Momma safely into her bed. He hated to suggest that Darcy quit her job so soon, but he didn't want his mother to be left alone, either. He held the screen door open as they walked out to the porch.

"I think I've got that covered," Darcy said, settling into the porch swing. "Earline told me that Leah thinks she can deal with it. She's free to be here all day. She can even sleep over sometimes so Earline doesn't have to bring her here every day.

Bill took his position at the porch rail. He propped his elbows against the rail, leaned back and crossed his feet at the ankle. He'd come to think of the porch as safe territory. Neutral. As long as he didn't sit next to Darcy on the swing.

That would be too close.

He wouldn't be able to keep his hands off her if he was close enough to smell her perfume.

"What if Momma…needs help?" he finally said, trying not to think about what he'd started to say. "Will Leah be able to handle it?"

Darcy leaned back on the swing, and gave it a good push with her foot. "I've already arranged to take the rest of the week off, and I'll give her a crash course in what to look for." She paused for a moment, seeming to enjoy the swaying of the swing, then she continued. "Let's face it, Bill. Even if I were here, there would be nothing I could really do but get her to the hospital.

"If I put Leah in charge and instruct her not to let Nettie talk her out of calling for help as she did last time, she'll be fine." Darcy put down her foot and stopped the swing from undulating. "More than anything, your mother needs Leah to make sure she takes her meds, to make sure she eats, and to keep her company. Leah's a bright girl. She can do that as well as I can.''

Bill chuckled, remembering the way Leah had learned to wrap him around her little finger by the time she was a year old. ''Yeah, I reckon she can, at that.''

He pushed himself away from the porch rail and heaved a big sigh. ''I have to go,'' he said reluctantly. ''I've got a class tonight, and I already missed it last week because of the night jump. It'll be a bear to make up if I miss too many.''

''Yes, I suppose so,'' Darcy said, pushing the swing back, then springing out of it as it swung forward. ''Do you have time for lunch before you go?''

''Wouldn't miss it,'' he said with false cheer. He might not miss lunch, but he'd definitely miss Darcy when he got back to Florida.

THOUGH THE DOCTOR had recommended bed rest for a few days, Nettie had insisted on coming out to the porch swing and watching the fireflies.

''I do love settin' out here this time of the day and reflectin' on what the day brung,'' Nettie said, her voice weaker than it had been prior to her recent illness. ''I surely did miss watching the night come in when I was stuck down there in the hospital. A person needs to be outside in the fresh air to breathe.''

Darcy set the swing into motion, but didn't respond to Nettie's comment. What could she say? After all, she agreed with her sentiments. Nettie might have limited time left, but she certainly wasn't wasting it feeling sorry for herself. Darcy hoped that when it was her time to go she would face it with the same dignity as Nettie.

''Reckon our Billy will call us tonight to let us know he got there safe?''

Darcy loved the way Nettie had taken to calling Bill "our Billy." It wasn't really accurate, but it was sweet. Billy might be Nettie's, but he wasn't hers. "I don't know. He said he had a class tonight, so he might not call because he wouldn't want to wake you."

"Psh. I can sleep through anything these days. Once I get to sleep. I reckon if he calls to talk to his bride, it won't bother me if I don't get to speak to him."

Darcy swallowed and blinked back a tear. If Nettie only knew the truth.

"Now, you know our Billy would be here if he didn't have to go back to his base and get ready for that Sergeant's Academy or whatever it is. And even if you could have gone with him, he wouldn't have much time for you until it's over," Nettie said, trying to be soothing.

Darcy choked back a sob.

It would be weeks before Billy would be able to come home. An early slot for NCO Academy had opened up, and he couldn't afford to let it slip away. Once the class started next week, he'd surely be too busy to call. So, maybe she'd be able to get back to her regular routine—whatever that was—and pretend.... What? That they had a future together as husband and wife?

"Now, now, Darcy girl. It'll be over soon. Then you and Billy can start your life together, and you won't have to worry about me." Nettie worked her arm around Darcy's shoulders and drew her near.

That gentle hug was almost more than Darcy could bear. Nettie was waiting to die, and all the woman could think about was her and Billy's happiness. She let all her misery and sadness go and wept in Nettie's arms.

She was so glad that Nettie couldn't possibly know why.

Finally, she cried herself out.

"Are you going to be all right now, Darcy?" Nettie patted her lightly on the shoulder, her weathered face a mask of concern in the yellow porch light.

Darcy nodded, her grasp on control too fragile to allow her to speak.

"Then I'll just go on to bed now." Nettie pushed herself up out of the porch swing. Smiling, she caressed Darcy's cheek. "It'll all work out, Darcy girl. What's meant to be will happen." Then Nettie slowly made her way back inside, leaving Darcy alone with the night.

BILL CAME IN from PT and his morning run in a sour mood, and it wasn't because of a bad workout. That had been happening too often lately, and it didn't take a degree in psychology to figure out why. He struggled with the combination of his gym locker and when it wouldn't open, slammed the metal door with his fist and muttered a pungent curse.

"Hell, boy, if you was a married man, I'd say you wasn't gettin' any," Runt Haggarty commented from the locker next to Bill's.

Clenching his towel tightly with his fist to keep from smashing Runt right in his smug face, Bill gritted his teeth and pretended he hadn't heard and worked at opening the lock. But, he had heard. And if Runt only knew how close to the truth he was.

He chuckled bitterly. Hell, he *was* a married man. And he damned sure wasn't getting any. That was as much the problem as anything. The only problem bigger was that he wasn't sure he ever would.

He'd made a promise to Darcy. And it hadn't been

to have and to hold forever. Only to make his mother happy.

Well, damn it. *He* wasn't happy. And he wouldn't ever be. Not as long as Darcy was two hundred miles away pretending to be single, and he was here doing the same.

He was going to have to come up with a way to convince Darcy to give him a chance. But, damn it, he couldn't do it from here.

And he couldn't go home.

Not until after he'd completed NCO Academy. And that didn't start till Monday and wouldn't end for four long weeks.

But maybe he could do something to get Darcy to see how he felt about her. He'd call her. Tonight. Every night. Hell, he'd send her flowers. He'd do everything he could think of to show her how he felt.

To show her that he loved her.

THE PHONE RANG and Darcy knew without answering that it was Billy. He'd taken to calling every night and inquiring about her day. Both she and Nettie looked forward to their nightly talks. She dried her hands and reached for the phone on the kitchen wall.

Pasting on a smile he couldn't see, but Darcy knew Billy could hear, she answered.

"Yes, she's fine. She still hasn't regained her strength, but her attitude's good." What else could she say? They both knew that Nettie wasn't getting better.

Though they never said anything intimate, Darcy looked forward to chatting, to hearing his rich, masculine voice. Hearing it every night was the cherry on top of her day.

She'd asked about Ski and Block, the men who had

been injured in the night jump. He told her that Block would make a full recovery, but Ski's progress had been slow. Ski was expected to walk again, but he'd never be the active, athletic man he'd been.

Finally they ran out of things to say. "Yes, she's out in the swing. I'll take the phone out to her."

She carried the cordless phone outside, stopping to sniff at the vase of yellow roses on the end table next to the sofa as she passed. She left the phone with Nettie and went back inside. Darcy let Nettie think that they'd shared their sweet nothings. It was the only way.

When she finished the dishes, she went out to the porch as was her habit and settled next to Nettie, who was staring off into the evening. The phone was turned off and rested in Nettie's lap.

"Did Billy say how he was enjoying his training course?" Translation: did he ask about me?

Nettie shrugged. "He didn't say too much. Said he'd be glad when it was over. He's anxious to get back to you."

Darcy's breath caught. "Did he really say that?" she asked, too eagerly.

"Well, not in those words, but I could tell that's what he meant," Nettie said. "I reckon you two spend too much time with I love yous to talk about much else."

Darcy blushed. If Nettie only knew.

She'd gotten to know Billy much better through their nightly chats. But the word *love* never came up, though she strained to hear it, if only between the lines. Darcy swallowed a lump of disappointment, but she managed to smile at Nettie.

"I reckon I'll just go on to bed. I do declare I get so tired these days." She patted Darcy's hand and Darcy couldn't help noticing how cool Nettie's fingers were in spite of the warm summer night.

"Do you need any help?"

"No, hon. I'll be fine." Nettie squeezed Darcy in a weak hug, then pushed herself out of the swing. She smiled. "We'll finish our story in the morning. I'm just too sleepy tonight."

Darcy squeezed back. "Don't worry, Nettie. I'll keep after you until I've heard every word of the Hays family history." She loved the tales of Nettie's youth and how she and Raymond had fallen in love and struggled to work the farm.

"You are goin' to be so good for our Billy," Nettie said. "He needs you, you know?"

Darcy just smiled, sadly, she supposed. Nettie might think Billy needed her, but Darcy knew the truth. If only she didn't.

BILL LAY BACK in his lumpy bunk and tried to sleep. It seemed so stupid to him that he had to stay here when he had a perfectly good apartment in Fort Walton Beach. But, rules were rules, and regs were even worse. The regs said you attended NCO Academy in residence, and it didn't matter whether you lived across country or across town.

He just wished he were home.

And he didn't mean the apartment on the other side of town.

The only thing that was keeping him going was that he had his dreams. Dreams where he and Darcy were married and happy, and the marriage was real.

He punched his pillow and wadded it up and wrapped his arms around it. It wasn't the same as holding a real, breathing woman—Darcy—but until he could make her his it was the best he could do.

DARCY HAD OVERSLEPT, trying to cling to a few extra moments of a wonderful dream about how it could be for her and Billy if... And now she was running late.

To make matters worse, Earline had called to say that she and Leah would be late, too. The only saving grace in all this was that after Darcy had slept through an entire hour of morning chatter from the clock radio, Earline had called and that was what had woken her up.

She hurried toward the bathroom, pausing in flight to knock on Nettie's closed door. "Nettie, I'm running late. Are you up?"

"I'm awake, sugar," Nettie answered. "I just seem to be having a hard time getting moving this morning."

"I hear ya'," Darcy called back. She smiled grimly. Apparently, that particular bug was contagious. Seemed like everybody was suffering from it this morning. "I'm just going to take a quick shower, and then I'll get your meds and start breakfast."

Nettie didn't respond, but no response was necessary, so Darcy hurried into the shower. She showered quickly and dressed in record time. One good thing about wearing a uniform to work, she thought as she slipped into her white slacks: there was no need to stare into the closet trying to figure out what to wear.

She swiped at the cloudy mirror until she'd cleared a small patch of fog and made quick work of combing her hair. She was grateful for her simple short do that made getting ready easy. Most of the time she was envious of women with lovely, styled hair, who always looked as if they'd just stepped out of the beauty parlor, but not on mornings like this.

Maybe, if she'd let it grow out a little, change the color, try a little curl, Billy might look at her as someone other than his mother's caretaker.

That thought made her laugh. Billy probably had his pick of any number of squared-away military women, not to mention stylish secretaries, bar girls and every other woman he passed on the street.

"Get a grip, Stanton," she muttered to herself as she stepped out into the cooler, dryer air of the hall. She didn't have time for a pity-fest this morning. She had to get Nettie ready for the day. Then she had to get to work.

People were counting on her.

She dashed into the kitchen to make Nettie's oatmeal. While the water boiled she poured a mug of coffee, doctored it, and took a sip. Finally! Now, she felt human.

There was no time for bacon and eggs today, so she popped a couple of pieces of bread into the toaster and grabbed a processed cheese slice from the fridge. She could eat a toasted cheese sandwich on the way, and maybe she'd get to work on time, in spite of spending too much time lying in bed clinging to a dream that she was realistic enough to know wasn't likely to ever come true.

Still, she thought, smiling to herself. It had been a very nice dream.

Too bad she didn't have all morning to think about it.

The water boiled and she added the rolled oats and stirred quickly to keep them from boiling over. If she had a little more time, she wouldn't mind having some herself. But once she had Nettie up and had doled out her meds, Darcy had to go.

"Nettie?" she called after she realized that Nettie hadn't made her usual prompt appearance in the kitchen. "Breakfast is served."

Darcy peeled the plastic off a slice of cheese and placed it between the two pieces of toast she'd plucked from the toaster. She took a bite while she waited.

She swallowed her dry sandwich, took a swig of coffee to wash it down, then hurried down the hall. She guessed she was going to have to light a fire under Nettie this morning, something she'd never had to do before.

"Come on, Nettie," she called as she hurried down the hall. "You're holding me up." She glanced at her watch. "Fudge," she murmured. Later than she thought. "Let's move it. I've got to go," she called as she rapped lightly on the door.

There was still no response from inside the room.

None at all.

"Nettie?" Darcy called softly, a wave of panic surging through her. She knocked again. Louder this time.

"Are you up?" The bathroom was empty, so Nettie couldn't be in there. Darcy tried calling one more time. "Come on, sleepyhead. It's time to get up."

Still no response, and it worried her.

Darcy pushed the door open and it glided silently inward as if pointing to the woman lying in the bed.

Nettie lay there, eyes closed as if asleep, peaceful as could be, her worn features softened and smoothed in repose. Darcy registered a short glimpse of the beautiful, young girl who had once loved a boy named Raymond and had worked so hard to make a go of this farm.

Darcy called again, with difficulty this time because of the lump in her throat. "Nettie? Are you all right?"

She crossed the room, touched Nettie's forehead, and quickly drew her hand away.

Chapter Fifteen

Nettie's skin was warm, but then why wouldn't it be? It was July and they had spoken not fifteen minutes earlier. Darcy swallowed, took a deep breath and reached for Nettie's hand. It, too, was still warm, but deceptively so. There was no life in the papery skin. No blood pumped through the veins. There was no response to Darcy's touch.

There was no sign of life in the hand that had squeezed Darcy's so lovingly just the night before.

As she'd known there wouldn't be.

Darcy had thought she was prepared for it, but she wasn't. Not when it was Nettie. Student nurses didn't get many opportunities to look at death up close, and this was more painful because it was someone she loved. She was the only one there to deal with this now. It was up to her.

She knew in theory what she had to do, and her training kicked in, overriding her emotions. Tears sliding silently down her cheeks, she tucked Nettie's hand back under the covers, noted the time, and whispered a silent prayer.

"Goodbye, Nettie," she murmured. "I love you."

Then she went back into the living room to make it official.

As if on automatic pilot, Darcy picked up the phone. She dialed Doctor Williamson's pager, then slowly placed the receiver back on the cradle. She barely had a chance to wipe her streaming eyes when the phone rang again, the doctor returning her call.

Darcy cut in before he could speak. "Nettie Hays died about fifteen minutes ago," she said quietly.

She didn't hear what he said in response, and it didn't really matter—she knew he'd take care of the details. Someone behind her gasped, and she jerked around in time to see something crash to the floor.

She hadn't heard Earline and Leah come in, and one of them had knocked over the roses from Billy. The flowers didn't matter now. The people did.

Darcy would have liked to soften the blow, but that couldn't be helped now. She did the only thing she could do. She gathered Leah and her mother in her arms, held them close and wept with them.

The only thing remaining to do was to call Treadwell's Funeral Home. And that could wait until....

...after she called Billy.

And she couldn't help thinking that, somehow, she'd let him down.

ANOTHER MAD DASH through the back country roads to get home. Bill wanted to weep, to gnash his teeth and roar in anger, in pain, but all he could do was drive.

The news had reached him about midday. Captain Thibodeaux had come to him, pulled him out of class and delivered the news personally. He shouldn't have been surprised by it, but he was. It was something a man never wants to believe, to accept.

It was another reminder of his own mortality.

He'd checked out of the academy and stashed the same dress uniform he'd worn to marry Darcy in in the plastic garment bag. He hung it on the hook behind the driver's seat, then headed north.

He'd been so overwhelmed with grief that he had barely seen the countryside he'd driven through. Now he was about to merge onto the interstate, and he wasn't sure how he'd managed to get here, much less driven all that way without killing himself or someone else. Thank God, it was early enough in the afternoon that the traffic was still light.

Just over an hour and he'd be home.

And he dreaded what was waiting for him. No matter how much he thought he'd prepared, this was something he wasn't ready to face.

DARCY HAD MADE IT through the afternoon on adrenaline and raw emotion. Nothing from the moment she'd found Nettie seemingly asleep until now had seemed real. She kept wondering if it was a dream and she'd wake up soon.

Somebody pinch me, she pleaded inwardly. Please, she prayed silently, but she knew that wouldn't happen.

By noon neighbors had begun streaming in with love offerings of food and kind words, and it had helped a little, but not enough. Food and words would never heal the fathomless pain of such a devastating loss. Even one she should have been prepared for. Only time would do that.

And Billy.

Was she expecting more than she truly deserved?

"So, do you know when Bill will be able to make it in?" Mrs. Scarborough asked.

It wasn't the first time she'd heard that question. Darcy recited the same answer she given everyone else. "I notified his commander first thing this morning. As soon as he gets his orders to leave the base, he'll be here."

"Humph, a man ought not have to get permission to go to his own mother's funeral," Mrs. Scarborough complained, wearing her indignation on her sleeve.

Darcy didn't disagree, but she was well familiar with the way military bureaucracy worked. And at times like this, it did move faster than usual. "Yes, ma'am." What else could she say? She accepted a yellow squash casserole from Billy's old teacher and placed it on the groaning dining-room table.

How anyone could think of food at a time like this, she didn't know.

Another woman approached, someone she didn't recognize. She offered simple condolences, and Darcy responded by rote. The woman left a baked ham and moved on to another part of the room. At least they wouldn't starve.

Her head throbbed and the jumbled babble of voices in the room didn't help. For the moment, she was alone, and she sank gratefully onto a chair, closed her eyes, and pressed her fingers against her temples.

Blessed relief.

If only for a moment.

The garbled sound of so many voices seemed to fade away, and Darcy drew in a breath of welcome fresh air.

The peaceful feeling grew until she realized that the room was silent. It wasn't the absence of sound she felt, but a feeling of expectation. Someone had come in. Curious about who could have caused such a change in the noisy room, she opened her eyes and slowly lifted her head to see.

Bill. Her Billy was home. Still in his light-blue uniform shirt and dark blue slacks, he was standing there in the open doorway from the porch into the little parlor. He seemed to be looking for someone.

Darcy held her breath as she watched him scan the room and finally settle his gaze on her. Their eyes locked, and Darcy gasped for air as the crowd parted between them.

She didn't realize when or how, but Darcy was on her feet. She stepped forward to meet him, her Billy, but he crossed the small room in three long strides.

Billy swept her into his arms and kissed her long, hard, and possessively. With a ragged groan, he dragged his lips away. "Thank you for being here," he murmured loud enough for only Darcy to hear. "I feel better knowing that you were there for my mother," he added huskily.

"I did what I could," Darcy said simply. Her words caught in her throat. She had done nothing. How could he be thanking her when she might have been able to save her if she'd gone into that room a few minutes sooner?

He kissed her again, then seemed to remember that they were not alone. He stepped away, and Darcy's arms felt empty without him there. Would he ever hold her like this again? Or was this the beginning of the end?

Bobby and Lucy Carterette came toward them, and Darcy almost felt relief that they would dilute the powerful magnetic field around Billy, drawing her to him.

Now was not the time to be exploring that attraction, even if her body craved it.

Billy had not come here for her. He had come home because his mother had died, she had to remind herself. He had come here to say his final goodbye to Nettie. He had only come to her seeking comfort.

She had to remember that if she was going to make it through the next few days.

FINALLY, they were gone.

He could breathe again.

Bill stood on the front porch, leaning against the support post, and watched as the red taillights of the last car disappeared down the lane. He knew the family and friends had meant well, but he'd had enough of his kind and generous neighbors. What he really wanted was to be alone. With Darcy, his wife.

He considered going out for a long run. Anything to assuage the pain, but his pain was too deep for that to help. Too open, too raw.

He heard the screen door squeaking behind him, but he didn't turn. He knew who it was. Darcy. She had stayed inside to deal with the remnants of the bountiful feast that his friends and neighbors had gifted them with.

"I don't think I'll have to cook for a week," Darcy said quietly as she stepped outside.

Bill listened for the familiar creak of the porch swing as Darcy settled into her usual place, but instead he felt her small hand on his arm, and a river of warmth flowed through him. Odd how cold he felt in spite of the clinging, July heat.

He liked Darcy's touch. He liked the way she felt in his arms.

"As much as I wish your mother were still here with

us," Darcy said softly, "I know she's happy to be re-united with your father."

"Yeah," Bill said thickly, his throat tight.

"They didn't have much time together on this earth, but now they'll have the rest of eternity," she whispered, her voice cracking with unrestrained emotion.

Bill turned and, as if it had been choreographed, Darcy melted into his arms. He hadn't had to ask her, or beg her, or pull her to him.

She was just there. Right where he needed her. At the right time.

"God, I missed you," he breathed, not sure he'd even said it aloud. He tucked her head under his chin and held her close to his heart and felt her rapid heartbeat, like that of a frightened bird, beating against his. That should have been enough.

But it wasn't.

He kissed the top of Darcy's head, but that wasn't enough, either. He placed two fingers under Darcy's chin and tipped her face up to his. He wanted to kiss her. He wanted her to kiss him. And this time, not for show.

It would all be for him.

Only him.

She accepted his unspoken invitation and kissed him, gently at first, her mouth firm, but yielding. As he took more, she gave, meeting his thrusting tongue with her own, asking and taking and seeking.

She trembled in his arms. Or was it he?

His groin tightened, and he caressed the small of Darcy's back, her breasts through the thin fabric of her summer dress. Her skin was damp and begged for his touch, and her breath came in short, hot gasps.

He should stop this now, Bill thought abstractly, but

he couldn't bear the thought of ending it. Of tearing himself away from her.

Of spending the night alone.

He swept her up into his arms and carried her to the door.

She didn't protest, just nestled in his arms as if she belonged there.

If she wanted him to stop, he would.

But she was his wife, and he was hungry for her, he needed her. Please, he prayed. Let her want me back.

DARCY KNEW that Billy was only doing this out of need, out of the ache of loss, but she needed it, too.

Maybe for the same reasons, maybe for some of her own, but she needed him, and it didn't really matter why. She wanted him. And he wanted her back.

If only for now.

Billy paused at the entrance to the short hallway as if he couldn't decide which way to go.

The only room with a double bed was Nettie's, but they couldn't go there. They could not make love, celebrate life, in the room where Billy's mother had died.

And the bunk beds in the tiny room where Billy always slept wouldn't work, either. There was only one other choice: her room with the pink chenille bedspreads where his sisters had slept when they were children.

Decision made, Billy strode purposefully to her room, the room where he had stood and watched her dress until she had closed the door. The door outside which Darcy was certain he had stood on their wedding night, but not come in.

The time hadn't been right then, but now it was.

He laid her gently on the bed, then perched on the

mattress beside her. Billy started to say something, but
Darcy stopped him. She didn't want him to take the
time to think, or to give her a chance to change her
mind. She wanted to do this. She wanted to love him.

She wanted him to make love to her.

"Please, Billy," she whispered, her voice hoarse,
strange, not sounding like herself. "Don't stop. I need
you."

"Oh, Darcy. You don't know how I've dreamed of
hearing you say that," he murmured as she drew him
to her.

She pressed her fingers to his lips and shivered with
delight as he kissed them. "Don't talk. Don't think,"
she told him softly. Then she fumbled with the buttons
on his starched blue shirt. "Just live."

He turned away from her and made short work of the
buttons while she struggled with the long zipper down
the back of her dress. Finally, the zipper gave, and as
the slide rasped slowly down the long track, she forgot
to breathe while she listened to the sensuous duet as
Billy's zipper joined the chorus.

Then they were naked in each other's arms.

Billy kissed her, caressed her, and pressed against her
with his strong, firm body, but it wasn't enough. She
could feel his need pressing insistently against her. Why
was he holding back?

"Please, Billy, please," she wanted to beg. Or had
she really said it aloud?

He must have heard her or read her mind, for he
positioned himself over her, his solid, hard body so
near, yet still so far away. He trembled as he hovered
over her, holding himself aloft, holding back.

Darcy held her breath. She wouldn't beg again. If he
wanted her, he had her. If he didn't...she'd die.

Billy took a deep breath, then let it out, his warm, damp breath setting her on fire. Then he kissed her, and pushed her legs apart with one knee. He settled into place, and she could feel him pulsing against her. Another breath, then he surged into her in one swift thrust.

They were one.

And nothing would ever be the same.

THE SUN was just as insistent in Darcy's small room as it always was in Bill's, and he tried to shut it out. But the finger of light was persistent, and it poked at his tired eyes until he finally forced them open.

Morning. Too early. Too soon.

At least, Darcy was still asleep, tucked in against his chest, her petite body soft and warm. He should feel like a million bucks, but he felt like a heel.

He knew that he and Darcy had made a deal, and this hadn't been part of it. It complicated things. But only if she still wanted to get out of it.

Darcy could now. His mother was gone, as were Darcy's reasons for being here. In his home, in his bed, in his arms.

He didn't want it to end. He wanted it to last forever. They might have married for a different reason, but why couldn't they remain so? He loved her. And he felt sure that she loved him, too.

This small, capable woman had disproved all his good, well-thought-out reasons for not marrying. Maybe his mother hadn't been prepared to raise five kids alone. Maybe Lougenia had been unprepared for the emotional blow her divorce had sent her, but Bill sensed that Darcy could handle anything. He loved her for that, and he couldn't bear the thought of living without her.

Darcy stirred in his arms and whimpered in her sleep.

He'd heard that sound before—when he'd lain over her and she'd come apart in his arms. He felt that familiar tightening in his groin, and he yearned to wake her and plunge inside her to hear that sound again.

But he didn't.

He lay still with her nestled in his arms and watched Darcy sleep. He listened to her breathe and wondered what the day would bring.

They were in for another long day just like yesterday. Only today, the action would shift to the funeral home, and he wasn't sure whether that would be easier to take. No matter what the location, it wasn't going to be easy.

It was never easy to say goodbye to someone you loved.

He looked again at Darcy, so beautiful in slumber, and closed his eyes as a shard of pain splintered his heart. He didn't want to have to say goodbye to her, too.

Dare he hope he wouldn't have to?

THEY'D SURVIVED the funeral, and if they could only make it through this last gathering of family and friends, the worst would be over. Darcy sighed as another mourner arrived with yet another covered dish of God-only-knew what. She smiled and murmured her thanks and found a space on the overloaded dining-room table.

"Do you think they'll ever leave?" Billy whispered into her ear as his hand found the curve of her waist.

A warm shiver worked its way through her and Darcy smiled. "It's wonderful that your mother had so many friends, but I'm ready for all this to end," she said under her breath. She smiled again, this one genuine, as someone else came in—empty-handed.

"Isn't it odd that they never hang around for the

cleanup?'' Billy muttered dryly as Earline came in from the kitchen with a huge stack of paper plates and napkins.

Darcy pretended to be shocked at Earline's burden. ''Mrs. Scarborough would be scandalized,'' Darcy murmured. ''Paper plates instead of the good china.''

''I heard that,'' Earline said. ''As it happens, Mrs. S. brought them. ''Now if we could just get all these good folks fed, we could send them on their way.''

''Amen to that,'' Billy said and squeezed Darcy up against him in a half hug.

Darcy had come to enjoy these intimate moments, and they had come more frequently since they'd made love. But she had to remind herself, it wasn't permanent.

In times of grief at the death of a loved one, it was a natural instinct to want to reaffirm life, to defy death. And what was more life-affirming than to make love?

Too bad it wasn't real.

If only Billy would say something, anything, to show that he loved her, she'd stay with him with no reservations. Of course, he had to invite her to stay.

If he loved her as she did him, they'd have something to build a future on. A life. All he had to do was tell her in three little words.

They'd slept together as man and wife for the past two nights, and would probably do so again tonight. In the eyes of the law, they were married. In her heart, they were married, but she still didn't know what was going on inside Billy's head. Or his heart.

She breathed a long, weary sigh.

Earline nudged her. ''Come on. The sooner we serve dinner, the quicker they'll go.''

Darcy fell into step beside Billy's older sister. She

wasn't sure she wanted to rush everyone out because then she and Billy would be alone. If she were alone with Billy, she'd be face to face with her questions.

And one she was terrified that Billy wouldn't ask.

BILL SQUEEZED Darcy's hand as they stood on the porch and waved goodbye to Earline and Edd and the kids. They had stayed long enough to help with the mess, and Earline and Lougenia had relieved them of a good portion of the leftovers. Still, once Billy went back to Florida tomorrow, Darcy would probably end up tossing most of it out.

Once the minivan was out of sight, Bill drew in a long breath and turned to Darcy. They needed to talk, and it was better to do it now in the light of day than wait until tonight when they were in bed. Of course, if this didn't go right, they might not be in bed. Not together, anyway.

He exhaled and drew her toward the swing and beckoned for Darcy to sit down. She arched an eyebrow, but said nothing as he seated himself beside her.

"We have to talk," he said, and wished he hadn't been so blunt. Darcy stiffened, and her breath caught in her throat.

Bill didn't know whether that was a good sign or not, but he had to go on. He inhaled, then let it out slow. "I know we agreed that we were only getting married for Momma," he said slowly. "But things have changed."

Darcy opened her mouth to say something, but Bill stopped her with a finger to her lips. "Let me finish. We got ourselves in a little deeper than we'd intended. We didn't think to use protection, so you could be pregnant. But, I still think it's okay. We were good together.

I don't want it to end.'' He swallowed and moistened his lips and waited for Darcy to respond.

She gasped and lifted her hand to her mouth. Her fingers trembled. She looked at him, her brown eyes bright and wide. Had she been expecting something else?

A real proposal?

Bill slid to the floor, setting the swing into wild motion as he went. He put a hand out to stop it, then positioned himself on one knee. He took Darcy's hand, the one on which he'd placed his mother's ring. ''Darcy, I want you for real.''

She looked at him, her eyes wide, for a long time. Then she blinked. ''I—I don't know,'' she murmured. ''I wasn't prepared for this. I need to think.'' Then she yanked her hand out of his grasp and ran inside.

Bill looked after her and tried to understand. It wasn't exactly hearts and flowers, but he'd said it from his heart. What had he done wrong? Why had she run away?

Chapter Sixteen

Pregnant?

He wanted to cover his bases in case she was pregnant!

Darcy slammed the door shut and flung herself down on the bed covered in silly pink chenille. She wanted to cry, but she clenched the soft fabric in her hands and balled it up in her fists instead. She wanted to scream, to pound something, to hurt Billy as much as he had her.

Pregnant, indeed. Shotgun marriages had gone out of style half a century ago, and besides, they were already married.

Men were so...stupid.

All she had needed to hear was that Billy loved her. Three little words. Did he seriously believe she would force him to stay married because they'd created a child?

He'd almost had her, then he'd ruined it all.

Darcy's eyes filled with tears, but she blinked them away. She would not cry. Weak women did that, and she was not weak. She could deal with this.

She knew what to do. She wouldn't give Billy his

answer now. She'd wait to see if she really were pregnant. If she wasn't, she'd tell him no. If she was....

Well, she'd have to think about that.

But she had plenty of time. Billy would be leaving tomorrow, and he wouldn't be home again for weeks.

By then, maybe, she'd know the answer to both questions: was she pregnant? And did he love her?

DAMN, women were hard to figure out, Bill thought as he headed to Florida and the remaining two weeks of the NCO Academy course.

He'd have given anything to stay in Mattison and try to work it out with Darcy, but he had to get back. And Darcy had barely spoken to him since he'd asked her to remain his wife.

What the hell had he done wrong?

Had she truly meant it when she'd told him weeks ago that she had wanted to make her way herself and not depend on someone else for everything?

Why?

Bill clenched the steering wheel and wished he could squeeze it in two.

Then he relaxed.

At least she had given in and agreed to think about what he'd said. She said she'd tell him when he returned.

He'd promised not to press her, and he meant to keep his word. In fact, he'd already made up his mind not to call her at all until the class was over. He'd miss hearing her sweet voice over the phone, but maybe she'd miss him, too. Maybe if he played hard to get, she'd come running.

The dry summer scenery whizzed by as he drove, every mile taking him farther away from Darcy.

Bill only hoped that absence truly did make the heart grow fonder. Darcy's heart, not his. He already knew how much he loved her.

He just wasn't sure she loved him back.

DARCY SAT in the porch swing, an album filled with fading photos and yellowed newspaper clippings in her lap. She wished that Nettie were still there to tell her about the pictures, the people who populated the book, but they'd never gotten around to it.

She turned another page and sighed.

A week had passed since Billy'd left, and Darcy already knew she wasn't pregnant. She wasn't surprised, and she should have been happy that the complication hadn't come to be. But in a dark little corner of her mind, she couldn't help feeling sad. She sighed again and looked off into the deepening twilight.

It would have been wonderful to have Billy's child, a new little human being to love, a new soul to take Nettie's place on this earth. But that hadn't happened, and Darcy supposed it was just as well. She didn't want to stay married to Billy by default. She wanted to know that he loved her as much as she did him.

She had returned to work, and her days were busy enough to keep her from thinking about Billy. Every night she busied herself sorting through Nettie's belongings, preparing them for...what? Billy?

Billy had been uncharacteristically silent since his return to Florida, and that worried her. He hadn't called once, and Darcy missed their nightly chats. She missed the sound of his voice.

Darcy tried to rationalize that he was busy and that his schedule hadn't permitted the time for him to call, but she knew it wasn't true. He was making a point.

She had hurt him by not trying to explain why she'd turned him down, but she hadn't tried, and now she missed him.

She just hoped he missed her, too.

Darcy knew beyond a shadow of doubt that she loved him. She had already decided that if he asked her again to remain married to him, she would accept. How important were those three little words, anyway?

They were only words.

How could mere words stand up against a living, breathing man? In her arms. In her bed. In her heart. Why should she miss hearing those little words when she had Billy?

Why hadn't she said yes?

She closed the album and went inside to bed. Not to the bed she'd slept in for almost a month, but the other bed across the room. She'd never be able to sleep in her old bed again. It felt too big, too empty, and she felt too alone.

BILL SAT with the rest of his class in a roped-off section of folding chairs and waited until he was called to accept his certificate of completion. He looked around to see wives, husbands and parents in another section of chairs and wondered how many of the other men had no one to share this day. He wondered if he was the only one who was alone.

The commandant called his name, and Bill stepped forward to accept the blue plastic folder that contained the proof of completion. He shook the man's hand, saluted, pivoted smartly, and returned to his seat. It was easy to know what to do when there were rules and procedures. What wasn't so easy was trying to figure out life.

The rules for life weren't in any reg book he knew about.

What the hell should he do about Darcy?

He'd halfway hoped that she'd be so bothered by the silent treatment that she'd call him. But she hadn't.

How many times had he gone to the pay phone in the hall and reached for it? And how many times had he walked away?

Why had he retreated?

Why couldn't he have taken the offensive? Combat controllers were tough. They took charge. Why was he letting a woman tie him in knots?

"…Dismissed!"

Bill pulled himself out of his thoughts as his class-mates tossed their hats in the air in celebration, caught them, and en masse surged toward their waiting loved ones.

He looked around. He was the only one still standing in the seats. The only one alone.

But, damn it, he vowed, he could do something about that. Not this time, of course, but next time, he would have someone waiting for him, too. If he didn't, it wouldn't be because he hadn't tried.

He loved Darcy, and damn it, he was going to make sure she knew it.

He took one last look at the men and women being congratulated by their loved ones, then he turned and headed in the opposite direction. He had to clear quarters and then he was free.

Free to do everything he could think of to convince Darcy that he was the man for her.

He had no intention of ever being alone again.

He passed by a newspaper stand on the way out of the academy billets and a headline caught his eye. Missing Woman's Car Found in Abandoned Car Lot: Foul Play Suspected!

But the headline wasn't what had him digging in his pocket for a quarter. It was the small head shot that accompanied the article.

It was a dead ringer for Darcy. The woman he'd married.

He inserted the coin with fumbling fingers and snatched up the last copy in the rack. He started to read the article as he walked to his car, his anger growing as he read each sentence.

Darcy Stanton Hays, his wife, was in reality Tracy D'Arcy Harbeson Stanton, the missing niece of his commanding officer. The one who'd climbed out the window of the chapel and left old Dick What's-his-name standing at the altar.

How could she not have told him who she was?

Bill unlocked the car and slid behind the wheel. The afternoon was hot, and he turned on the engine so he could use the air conditioner, but he didn't drive. Not until he'd read every word of the article.

No wonder she hadn't wanted to remain married to him. He hardly traveled in her circles. Her father was a general, for God's sake. Her mother was the daughter of one of the most decorated heroes of World War II, and the rest of her family was a veritable Who's Who of American military history.

Why the hell hadn't he made the connection?

She'd told him she'd backed out of a marriage that her family had practically arranged. He didn't realize that it had been just a matter of hours prior to him finding her on that deserted road.

Had she been laughing at him behind his back? Was

she having a merry old time thinking she had him wound around her little finger?

He looked back at the photograph. It was apparently a college yearbook shot, and not the most flattering picture, but it looked like her, the woman he'd fallen in love with. Then he opened the paper to read the rest of the article.

Apparently, her family called her Tracy, and he'd known that the missing bride was Colonel Harbeson's niece and assumed that she was Tracy Harbeson. The girl he'd picked up on the road had a different name. No wonder he hadn't made the connection.

He had to get home. He had to figure out what to do. Hell, could he be accused of harboring a fugitive or something? Had he done something against the law?

He slammed his fist against the steering wheel, causing the horn to blow. Damn it. He was more confused than ever. And the only one who could clear it all up was Darcy.

He had the weekend, forty-eight hours, before he had to report back to the squadron. He would go home, and he would demand answers. He would find out why she had played him for a fool. Then he would let her go.

Even if he'd regret it for the rest of his life.

DARCY'S DAY had started slowly enough, but just when she'd thought she'd made it through, a flurry of minor emergencies that all had to be attended to had come in in the last hour. She'd been ready to pack up and leave early and had ended up staying. She finally headed home from work an hour late.

She was tired and hot and cranky. She hadn't been sleeping well lately, and all she could think about was preparing a light supper and going to bed early. And to make matters worse, the air conditioner on Nettie's old car had given up and died.

A thunderstorm was forming off in the distance and the hot air was thick with humidity. Lightning flickered against the backdrop of purple-gray clouds. Maybe the impending storm would help to cool things off.

She steered the car into the driveway with nothing more pressing on her mind than a cold shower and a light snack. Then she realized that there was another car in her usual parking spot by the old tool shed.

Darcy's heart did a back flip when she realized it was Billy's dark green Cherokee.

He was home! He'd come for her!

Excited, she parked beside the dusty Jeep and hurried toward the house.

Billy, leaning against the support column, was waiting for her in the shade of the porch. Darcy grinned and started to wave, but her smile faltered as the grim expression on Billy's face registered. He looked as dark and as threatening as the thunderstorm building in the distance.

''What's wrong?'' Darcy tried to temper her alarm, but the expression on Bill's face was frightening. This was a side of the man she'd never seen before.

''Oh, that's rich,'' Bill snarled. ''You spend weeks laughing behind my back about how you...'' He stopped, apparently too angry for words. He had a wadded-up copy of a newspaper in his hands and he threw it at her, the pages separating and fluttering out onto the lawn in the cool breeze that carried the smell of rain.

''How could you not tell me who you are?'' He turned and marched inside, leaving Darcy standing, stunned, at the bottom of the steps. "How could you make me love you, then play me like a fool?"

"Who I am?" Darcy still didn't know what he was talking about, but she guessed the newspaper would clear up the mystery. And she couldn't defend herself until she knew what this was all about.

As fat raindrops spattered against the tin roof of the porch, she gathered up the scattered sheets of newsprint, polka-dotted with wet spots. She barely made it to the shelter of the porch before the sky opened and rain fell in blowing sheets.

PACING LIKE an angry tiger, Bill waited inside, his rage growing with each moment it took. How the hell long did it take to read one damned newspaper article?

Lightning struck nearby and with it came the acrid ozone smell. His skin tingled as the electrical charge ripped through the air.

Darcy was still on the porch! He had to get her inside where it was dry. Where it was safe.

Bill hurried to the door and a gust of wind ripped the screen out of his hands and set the door flapping against the wall. A volley of raindrops mixed with hail rattled against the tin roof, sounding like machine-gun fire. Why was she still sitting out there?

He pushed outside. Darcy was in the swing, the newspaper clasped tightly in her hands. Her face was wet and her eyes clouded, her expression miserable. She was soaking wet and shivering, whether from the cold rain or something else, he didn't know.

"I—I'm sorry, Darcy," he said, holding out his hand, but wanting to scoop her into his arms, though he didn't dare. He had to make it right first. "Come inside."

Apologies didn't come easy to him, but he struggled for the right words. "I didn't mean to take it out on you."

She looked up at him and took his hand. A little of the light had returned to her eyes, but her expression was wary. "I guess I owe you an explanation," Darcy murmured, shivering as Bill led her inside.

"That would be a good start," Bill said, grabbing a kitchen towel and rubbing the excess water off her skin, skin he'd rather be kissing. No, he had to harden his heart. At least, until he'd heard what Darcy had to say.

"I don't know where to begin," she answered weakly. "I was so confused."

"Go on." It was hard not to drag her to him, not to crush her in his arms, but Bill determined he would remain aloof, objective, until she'd had her say.

"Looking back on it, I'm not really sure why I agreed to marry Dick," she said simply. "He had given me a long list of good reasons that had more to do with pedigrees than affection. My mother had gone on and on about the wonderful match, and it seemed easier to go along with everyone than to make waves. I'd known Dick forever, we'd dated on and off in high school and college, and I hadn't had that much experience with other guys." She shrugged. "What did I know? I didn't know how love was supposed to feel.

"Until I met you," she said, so softly that Bill wasn't sure he hadn't wished it.

"I—I guess it was just easier to go along with it than to disagree." She smiled wanly through a sheen of moisture that Bill knew this time was from tears. "I figured that if all the other things were right, then love would grow. And, to tell the truth, I was ready to get out from under my parents' influence and be on my own.

"Only Dick just proved to be a younger version of my parents. He didn't want me to work." She looked up, her eyes bright with indignation. "How could he expect me to go along with that after I'd knocked myself out to succeed in nursing school?"

Bill drew in a deep breath and wondered if he was supposed to respond. How had this woman, who seemed so strong, been so easily led by her parents and fiancé?

"My parents didn't understand me. My mother certainly didn't. She didn't seem to realize that the world had changed since she married Dad. That women were no longer content to play the dutiful military wife, to attend teas and to entertain generals when they happened to be in town. I felt like everyone expected me to be a Stepford Wife.

"So there I was, full of doubts, waiting for the ceremony to begin. My mother was fiddling with my hair, my attendants were giggling about how manly Dick was, and I suddenly felt like the walls were closing in around me."

Darcy drew in a deep sigh as another gust of wind blew more rain against the windows. "I asked them to leave me alone for a few minutes to collect myself, and as soon as they were gone, I climbed out the window and dashed to my car. I changed clothes in a gas-station bathroom, stashed the dress in the back of the Volkswagon Bug, and you know the rest...."

She chuckled. "I cut my finger on a safety pin and got some blood on the dress when I was rolling it up. I guess that's why they think I was the victim of foul play." She shrugged and raised her hands in a placating gesture. "So that's the condensed version.

"I'm sorry if you were caught in the middle of it. I didn't know your connection to my uncle at first." She drew in a deep breath. "By the time I did, it was too late. I was already in love with you."

Bill couldn't think. Not with Darcy there in front of him in full and glorious color. Her explanation seemed so logical, so reasonable, but still.... It could be the sheer closeness of her impairing his judgment.

He had to get out of here. He had to think. He had to go someplace where he wouldn't be distracted by her. Maybe it was a coward's way. Maybe it wasn't the way any of the other guys on the team would do it, but he couldn't think clearly when Darcy was so close.

He turned and walked out the door, the wind slamming it behind him.

Darcy watched him go and tried not to jump to conclusions, but Billy's response was crystal clear. The slamming door had illustrated it plainly.

Why couldn't Billy see that she hadn't intentionally set out to deceive him? Why was he so eager to get away from her that he'd stomped off into a thunderstorm?

At least, he'd taken the Jeep. She'd heard the engine start through a lull in the wind and seen the taillights as he'd torn down the lane. She whispered a prayer that he'd be safe, then set her mind to doing what she knew she must.

She'd call her family to tell them she was safe, then she'd be packed and ready by the time Billy returned. She'd take nothing that wasn't hers. One thing was certain, she wouldn't stay another night in this house where she was so obviously not wanted. Where she no longer belonged.

BILL DIDN'T KNOW how long he drove or why he ended up in the Reflection Garden in the Old Confederate Memorial Cemetery.

Maybe it was because his mother had devoted so much time to it when his Boy Scout troop had adopted the neglected graveyard as their community service project. The boys had only intended to clear the brush and keep it trimmed, but Momma had insisted that there had to be something pretty, something for the living to enjoy.

She had kept them busy for weeks, shoveling dirt, laying out paths, planting shrubs, flowers and bulbs. They hadn't been too crazy about it at first, but once the project was finished they'd loved it, too.

But never as much as Momma had. She'd always said that besides her young 'uns, it was the only thing she had to speak for her, the woman she'd been. And it spoke well.

The storm had finally rained itself out and all that remained of it was the occasional flicker of lightning in the distance and the steady patter of rain as it dripped from the trees. Already the clouds were racing away, scudding across the sky and letting the stars peek through the breaks.

He stepped out of the car and found the path that led to the garden. His clothes were still damp from his dash through the rain, and when the cool breeze left by the storm blew, it chilled him. It didn't matter. All that mattered was working this out. Making the right decision.

He found the concrete bench in the middle of the garden. It was wet, but he brushed the water off and sat anyway. It wasn't as if he weren't wet already. And he had to be here. He had a lot to think about. And maybe here, he could get it right.

He sat for a while listening to the drip drop of the

water sifting through the leaves. He heard the night birds and the crickets and the occasional call of an owl.

He heard his mother's voice. "She loves you, you know," she seemed to say. "She didn't mean to lie to you." Momma chuckled. "But you pure railroaded her into everything you two done."

Bill could almost see his mother's smile. "I reckon I ought to be mad as a wet hen about how you two fooled me, but your reasons were good. Darcy got caught up in everything, and then she didn't know how to get out of it."

"What about her family?"

"I reckon her family would surely be grateful to know that she's alive and well and married to you instead of what they must think now. Go to her, son. Go to her. Before it's too late."

Bill was a logical man. He knew that he couldn't possibly have heard his mother speak, but wherever the words of wisdom had come from they were the right ones. Why was he letting pride and hurt get in the way of the real thing? He loved Darcy, and he wouldn't let her go without a fight.

Maybe he hadn't told her so, but he did love her. And maybe if he told her, she'd respond in kind.

He stood up and looked around. The place was as still and as empty as it had been before, but he really did sense his mother's presence. "I'm going, Momma. I'm going to tell her. Thank you." He started to go, but he stopped.

"I love you, Momma," he whispered to the wind.

DARCY WAS ALMOST packed when she heard the car. She stiffened her spine and steeled her resolve not to let him get to her. She wouldn't let Billy see her cry.

She'd have plenty of time to cry the rest of her life.

She heard him fling open the door and come inside, but she wouldn't give him the satisfaction of going to him. Let him come to her.

Finally, he found her.

"I'll have everything packed in a couple of minutes," she said stiffly, without turning around. "You can take me to a motel like you promised that first night. Then I have no intention of taking up any more of your time."

"What if I don't want to take you?" Billy said, his voice husky, thick.

"Then I guess I'll borrow Nettie's car one last time. I'll return it," she answered sharply to cover the lump in her throat. She couldn't look at him. She wouldn't. Not yet, anyway. If she did she would cry.

"What if I don't want you to go?"

Hope soared, but Darcy knew better than to count on it. "What do you mean?" She knew she sounded wary, but she had to know exactly where she stood.

"I love you, Darcy. Maybe we didn't go about it in the normal way: love first, then marriage. But, I do love you."

Darcy's heart caught in her throat, and she couldn't speak. Didn't know what to say if she could. She turned to look at him, her eyes swimming with tears.

"I see now that most of the misunderstanding is my fault. I made assumptions I shouldn't have. I didn't ask enough questions. I just looked at you and assumed I knew who you were." He chuckled wryly.

"Maybe I did. The real you, anyway. And if I'd known about your family tree, I might never have dared to look further. Much less touch." He paused for a moment, then stepped nearer. "I think I remember you saying that you love me. Is that true or was it just the heat of the moment?''

''No. Yes. Both, I guess,'' she answered, her heart beating so rapidly that she could barely breathe much less think. ''I do love you. I love you for the way you cared for your mother. I love you for the way you made me feel important, like I mattered. Yes, Billy Hays, I love you.''

She could see the relief on Billy's face. ''What do we want to do about it, then?'' He stepped closer, but still a little too far.

Darcy drew a deep breath. ''We-e-ll,'' she said. ''We could invite everyone to another wedding, and pretend it was our first...''

Billy shook his head. ''No,'' he said. ''Then I'd have to pretend to wait to be with you. I want to shout it to the rooftops that I love you and you're mine.''

''I guess this means I'll have to quit my job.''

''Why?''

''I want to be more than just a weekend wife,'' Darcy answered simply. ''I want to live with you in Florida, and I want you to come home to me every day.''

''Hoo ah,'' Billy cheered softly, then gathered her to him and held her as if he'd never let go. ''There's nothing I want more.''

He kissed her, and when he was finished staking his claim, Darcy drew back and Billy tried to pull her back to him.

She placed her finger on her lips. ''One more thing,'' she whispered, her voice husky with need. ''Don't you worry about my uncle. He's the one man I really do have wrapped around my finger.''

''That's not true,'' Billy said as he lowered his head. ''There are two.''

Then he lifted her into his arms and took her to bed.

Author Note

MISSION

U.S. Air Force Special Tactics Teams

The mission of the US Air Force Special Tactics Team is to provide air traffic control and terminal guidance for aircraft operations under combat conditions.

Often a Special Tactics operator must parachute into hostile territory and secure the desired location before he can serve incoming aircraft.

Trained as air traffic controllers or emergency medical technicians, they receive extensive training in weapons and demolition, combat skills, survival and anything necessary to get the job done. They often provide support to covert, top-secret missions in far-flung reaches of the world.

Their motto is FIRST THERE

Special Tactics operators wear the same uniforms as regular members of the air force, mostly the camouflaged battle dress uniform, but are privileged to wear the distinctive scarlet beret. The scarlet beret bearing a metal flash depicting the combat control shield and the motto, First There, is awarded only after the member earns the right to wear it after completing extensive physical and tactical training. Many men apply, but only a few are chosen and pass through the rigorous training regimen.

**Beginning in March
from**

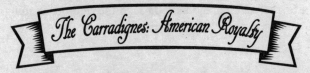

HARLEQUIN®

AMERICAN *Romance*®

The Carradignes: American Royalty

A royal monarch's search for an heir leads him to three American princesses. King Easton will get more than he bargained for in his quest to pass on the crown! His first choice—Princess CeCe Carradigne, a no-nonsense executive who never mixes business with pleasure...until she gets pregnant by her rival, Shane O'Connell.

Don't miss:

THE IMPROPERLY PREGNANT PRINCESS
by Jacqueline Diamond   March 2002

And check out these other titles in the series:

THE UNLAWFULLY WEDDED PRINCESS
by Kara Lennox   April 2002

THE SIMPLY SCANDALOUS PRINCESS
by Michele Dunaway   May 2002

And a tie-in title from
HARLEQUIN®
INTRIGUE®

THE DUKE'S COVERT MISSION
by Julie Miller   June 2002

Available at your favorite retail outlet.

HARLEQUIN®
Makes any time special ®

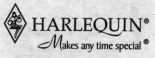

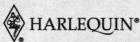